TALES OF THE CHAI MAKHANI TRIO

VOLUME I

KATE MACLEOD

1 A TANJO, TWO KNIVES AND THREE CUPS OF CHAI MAKHANI

IT'S NOT like Elyot could ever forget they were there, hanging ominously over the entire city, constantly keeping it in the shadow of one ship or another. But every afternoon when he emerged from the nook he called home - just a space where the eaves of one building overlapped the flat roof of another, keeping out most of the rain but none of the wind - the sight of those five ships lording over him and all of his fellow citizens of Adghal struck him anew.

He didn't really understand how they stayed up there. He knew it had something to do with their antigravity drives, but every ship on Adghal required wings and a propulsive engine to stay in the sky. The Commonwealth ships did not. They just dangled silently over the city, no roar of engines or jostling movement as they rode the air currents.

They always looked to him as if they were about to fall.

He didn't grasp the scale, either. They seemed close enough to touch, and the details of protruding sensors and lights and windows were so clear to his eye it was like there was nothing between him and them. And yet he knew they were in the highest levels of the atmosphere. And they were massive, truly massive.

An enforcer had overheard him referring to the largest of the five as the flagship once and laughed, laughed loud and hard until his face turned red. Then he had told Elyot that his planet was too tiny, too remote to bother with more than the smallest class of Commonwealth cruisers.

But even more disturbing than that thought was the constant question that never left his mind but that he was too afraid of the answer to ever speak it out loud: why was it that there were never any clouds between those ships and the city?

The idea that the Commonwealth just might have the power to control the weather was too spooky to dwell on. And yet he couldn't stop dwelling on it.

It was late afternoon, nighttime chilly already as his quarter of the city was once more in the shadow of one of those hovering ships. He carefully filled his pockets with his few meager belongings before climbing down from the nook that was now his home and dropping to the rough packed earth of the alley below.

He never left anything behind. He was pretty sure at least one other person was squatting in his nook when he was away. The day might come when he would have to fight for the last bit of shelter he had left. But today was not that day.

His stomach growled as the smell of meat grilling on street vendor's carts filled his nostrils. He hadn't had meat in ages. Not since the day his mother had gone out to see a friend and never returned.

He closed his eyes and inhaled deeply, the smell of dripping fat and charred flesh so rich in the air he could nearly taste it on the back of his tongue. If only to have even the most gristly bit...

The sound of a loud voice shouting orders had his eyes open in a flash, and his feet changed directions quicker than he could even think about it.

Which was good. It would look more natural that way, like he was going about his business down this side street and not avoiding yet another Commonwealth enforcer patrol.

He still had his identcard in his pocket; that hadn't been stolen from him yet. But every time he was caught by a patrol and presented his card for inspection, that inspection had taken longer and longer. It was agony, trying not to squirm or shift suspiciously as the foreigner scrutinized his name, then his mother's name, then the blank that was meant to be his father's name.

Every time he was confused why they were lingering over his mother's name, as if it were familiar to them. But every time they had just thrust his card back into his hands and sent him on his way.

Where was she? Why had she never come home that day?

Elyot kept to the back ways the rest of the way to the tavern, but he was still early for his shift. He always was. He never knew when he was going to get lucky, to find it busy, to find his employers needed him to start early, to work extra.

But he seldom got lucky, not these days when the citizens preferred to avoid the patrols, to stay out of sight in their own homes. Mostly he got sent home early with only a coin or two in his hand for his troubles. Enough for a piece of a vat-protein bar, not enough for proper food.

How he longed for proper food.

But today wasn't a lucky day. As he slipped inside the tavern's dark interior and walked down the steps to the sunken main floor, he saw only the usual spattering of customers. A group of dock workers were sitting close together at one of the tables near where the heating coils met, the warmest spot in the cave-cool room. They shared a pitcher of dark ale, but they spoke little. Their vibe was more of sullen defiance than bonhomie. Elyot recognized them, part of a much larger group that had once come to the tavern every day at shift's end to drink an ale or two before going home to their families. Their visits were rarer now.

A girl in a tattered cloak with her hood drawn close around her face sat in one corner, a menu sitting neglected in front of her. She looked like a local, with a touch of red in her brown hair and a smattering of freckles across her cheeks. And she dressed like a local, albeit one as down on her luck as Elyot was on his. Her shirt sleeves and pant legs both stopped well short of her wrists and ankles and the fabric was worn so smooth it was about to be nonexistent in places. Her darting eyes caught Elyot looking her way and she jumped then bent over the menu with too much concentration.

Another girl sat at a nearby table, looking around the tavern as if she were in a museum filled with fascinating artifacts from a forgotten age. She wore a long cape, although the material of her pants and jacket looked warm enough for her not to need one. The sheen suggested they were windproof as well. Elyot knew some of the merchant families on Adghal were doing quite well working with the Commonwealth, but although her clothes spoke of wealth she was definitely not a local. Not with that honey-colored skin so perfectly complected and that sleek, shiny silver blonde hair pulled back into a loose braid that fell to the middle of her back. No, definitely not local.

"Hello, Elyot," Mama Scotti said as she emerged from behind the bar with another pitcher of ale for the dock workers. "I'm not sure if we're going to need you today," she added regretfully.

"It doesn't look like it," Elyot agreed, trying hard not to sound disappointed. It wasn't Mama Scotti's fault her tavern did so little business these days. He knew she already paid him more than she could afford. "I'll just sit at the bar there in case something changes."

"You're a good lad," she said with a warm smile, then crossed the room to set the pitcher on the dock workers' table.

"We didn't order another," one of them said.

"It's on the house," Mama Scotti said, smiling down at all of them. They shifted uncomfortably. Elyot knew that Mama Scotti was trying to lure them into staying longer, to make her tavern look homey and inviting to anyone else that might drop by. But he also suspected the men were using up all their gumption staying for the one pitcher. Two might ask more of them than they had to give.

Finally the biggest of the group, a fellow Elyot only knew by his nickname Ox, took the newly arrived pitcher and topped off his own mug with the foaming ale. Then he raised his glass to Mama Scotti and drank the whole thing down, slamming the mug back down on the table and giving a loud belch that set a few of the others laughing.

It was almost like old times.

But then the door banged open - caught by a gust of wind and tearing free of some poor customer's hand, surely - and they all jumped.

For a moment, just a single moment, Elyot felt his heart start to swell. Customers! From the sounds of feet coming down the stairs, lots of customers! And the look on Mama Scotti's face said she was thinking the same thing.

But the footsteps had a ring to them, a certain harsh sound to the heels, and when the sight of black boots became black jumpsuits became a squadron of Commonwealth enforcers, he wasn't even surprised.

"Is this the right place?" one of them asked when they saw the nearly empty room.

"It'll do," the one in front grumbled, and they all took chairs around the largest table.

The table right at the bottom of the stairs. They were now between everyone in the tavern and the only way out of the building.

The dock workers started drinking their ale with as much speed as they dared. Mama Scotti clutched her hands together but mustered up a smile before approaching the enforcers' table.

The girl with silver-blonde hair had turned in her chair as if suddenly engrossed by the array of bottles displayed behind the bar, but Elyot suspected she was really hiding her face from the enforcers.

The other girl, the local girl in the hooded cloak, was clutching the menu in trembling hands.

"Elyot, I just might need you this evening," Mama Scotti said as she slipped behind the bar. "I need to set some meat skewers to grilling and fry up a couple of baskets of potato pop-pops. Can you bring four pitchers to that table, then check if those two girls are ever going to order?"

"Sure thing, Mama," Elyot said. There wasn't much room behind the bar, so he had to wait until Mama Scotti was in the kitchen before he could fill four pitchers from the tap and carefully carry them over to the table at the bottom of the stairs.

There were only eight enforcers there. A half a pitcher of Mama's signature ale was enough to knock even a seasoned dock worker for a loop. These reed-thin foreigners didn't stand a chance. And he suspected the red flush to their cheeks was not from the ever-present wind outside. This was not their first tavern of the evening.

"Expecting more?" Elyot asked as he set the pitchers around the table.

"What's it to you?" one of the enforcers snarled at him.

"I'm just wondering if you need me to pull over a few more tables and chairs," Elyot said, his cheeks flaming. He honestly wasn't sure what was worse: a small band of very drunk enforcers, or a larger band of only tipsy enforcers.

He would prefer no enforcers.

"We can move furniture when they get here," said another of the enforcers. This one was younger than the others, but that wasn't the only thing that set him apart. His cheeks only had the slight pinkness from wind exposure, and his tone was quite mild, not the belligerent barking that Elyot had come to assume was the only way enforcers could talk.

"Very good," Elyot said with a little bow then quickly rushed away. Somehow that last fellow with his soft voice and quiet demeanor scared him more than the others.

"What will you have?" Elyot asked, making the girl in the hooded cloak jump.

"Um," she said, clutching the menu more tightly, which only seemed to make her hands tremble more.

Her hands were in bad shape. They looked like she had been feeding a long-toothed mountain cat by hand and hadn't been quick enough to avoid getting half-chewed herself. What had she been doing?

Elyot looked around at the enforcers then towards the kitchen door. No sign of Mama Scotti. He leaned in to whisper to the girl, "I know it seems dead in here, but really Mama isn't going to let you stay if you don't order something."

"Um," the girl said, looking from her menu to the stairs up to the doorway, now blocked by increasingly raucous enforcers, then back to the menu. "Um."

Elyot was afraid she was about to burst into tears.

"Two chai makhanis," the girl with silver blonde hair said as she moved from her chair to the one opposite the hooded girl's. Now she had her back to the enforcers, and was no longer alone.

"I don't have any money," the hooded girl said.

"Never mind, I've got it," the other girl said with a wave of her hand. "The menu says they are the specialty of the house, but I'm keeping my expectations low."

Elyot gathered up the menus and avoided telling the imperious snit just what he thought of her. He rather hoped she would repeat it later, when Mama Scotti was in hearing range. That could be fun.

Elyot poked his head into the kitchen and saw Mama Scotti plating up an array of meat skewers then adding little bowls of sauces. She saw Elyot in the doorway and thrust the platter into his hands then shooed him out of her kitchen with a sweeping motion of her hands.

"Two chai makhanis," Elyot said before retreating from her space. He set the platter into the center of the enforcers' table and was once again reminded of someone feeding long-toothed mountain cats. They fairly pounced on the offering of meat, tearing it from the wooden skewers with visceral delight and far too many of them chewing with their mouths open.

The two girls were making no effort to engage each other in conversation. The one with silver blonde hair was examining the heat coils as if trying to puzzle out how they worked. The hooded one was staring fixedly over her shoulder at something behind the bar.

He went back into the kitchen and scooped up the waiting chai makhanis then brought them out to the girls. The hooded one took a large gulp from hers, apparently not expecting it to be hot. She somehow managed to swallow and he could just imagine the burning sensation traveling all of the way down her throat to settle in her stomach. But then a huge grin spread across her face.

"What's in this stuff?" she asked, peering into her mug.

"It's suppose to be strong, black tea with butter, salt, cinnamon, cardamom, ginger and pepper," the other girl told her, taking a hesitant sip. She grimaced.

"What?" Elyot asked, not particularly kindly.

"The butter is off," she said.

"It's fresh," he said.

"From a cow?" she shot back.

"Yak," he said.

"The menu didn't state that," she said with a dissatisfied frown.

"And the spices are so weak they must be positively ancient. But I guess that's to be expected in such a backwater planet."

He was about to ask her just where she was from, as offworlders were rare or at least had been before the enforcers had arrived, but before he got my chance the door above banged open again and another pair of boots clomped down the steps at a run.

"You found her!" the man cried as he spotted the others at the bottom of the stairs.

Both of the girls beside me stiffened at once. The hooded girl drew her hood more closely around her and turned her face away, although whether to turn it away from the enforcers or towards whatever fascinated her behind the bar Elyot couldn't tell. The other had her hand on her thigh. Elyot belatedly realized she wore some sort of weapon there, a long, straight club that attached at her hip and just above her knee. She stroked the length of it with her gloved fingers but didn't pull it out of its holster.

But one of the enforcers hopped to her feet, a heavy set woman who greeted the newcomer with an aggressive handshake and many slaps to the shoulder. Apparently she was the "her" who had been found, but neither of the girls was relaxing in the slightest.

"Another round!" one of the enforcers called out. Elyot rushed behind the bar to take down another four pitchers from the shelf, but the minute he left the girls' table the quiet enforcer approached it, settling himself comfortably in a chair between the two girls and looking them each over carefully. The silver-blonde girl took another sip from her chai makhani and grimaced again. The hooded girl seemed to see the wisdom in the distraction and grasped her mug in both hands, drinking deeply.

"This is a local beverage?" the enforcer asked, taking the hooded girl's mug from her to sniff at its contents.

"It's meant to be chai makhani," the silver-blonde girl said.

"Ah," the enforcer said, then waved a finger at Elyot, who was heading to the other table with his hands full of ale. "One of these chai makhani concoctions for me."

"Right away," Elyot said, and reached the kitchen just as Mama Scotti was emerging with baskets of potato pop-pops. That meant he had to go into the kitchen and mix up the chai makhani himself. It only took a moment: the spices were premixed, the tea kept hot in a massive urn. He only had to wait for the yak butter to melt enough to stir it all together, but still. Every moment was agony. Why had that enforcer sat down with those two girls?

"Ah, thank you," the enforcer said as Elyot set the mug before him. He took a sip, but whatever he thought of the drink was a mystery as he merely wiped his lips delicately then turned his attention back to the silver-blonde girl.

"Alextra is not a terribly common name," he said to her. She shrugged disinterestedly. "It's tradition in the Commonwealth to stop using girl names after the Empress bestows it on one of her seventy-seven daughters."

"I was born just before the daughter in question," she said. "On the twelfth day of the fourth moon of the year 37887."

The enforcer's eyes moved up and to the left as if consulting some mental list. There was no way anyone could memorize the birthdays of seventy-seven daughters, but this man acted as if he had. "Yes, that checks out. Very good."

That sounded less like the usual dismissive "very good" Elyot received after the scrutiny of his identcard and more like the sort of "very good" one would hear from someone appreciating how another pulled off a clever trick.

But if he suspected this Alextra of anything, he didn't act on it. Instead he turned his attention to the other girl.

"And you?" he asked.

"Keani," she said, lifting her chin.

He reached over and plucked the back of her hood until it spilled down her back. Her red-brown hair was wind-tossed despite the elaborate network of interconnecting ties she had caught it all up in.

"Local," he said, not really a guess. She nodded.

The enforcers were getting louder by the moment. Mama Scotti emerged from the kitchen with yet another platter of grilled meat, but no amount of protein was going to absorb all the alcohol they were kicking back.

The dock workers had made themselves scarce. When the enforcers got belligerent, there'd be nobody around for them to fight but each other. Elyot gathered up the empty pitchers and carried them back to the bar, passing the threesome at the smaller table as he went.

"And what is your name?" Alextra asked in a haughty tone. The enforcer quirked an eyebrow in amusement.

"Captain Koltn Ward of the Empress' Enforcers of the Commonwealth of Planets of the Third Quadrant of the Kullab Galaxy," he said airily. "Fourth Squad, third division," he added.

"Captain Ward," Alextra said. "Are you aware that detaining a citizen without cause is unconstitutional in the Commonwealth?"

"Ah, but we're not in the Commonwealth," he said, taking another sip of his chai makhani then making another delicate wipe of his lips. "Not yet."

"Surely the rules still apply to you as a representative of the empress wherever you happen to be," Alextra said.

"As they do to you," he countered. "You seem to know the law well, and yet you openly carry a tanjo, a ceremonial object forbidden to be so much as touched by any but the imperial guard." He gave her a mock assessing look. "You don't look like imperial guard to me."

"I have earned the right to carry this weapon," Alextra said coldly.

"If that's true," Captain Ward said, raising from his chair. "Then I do have cause to detain you." Alextra said nothing, just gave him a withering look, but Keani for whatever reason decided that was the moment to make a run for it. She looked back over her shoulder again, at Elyot refilling pitchers at the ale tap and then something behind him, something she desperately wanted to get to.

But she was only half out of her chair when Captain Ward's hand caught her wrist, pulling her with a jerk so that she spilled against him. She looked up at him with wide, startled eyes. "And just where do you think you're going?" he asked.

"Let her go," Alextra said, springing to her feet with her hand at the ready over that club at her hip but still not pulling it out.

"No, I think I'll be taking you both in," Captain Ward said, still looking down at Keani who stared up at him like a panicked rabbit.

He was going to arrest them, both of them. People in Adghal who got arrested by the enforcers were taken up to those ships up in the sky. Most were never heard from again. The few who did return never spoke of what happened to them, never spoke of much of anything at all. They just wandered the streets, broken people.

Was his mother up in the sky? Or was she even now wandering the streets, mind broken, unable to recall her home and the son who waited for her every day?

Elyot doubted if he got arrested he would ever see her. Those ships were massive, the odds of their paths crossing even if she were up there were infinitesimally small.

No, he didn't want to get arrested, but he couldn't stand by and watch two girls his own age taken away. Not if there was some way he could help them escape.

It wasn't hard to do. There were so many chairs scattered about, so easy to trip over. Never mind that navigating the room even when crowded with jostling bodies while carrying four pitchers in each hand had been commonplace for him back before the enforcers came. They didn't know that.

"Oops!" Elyot cried, stumbling away from a chair that just might have tripped him, and sending the contents of all four pitchers flying towards Captain Ward.

Captain Ward spun out of the way in time, but he had to let Keani go to do it. He didn't so much release her as thrust her away from him, and she nearly fell to the ground before getting her feet under her and scrambling away to hide behind the bar.

Then he drew his needler and aimed it right at Elyot's face. Elyot dropped the now-empty pitchers and held up his hands. He saw the finger start to slowly pull back on the trigger.

Like everyone else in the city, he had seen people peppered with the enforcers' needle guns. It didn't look like a peaceful way to die. There was no way a faceful of needles wasn't going to hurt. Elyot closed his eyes.

Then there was a cracking sound, and the clatter of a gun across the tiled floor. Elyot opened first one and then the other eye. Captain Ward was nursing the wrist of his gun hand, turning away from Elyot to glare at Alextra.

Alextra had kicked her chair out of the way and was standing on an open patch of floor. The club that had been attached to her thigh was now in her hand, although it was no longer just a club. It had extended out into a long, straight staff, only the ends weren't wood like the central piece. Elyot didn't know what they were. They were the blackest of blacks, as if all color were pulled deep inside and never allowed to escape. They looked solid, and yet had a shimmery glow to them like a hologram. As he watched the top one morphed from blunt staff end to a pointed spear head.

"Enforcers!" Captain Ward called out. "Arrest them!"

The enforcers around the table were on their feet at once, pulling uniform caps out of pockets and snapping them into shape before putting them on their heads.

Not a one of them looked remotely worse for the bottomless mugs of ale they had been consuming. How did they do that?

Alextra took a step back, not a retreat so much as a change to a more defensive stance, the spear held out before her as the enforcers closed in. They had short billy clubs of their own, inelegant but brutally effective weapons. Her eyes moved from one to the next as they formed a circle around her. She made a few testing jabs to see if she could force them to back off, but they closed in tighter.

Then she made a sound between a song and a battle cry, words Elyot didn't understand. She raised her weapon high and the blunt staff end and the pointed spear end both morphed, changing into crescent-shaped blades.

Then she dropped low, swinging the weapon around her below knee-height at the enforcers.

Some of them fell back in time. Some didn't. And the cave-like tavern was suddenly echoing with the sound of their screams.

Elyot looked around for the fallen needle gun, but Captain Ward already had it back in his hand. He took aim at Elyot again and Elyot leaped away with a cry, stumbling into Alextra and knocking her off her stance.

"Get out of the way!" she grumbled, throwing him off her. He stumbled back into the bar and watched as she slashed at three more of the enforcers as they slipped on the ale from the fallen pitchers.

Mama Scotti was nowhere in sight. Elyot pulled himself along the bar, eyes on the fight around him until he reached the point where he could dive behind the counter.

He pulled up short on that dive when he saw two blades gleaming in the shadows behind the bar.

"Stay back!" Keani hissed. Elyot knew what she had been staring at so fixedly before. Mama Scotti's paring knives. They weren't good for much more than peeling or slicing drink condiments, but Keani looked prepared to peel and slice him if he came any closer.

"I'm not the enemy," Elyot said, hands raised.

"Why did they come down here?" Keani demanded.

"They go where they please!" Elyot said.

The Mama Scotti started to scream, a sound that made Elyot's insides go liquid. That wasn't a cry of alarm or surprise, that was a shriek of real pain. And it went on and on.

Elyot left the bar and ran to the kitchen door, which hung half off its hinges. A long carving knife lay abandoned on the floor and Elyot suspected that like Keani Mama Scotti had been trying to use it to protect herself. Now she was bent over, up to her waist in the cauldron of boiling fat she used to fry the potato pop-pops.

Her screaming had stopped.

Elyot fell back against the doorframe, hand to his mouth as he fought the urge to vomit. One of the two enforcers who had charged into the kitchen had pulled on the elbow-length heat-resistant gloves Mama Scotti used to pull hot things out of her oven. He reached into the cauldron - the gloves not quite heat-resistant enough to judge by the grimace on his face - and caught hold of the back of Mama Scotti's apron and hauled her out of the boiling fat.

The smell of deep-fried Mama Scotti was too much like the grilled meat Elyot was constantly craving. Which only made the urge to vomit worse. The enforcer let her body drop to the floor. Then he noticed Elyot.

"Freeze, boy," he said, peeling off the gloves. But Elyot couldn't take his eyes off Mama Scotti. He had known her all his life. His mother had worked at this tavern tending the bar for years and years. When she had disappeared, Mama Scotti had given Elyot a job. She had paid him even when she had too little to keep her own business out of debt. She had been like an aunt to him, or a grandmother.

Wait, was she still moving?

"Identcard," the enforcer said, finally having extracted himself from the gloves. But Elyot's eyes were still on Mama Scotti ever so slowly writhing across the floor. What was she trying to get to? The wood fire oven? Why?

"Identcard," the enforcer said again, running out of patience. Elyot nodded, but didn't reach for his card. He just raised a hand, pointing at where Mama Scotti was pulling herself up onto her elbows and reaching for the latch on the oven door.

"I'm not in the mood for this," the enforcer growled, and his hand closed around Elyot's throat, holding him pinned against the wall and rapidly running out of air. Only when he was sure that Elyot was immobilized did he turn his head to look where Elyot had been pointing.

Mama Scotti was collapsed back down on the foor. But she had achieved her objective first. The oven door stood open, the wood fire within banked down to warm embers as it always was when there were no food orders that called for it.

But in her hand was a single burning brand, a brand that glowed back to life in the more oxygen-rich environment of the open kitchen. Mama Scotti held it up for a moment until a flame emerged and began to dance.

Then she dropped it into the long trail of oil and fat she had dragged with her from the cauldron. And that one flame became a roaring wall of fire.

"Fire!" the enforcer called, pulling Elyot by the throat out of the kitchen and back into the common room where Alextra still spun and danced with that strange weapon in her hands. Most of the enforcers were staggering away, bleeding from cuts all over their bodies, but a few were still on their feet, circling around behind her as Captain Ward stood before her, aiming his needle pistol at her. He fired a barrage of shots, but Alextra merely spun her weapon on her hands like a fan, the blades that glowed like holograms catching the needles and sending them in all directions. The enforcers around her cried out and covered their heads with their arms as the needles rained down on them.

"Fire!" another enforcer cried as the flames from the kitchen advanced to the doorway and found the nearest ale-soaked chair.

Elyot was starting to black out, the hand on his throat never loosening even as the enforcer it belonged to just gaped at the growing carnage around him. Then suddenly he jerked upright as if he had been shocked. Elyot stumbled away the moment the hand's grip eased off his throat, gasping for breath as he collided with someone standing behind him. An arm wrapped around him, offering support as he and his new companion fell back behind the bar. His last glimpse was of that enforcer slowly crumpling to his knees and then to the ground, the worn handle of one of Mama Scotti's paring knives just visible from where the blade was buried deep in his temple.

Elyot blinked as the world came back into focus and he saw Keani crouched beside him, the other knife still in her hand.

"We have to get out of here!" she hissed at him.

Suddenly Alextra was there beside them, fighting to catch her breath. "They've fallen back to the door," she said. "We'll never get out that way."

"There must be another way out!" Keani said.

Then they both looked at Elyot.

Elyot bit his lip. He knew of another way out, but he really, really didn't want to go that way. The enforcers outside would be preferable. Arrest, torture, endless questioning and eventual execution, all would be preferable compared to what lay beyond that other door.

Then there was an explosion of glass and he realized the walls around the bar were on fire. Soon the tavern would be nothing more than a cave tucked under the walls of the oldest quarter of the mountaintop city.

He could feel the heat from the flames blistering his skin, scorching away the fine hairs of his eyebrows and eyelashes, consuming all the oxygen in the air so that it was real work to breathe.

As bad as the tales were, someone must have survived to tell them. There was hope.

"Down here!" Elyot said, grasping the ring that lifted the trapdoor behind the bar. He had never opened it before, had never even seen it opened. It felt like time had welded it shut. But then Keani and Alextra were on either side of him, grasping the edges of the ring until they had lifted the door enough to slip their fingers under the edge of it and pull from there.

The smell that rushed up at them was repulsive. It spoke of slimy wet things that lurked in the cold, damp dark. Legless things that squirmed through trails of their own ooze, that fed on each other by vomiting out their own digestive juices then slurping up the softened remains of their prey.

But the girls didn't seem to mind. They didn't even wait to ask how deep the hole was. They just threw the heavy trapdoor back against the burning wall and plunged one after the other down into the darkness.

The splashes came some time later. Then they were calling up to him, calling for him to join them.

He wished he could be as lucky as they were, capable of being brave because they had no idea what they had just flung themselves into.

Then another bottle exploded, pelting him with shards of hot glass, and there was no more time for dithering.

Elyot plugged his nose against the repugnant smell and jumped into the darkness of the hell that was the city catacombs.

2   THE MAZE AND THE MAW

ELYOT HADN'T REALIZED how hot the air inside the burning tavern had gotten until the moment the blessedly cool water splashed up all around him. It was like a healing balm against his nearly blistering skin, soothing tortured nerve endings as it washed over him.

But it wasn't very deep. He still had a lot of momentum when one foot hit bottom then slipped, his bare ankle scraping across the rock even as it twisted painfully under his weight. He splashed face-first into the water, quickly righting himself but not before getting a generous mouthful of the stuff.

The foul, green-tasting stuff. The smell had been horrid from above. It was even worse down at the bottom, as if the odor had settled thickly here, undisturbed for centuries, growing more rancid with time.

But the smell was nothing compared to the taste. Elyot heaved again and again, desperate to be sure he swallowed not a bit of it. But without a drink of something fresher, there was no way to get the thick layer off his tongue, no way to stop tasting the foulness of it.

It was like someone else had been sick in his mouth after eating rancid meat and really old cheese. Just the thought had him heaving again.

He hoped the burning sensation that ran up his ankle wasn't a gash from the rocky bottom. The idea of an open wound in that water was too much to bear.

At last, he managed to stop heaving and was once more aware of the world around him. It was too dark to see more than the occasional reflection of the fire above on the waist-deep water around him, but the sounds of splashes as the two girls moved around echoed in a way that spoke of a very narrow space. The barman who had first shown him the hatch had told him it led down into the catacombs, and if Elyot didn't keep out of the way when the barman was working Mama Scotti would throw him down there and let the monsters have him, and not even Elyot's mother would be able to save him.

Elyot had never thought to ask in the intervening years what the hatch was actually for. He had assumed some prior owner had been a smuggler, but he doubted that now. Even if he wanted to, there was no way to get back up to that hatch. He had just taken a one-way trip into the unknown, not that he had had much choice.

The fire above was roaring now, consuming the alcohol-soaked wood of the bar itself. Soon there would be nothing left of the tavern but a scorched cave. Even if he found a way back up there, life as he knew it had just gone up in smoke.

"Watch out!" the girl named Alextra hissed at him, pulling him toward her with such a jerk he lost his footing and fell against her with a splash. He was about to protest when something hit the water where he had been with an angry hiss. The wave that rushed up his back was uncomfortably warm.

"It's all going to come down," she said, narrowing her eyes as she looked up at the hatch. "We have to get out of here."

She looked at Elyot for a long moment before he realized what she was really saying. "Well, I don't know the way out," he said. "I've never even been down here before."

"But there *is* a way out," she said, her hand still on his arm gripping him more tightly.

"I would assume so," Elyot said.

"It looks like we're at the bottom of a well," the girl called Keani said. "Wells don't have other ways out."

Alextra released Elyot's arm and brushed back her cape. It spun through the water around her, floating out of her way. Elyot had a sudden vision of her emerging from this foul, brackish water, of the droplets flying off of her as she walked as if anxious not to offend, leaving her as clean and dry as she had been before her dunking.

She definitely had the air of someone who didn't get dirty.

Keani, on the other hand… Well, Elyot suspected she might be cleaner now than she had been five minutes before.

Elyot was suddenly blinded by a silvery light, but only for a moment. The light quickly passed on, and when the stars faded from his vision, he saw it came from a small object like a crystal in Alextra's hand. She raised her hand higher, and the silvery light danced over the dripping stone walls around them.

"There," she said, pointing with her other hand. "That's an opening."

"I don't see it," Elyot said, putting a hand over his eyes to block out the flickering light from the burning hatch.

"I do," Keani said, and she pointed as well.

Elyot's stomach sank. "That's impossible," he said.

"We can squeeze through it," Alextra said.

"Assuming it actually goes anywhere at all," Elyot said, "how do you propose we reach it? It's halfway up a very wet wall with no handholds."

"I see handholds," Keani said, then splashed over to stand directly under the hole, careful to stay close to the walls and not cross the center of the well where burning bits were raining down with growing frequency. She put the paring knife she had been holding in one hand between her teeth then reached up as far as she could stretch. Alextra moved the light back down to illuminate the wall around Keani. Keani's fingertips skimmed over the smooth surface then somehow just gripped into it and she hoisted herself up out of the water.

"I'm never going to be able to do that," Elyot said. Judging by the frown on Alextra's face, she was thinking the same thing.

"No worries," Keani said through gritted teeth. She said no more, focused on digging the sides of her soft shoes into the wall then looking up and finding new holds for her hands.

Elyot didn't realize he had been holding his breath until it all came out in a whoosh as Keani pulled herself into the darkness of the tiny opening. She turned about in the tight space, and when her head and shoulders appeared again, she was holding one end of her long, tattered cloak.

"Can you reach it?" she asked as she got down on her belly and extended her arms as far as she could.

"Yes, I think so," Alextra said, moving around Elyot and tucking the crystal back out of sight. Elyot could just make out the outline of her body in the flickering firelight as she grasped the cloak and used her feet as much as she could to scale the wall up to Keani.

"Come on!" Keani called down to Elyot. "There isn't much time. That floor is coming down."

Elyot looked up and saw that she was right. Embers were still raining down, striking the water with pops and hisses, but the heavy floorboards were eaten nearly through by the flames. He could hear a creaking, cracking, settling sound, as the weight of what remained of the bar became too much for the floor to support.

Elyot threw his arms over his head and dashed across the well to the far side. He had never been waist-deep in water before; it slowed him down far more than he had expected.

"Quickly!" Alextra called down to him. He flailed around until he caught the edge of the cloak. He held it tight in both hands and tried to figure out what to do with his feet. How had Alextra done it, that walking up the wall motion?

Both girls were hauling on their end of the cloak, pulling him up and out of the water. He got his feet situated, and although it seemed to be more slipping and sliding than actual climbing he managed to get up the slimy wall.

Then two pairs of hands were grasping his arms. His feet slipped, and for a moment he thought he was going to go tumbling back down into the water. The floor overhead started to groan like a dying crea-ture, and the panic gave him a surge of strength.

He wasn't even sure how he used it, that strength. It felt like a mad scramble, but the next thing he knew he was inside the little tunnel, arms and legs all tangled with two other pairs of each in a much too small space to fit three people.

The dim light flared up behind him, and for a moment he could see the fear on Keani's face, the knife still clutched in her teeth. He saw Alextra's face too, her lips drawn tight and her jaw clenched.

Then the light was gone, and there was a splash and a hiss of steam that rose up to cook the flesh of his already hurting feet. The three of them struggled together, pulling themselves further along the tunnel until they were away from that heat.

"Now what?" Keani asked, tipping her head back to look further down the tunnel, her jutting chin catching Elyot at the corner of his eye.

"It gets bigger up ahead," Alextra said, her elbow jabbing at them both as she dug the crystal back out. "The echoes, can't you hear?"

"Yes," Elyot said. "You go first, with the light."

He and Keani helped Alextra extricate herself from the tangle of their limbs, and she crawled ahead. Keani clutched her wadded cloak to her chest and followed.

Elyot gave one last look back, but the well behind was in total darkness now. The fire had done its worst. It was all over now.

The tunnel was uncomfortably narrow, but at least it was short. Elyot tumbled out of the end of it, rolling to the middle of the gently sloping floor beyond. Alextra had set her crystal on the ground as she used both of her hands to wring the water from her long silver hair. Keani shook out her cloak and refastened it around her shoulders. She took the little knife out of her mouth then spit a few times on the ground. Just watching her do it brought the foul taste coating his own tongue back to the front of his mind.

He hoped a dunking in a public fountain would clean the smell out of his clothes. He didn't have any others. He checked his pockets to make sure he hadn't lost anything in the well. Identcard, a few tarnished coins not worth the cheap metal they were minted from, the image disc of his mother holding him when he was still just a baby.

All still there, nothing of any use at the moment. He wondered what else Alextra had in *her* pockets.

Alextra was running her hand over the tunnel wall. The entire space was curved around them like a tube, the top just within reach of her questing fingertips, the bowed bottom holding a bare trickle of what he hoped was water.

"What is this place?" she asked, touching a soft scalloping worked into the stone.

"Catacombs," Elyot said.

"Catacombs," Keani said in a bare whisper. The hand clutching the little knife tightened, her knuckles whitening.

"This doesn't look carved," Alextra said, peering closer at the stone. "This isn't geologically natural either."

"The tunnels were here when the city was founded, or so they say," Elyot said.

"Monsters," Keani whispered. Alextra threw her a skeptical look, but the other girl just raised her chin, not taking back the word.

"Catacombs," Alextra said. "That doesn't explain the pattern in the rock, but I guess it explains the smell."

"Don't be absurd. No one gets buried down here anymore," Elyot said.

"How long does it take for a body to stop rotting?" Keani asked, crinkling her nose as she sniffed the air.

"Depends on the conditions," Alextra said.

"Even when these catacombs were still in use, the bodies were incinerated first," Elyot said. "And if you go really far back in time, they were preserved."

"How?" Alextra asked with keen interest.

"I don't know," Elyot said, getting annoyed. "It was centuries ago. Maybe no one knows."

"Someone knows," Alextra said dismissively. "But say you're right. What do you think we're smelling?"

"I don't want to think about that," Elyot said. The cool air of the tunnel combined with his soaked clothes were starting to give him a chill, and he was anxious to get moving.

"Something is still down here," Keani said, still at a whisper. "Something hunts and something is left behind to rot."

"Maybe," Alextra said.

"Let's just get out of here," Elyot said.

"Well, which way?" Alextra asked, raising her hands to indicate their only two options.

"This way," Elyot said and started walking.

"You know the catacombs, then?" Alextra asked as she fell into step beside him.

"No, but I know the city," Elyot said. "There's a public square not too far from the tavern that has one of the old gates. I've seen it. No one uses them anymore. They'll be locked, maybe even rusted shut…"

"You let me worry about that," Alextra said, patting the weapon the enforcer captain Koltn Ward had called a tanjo. At the moment it looked like no more than a shiny stick of wood against her thigh. "You just get us there."

They didn't get far before the tunnel branched into two equal-sized tunnels, each veering only a few degrees off of the heading of the original tunnel.

"Which way?" Alextra asked, shining her light as far into each as she could.

"They are both going basically the right way," Elyot said.

"No," Keani said. "The one on the left is sloping up, but the one on the right is sloping down."

"She's right," Alextra said.

"Left it is, then," Elyot said, and they pressed on to the next branching. Here the new tunnels branched off at a greater angle, and Elyot was certain the one on the left would take them too far off course.

Keani caught his arm before he stepped into the tunnel on the right.

"No," she said firmly.

"This is the way, I'm sure," he assured her.

"No, it goes down," Keani said.

"I agree," Alextra said. "Does it matter where we come up as long as we're out of the catacombs? We should keep picking the branches that slope up."

"It *does* matter where we come up," Elyot said. "The enforcers are all over the streets, but not in the same numbers. The gate I'm thinking of is in a small plaza where a few narrow alleys meet. No one goes there but the people that live in the surrounding buildings. It's our safest bet."

"I too would prefer not to tangle with enforcers," Alextra said, then looked at Keani.

Keani's face was twitching as warring emotions fought. She clearly didn't want to go down, but she didn't want to run into enforcers either.

"I'll go your way," she said at last. "But make sure the next path goes up."

"I don't think that's up to me," Elyot said.

And indeed it wasn't. Branching after branching, none of the options were ever quite right. At first he was certain they were veering too far to the left, then to the right, but eventually, he had no sense of where they were in relation to the city at all. All he knew for sure was that they were way too deep beneath the city to find a gate out now.

"This isn't working; is it?" Alextra asked after the third overly-pondered choice.

"You don't know where we are?" Keani asked, almost a wail.

"Can you find your way back?" Alextra asked. She spoke with measured calm as if compensating for Keani's growing panic.

"Maybe," Elyot said. "But what would be the point?"

"I'm worried we might be going in circles," Alextra said, still with that eerie calm.

"That would be bad," Keani said, looking around as if something might be lurking in the shadows.

"I can mark the walls," Alextra said, searching in her belt pouch for something.

"No," Elyot said. He thought he heard something distantly, but so briefly that even that short word had kept him from being sure.

"Why not?" Alextra asked, but he motioned for her to fall silent. They all strained to listen. Somewhere in the maze of tunnels water was dripping. Something scuttled, stopped, then scuttled again.

Then Elyot heard it again: voices. Human voices. The first two were little more than murmurs: he thought perhaps a man and a woman speaking low. But the voice that answered them he recognized at once.

Koltn Ward.

"The tavern must have burned itself out," Elyot whispered. "He came down to find us."

Alextra gave a tight nod and closed her belt pouch.

"We should hurry," Keani said. "Just pick the tunnels going up, who cares where it ends?"

"No," Elyot said. "He's in the catacombs. He knows we're here. He'll have called for backup."

"We can hear them coming a kilometer away," Alextra said, her hand on her tanjo.

"Can we?" Elyot countered. "Could you tell how far away that scuttling came from? And from which tunnel?"

Alextra exchanged a glance with Keani then shook her head.

"But we know they're behind us now," Keani said.

"He'll have called for backup," Elyot said again. "All squads, all checkpoints."

"All gates," Alextra said, his point finally dawning on her. She held up a hand before Keani could speak and they all heard voices again, but these voices appeared to be echoing down from in front of them. Alextra gave Elyot a conceding nod.

"What do we do?" Keani asked. She looked down at the paring knife, so small in her hand.

"Only one thing to do," Elyot said. "We have to go down. Deeper. Hope there are places to hide there and wait for this all to blow over."

"Quickly but quietly," Alextra agreed.

They were all three wearing soft-soled shoes, and Elyot doubted the enforcers could hear anything over their own ringing footfalls and loud voices. But still, he moved from tunnel to tunnel as fast as Alextra's crystal could light the way.

This was made more difficult when Alextra paused to shine her light into the little alcoves that were beginning to appear at irregular intervals at the widest part of the tunnel. Some contained half-rotted wood boxes, some dull-colored urns, others still nothing more than mounds of ash.

"How barbaric," she whispered to herself but saw Elyot looking back at her and blushed. "Sorry."

"It was centuries ago," Elyot said. "Our bodies are recycled now, same as in the Commonwealth."

"The Commonwealth has been recycling all organic matter for

millennia," she said with something like pride in her voice. But that made no sense. Why would someone who was pro-Commonwealth be running from enforcers?

"No one comes down here anymore," he said as he resumed walking.

"Because of the monsters," Keani said.

"No, not because of the monsters," Elyot said, annoyed.

"There *are* monsters," Keani insisted. "What do you think made this tunnel?"

"Oh, interesting," Alextra said, brushing her fingertips over the scalloped wall once again. "A biological process? Tunneling through stone? That would explain that bile smell in the air, I guess."

"Not because of monsters," Elyot said again. "Our ancestors stored their dead here, but we don't do that anymore. One by one the gates rusted shut from disuse, the maps were lost, the smaller entrances forgotten."

"But if these tunnels are the work of subterranean creatures, why haven't we encountered any?" Alextra wondered.

"I'm glad we haven't," Elyot said with a shudder. "Imagine the size of the thing that could make this. Where would we go to get out of its way?"

Alextra peeked into another alcove. They were deeper now, among the dead from the early days of the city when corpses had been preserved, not burned. Elyot wished Alextra hadn't illuminated that alcove, lighting up the slightly waxy faces of a family of five laying side by side, hands folded on their bellies as if in sleep.

"They're all around us," Keani said in a whisper so faint she could barely be heard.

"The oldest citizens," Alextra said, whispering as well. "We must be in the oldest tunnels then. The center of the maze, maybe."

The voices behind them didn't seem to be drawing any closer, although it was hard to tell with the strange way things echoed through the tunnels. Perhaps not closer, but Elyot was certain they were more numerous. It sounded to him like every enforcer in the city was now in the catacombs, searching for them.

That seemed like an excessive use of force to catch him, even if they had his mother, even if she had done something truly terrible and they thought he was involved. Keani in her tattered clothes clutching a paring knife didn't look like a threat worthy of that response either. From the state of her hands, she had been up to something before she stepped into the tavern, but surely not so great a crime as all that.

Which left only Alextra. Alextra with her fine clothes and strange weapon.

"Who are you?" Elyot asked her, surprising himself to hear his thoughts out loud.

"What do you mean?" Alextra asked, unperturbed.

"I thought they were after all of us, but maybe it's just you?"

Keani's eyes widened as if that thought hadn't struck her.

"Are you hoping to take me hostage? Exchange me for your own freedom?" she asked, resting a hand oh so casually on her weapon.

"No," Elyot said.

"They might take that deal," Alextra said. "That Ward fellow has worked out who I am, I'm sure. Only he doesn't seem like he makes deals. Wouldn't be right, not for an officer with his responsibilities."

"What is that?" Keani asked. At first, Elyot was puzzled by the terror in her voice. Then he realized she wasn't referring to what Alextra had just been saying.

Something was moving through the depths. Something massive, slithering and slopping and moaning as if movement was all too fatiguing.

"That's the other option," Alextra said. "It's the enforcers or that. Personally, I vote for that."

"But what is it really?" Elyot asked. "There are a hundred children stories about what lurks in the catacombs, no two the same. But they're all really, really horrid." He shuddered. Some childhood nightmares never went away.

"Maybe," Alextra said with a little uplift to the corner of her mouth. "But better that than enforcers. Plus now I'm just curious to see what it is. Aren't you?"

Keani merely gaped at her as if her mind couldn't even process such a thought.

But Elyot was kind of curious too. "Let's keep going," he said. Alextra gave him a nod then looked to Keani.

"Are you with us?" she asked.

Keani clutched her knife as her face went through another cascade of facial expressions. She ended with her eyes screwed tightly shut, but she gave a curt nod.

As they continued on the alcoves grew fewer and fewer, mainly because there were so many cross tunnels there was nowhere left to dig such a space. Tunnels spun through in all directions, directly overhead or shooting out from the floor beneath them. The stone was so carved up there didn't seem to be enough remaining to hold up the mountain.

Then their tunnel ended, the ground falling away in front of them in a slope too steep to walk on, with no side path to take around it.

"Dead end," Alextra said, holding her crystal as high over her head as she could. It did little to illuminate the vast space before them.

"It's a cavern," Elyot said. "There are probably a million other tunnels coming out from here."

"The heart of the mountain," Keani said. "In our stories, we call it the maw."

"The maw, I've heard that one too. But it doesn't make any sense. How can the center of a thing be a mouth?" Elyot said. But then he wondered what she meant by 'our' stories. Who was she talking about?

He was about to ask her when Alextra suddenly said, "look!"

Elyot didn't know what he was looking at. At first, he thought the floor itself was moving, but the reflections of Alextra's light being thrown back didn't look like they were coming from stone. Perhaps a subterranean pool? Inky water, perhaps even fouler than the water in the well…

Then something clicked in his brain, and he realized what he was looking at. It was rather like a sea, but a sea of writhing creatures, not water. Blobby creatures who threw out long, dripping tentacles to catch hold of rock protrusions or other blobby creatures. They used those tentacles to pull their central mass across the sandy floor of the cavern, but slowly, as if they found themselves too heavy, the muscles in their tentacles too puny.

"What are they?" Alextra asked. She was still whispering, but the tone to her voice was pure wonder. "Are they aware of us up here? I don't see any ears or eyes on them, but they're pretty far away."

Elyot squinted down at the things. They were all on the move, but to where and for what reason he didn't have a clue.

"Oh!" Keani cried, falling against Elyot as she stumbled back from the cliff edge. Elyot had been certain they had been standing on solid stone, but the crumbling edge told a different story.

"Fascinating," Alextra said, picking up a large chunk before it could roll away down the steep slope. "Look, tiny tunnels, all the way through it. Probably through all of it right under our feet. Those little fellows below are too little to form the tunnel we're standing in, but some of those side tunnels are about their size. And when they were littler still - when they were hatchlings - I bet they could manage these."

"Um, Alextra?" Elyot said. Keani was gripping his arm almost too tightly, but Alextra was still examining the chunk of rock with the light of her crystal. "Alextra! They're coming this way!" he hissed, finally getting her attention.

She turned to follow Elyot's gaze down the slope. The blobby things below were now all moving in the same direction, making more of an effort to find solid holds for their tentacles and not yanking on each other.

Yes, they were definitely all working together for a common cause, and that cause was getting up to the tunnel where the three of them stood more or less helpless.

Then they heard the voices again, just as numerous as before but this time there was no question they were getting closer. It probably didn't even matter which tunnel they followed. Eventually, they all led to this chamber in the heart of the mountain.

"We have to get out of here," Elyot said, scanning the darkness around them. It was impossible even to say how large the space actually was. Judging from the way the sounds echoed, it was many times larger than the circle of illumination Alextra's crystal was capable of.

The blobs were making good progress up the steep slope. They looked awkward pulling their weight across the ground and were no less awkward climbing up the walls.

But they were no more awkward either.

One of the voices behind them was close enough for them to make out the words, "this way." Koltn Ward. And he wasn't shouting.

"I don't know if we should try fighting them," Alextra said, peering down the slope with one hand on her tanjo.

"The enforcers?" Elyot asked.

"No, those blobby things, They work as a group. They might swarm. Attacking just one might be very, very stupid."

"There's too many anyway," Elyot said. "You have your tango thing, but Keani only has the one knife left, and I don't have anything at all. Is there another way out?"

"I can find one," Keani said, eying the wall.

"I don't doubt you can," Alextra said, "but will we be able to follow you?"

"We can take it slow," Elyot said. "Look, the wall along this way is sheer near the bottom, but more jagged closer to the ceiling." He took hold of Alextra's wrist to guide her light, and she nodded.

"There must be a way across there," she said. "There are so many tunnels; there must be another entrance close by. I just hope their tentacles can't adhere to bare rock."

"Follow me," Keani said, then stuck the knife between her teeth and tossed her cloak back over her shoulders. She didn't even seem to look for handholds; they were just there when she reached out for them. She moved across the wall faster than Elyot could crawl on the ground.

He hoped it was at least half as easy as she made it look.

Alextra gestured for him to go next then stood guard, shifting her gaze from up the tunnel to down the cliff slope and back, her hand never leaving the handle of her tanjo. Elyot picked his way for several meters before looking back. The curvature of the wall bringing him around so that he could see further into the tunnel mouth behind Alextra. There were lights, silvery like her crystal but far more numerous.

"Alextra!" he hissed. "Come on!"

"Keep going!" she said, then put the crystal between her teeth before starting her own climb.

There was scarcely any light, but holds were plentiful enough that if he groped around, he could find one without having to see it. The footholds were wide enough for him to keep most of his weight in his legs or else he would be tiring by now, he was sure.

He couldn't see Keani ahead of him, but he could hear her little grunts of breath and the swish of her cloak against the stone. Then she gave a louder grunt, and he heard her land on two feet. She had found a tunnel mouth or at least a wider ledge.

"I need more light," she hissed back to Elyot. Elyot looked back behind him. Alextra's black clothing blended with the darkness, but the light from the crystal gripped in her mouth glowed through her silver hair. The way it swung and danced as she climbed when no other part of her could be seen was surreal, like a silk scarf caught in a wind.

She was moving along faster than Elyot; she would be on top of him in a moment. He turned his attention back to his own climbing until he reached a point where no amount of groping was finding the next hold.

"Just jump," Keani whispered to him. "Hurry, I can see boots coming."

Elyot couldn't see a thing. He mustered the last of his strength and flung himself away from the wall, towards the direction of Keani's voice.

His toes landed on solid stone, but his heels came down on nothing but air. He pitched his weight forward, and Keani caught at his arms, hauling him further into the dark, away from the ledge.

"Don't crumble it or they'll be on us!" she hissed.

"I can't see a thing," Elyot grumbled. Keani just moved him to one side so she could be there to catch Alextra as she landed.

"Did you drop the light?" Elyot asked. He could see their shadows moving, but he couldn't even discern a definite outline to their forms. Then he saw Alextra's face lit up in silver. Only for a moment, then she closed her mouth over the crystal again. "You can see without it?" he asked Keani.

"A little," she said. "There is a little bit of light coming in from somewhere."

"Can you see another way out?" he asked.

"Not a tunnel," she said, but before she could say more, they were all bathed in silvery light. The enforcers had larger, more powerful crystals than Alextra was hiding in her mouth. The light was quickly followed by a volley of needles, and the three of them dropped to the ground.

"This way!" Keani said, crawling on her belly to the back of the ledge where partially formed stalagmites offered some shelter.

One of the enforcers gave a yelp of alarm, and the shower of needles lessened. Elyot risked a peek around the side of his stalagmite. The enforcers had finally seen the blobby things, who were renewing their quest to climb the slope.

"Hold your fire!" Koltn Ward commanded. He was talking to two of the enforcers who had been taking aim at the blobs, but all of them stopped firing, and the rain of needles stopped. "We don't know what these things are or what their defenses are. Hold your fire while I call this in."

He stepped back from the ledge, comm in hand. The enforcers were disciplined. They kept their guns down but at the ready even as their heads swiveled everywhere, scanning the cavern. Their lights lit up a good sphere of space around them, but everything outside of that sphere was in deeper shadow than before.

For a moment all that could be heard was the low murmur of Koltn Ward's voice and the constant slurping, squishing sound of the blobs pulling themselves over well-worn stone.

Then the air was rent with screams. One of the enforcers was stumbling back from the edge, still screaming even as he fired a continuous stream of needles at a solitary blobby creature who had crested the edge. The blob cried piteously as it fell back, peppered with needles. Then it dangled there for a moment, a single tentacle still wrapped around the enforcer's ankle. The enforcer fell back on the ground, but his companions helped free him from its grasp.

The thing was quite dead as it fell to the bottom of the cavern, but the enforcer was still screaming. His boot was smoking, and there was a smell of burning flesh so strong it carried all the way to the threesome.

"Sedate him!" Koltn Ward barked, and one of the other enforcers pulled something from a belt pouch and pressed it to the injured man's neck.

The screams stopped, but the cavern was far from silent. The blobs were making a sound like a humming growl. Their earlier climb up the slope had been slow but steady, as if they had only been looking to satisfy a curiosity. Now they climbed in real earnest, and the enforcers gave shrieks of alarm as dozens of tentacles reached out for them.

The injured man's leg was still smoking. It looked like whatever substance had coated that tentacle was eating through his boot into his flesh, and it wasn't stopping.

"Permission to fire, sir?" one of the enforcers asked as several of the others started scrambling up the wall that the threesome had just scaled to get out of reach of those tentacles.

Koltn Ward looked at his silent comm and scowled. He gave a curt nod, and the enforcers started firing. Needles hissed through the air, barely audible over the pained cries of the blobs.

"We should get out of here," Elyot said to the others. "Now, while they're distracted."

"There are no tunnels on this side," Keani said. "The closest one is over there, but if we try to make a run for it, those enforcers are going to see us. I'm not sure they're distracted enough for us to make it so far."

"We can't stay here," Elyot said. "Those blobs don't stand a chance. Our only hope is that they run out of ammo, but even still they outnumber us by quite a bit."

"Their tentacles secrete an acid," Alextra said, stroking the stone floor beneath her. It had the same scalloped patterns as the tunnels.

"Knowing that doesn't help us," Elyot said.

"These blobs are too little to have carved all this," Alextra went on as if she hadn't heard him. "Something bigger did this."

"How much bigger?" Elyot asked.

A low rumbling sound echoed through the cavern all around them as if in reply to his question. Then they heard that slithering sound again, but it wasn't coming from a hundred little blobs. This was coming from one massive blob, pulling itself along a tunnel they couldn't see.

"Where is it?" Elyot asked. Keani was on her feet, oblivious to the risk of another needle attack as she crept closer to the ledge and peered down into the cavern. "Can you see it?"

She must have seen something from the way she jumped away from the edge, tripping over a protrusion of rock and landing sprawled on her back. Elyot half-rose to help her but then froze as several tentacles jutted up into the air in the center of the cavern. They were immense, too wide around for a human's arms to reach, long enough to stretch from beneath the floor to the ceiling far above. They wrapped around the thickest of the stalactites. Elyot could see the muscles inside them tighten and contract. The stone beneath their grasp was smoking, great thick clouds that made his eyes water even from that distance.

He supposed the thing emerging from the well hidden in the center of the cavern was a blob thing like the others, but that's not what he saw emerging from the ground. No, all that was visible of the creature with the immense tentacles was its gaping maw. Within that maw, there was nothing but glistening darkness.

Elyot flopped down flat on his belly. He fought the urge to cover his head with his hands as if he could somehow hide from that thing. Instead, he reached out and took Keani's hand. She laid as paralyzed as he, but she squeezed his hand back. Now they both knew why the oldest of the stories called the heart of the mountain a maw.

The gaping maw pivoted as if the creature could perceive the world around it through its open mouth. It passed over the three of them without pausing, but it stopped when it was facing the opposite ledge.

The enforcers held their ground, needlers trained on the beast but waiting for Koltn Ward's order. Koltn Ward looked completely unbothered by the massive thing looming up at them, just whispered a few more words into his comm.

For a long moment, no one moved.

Then one of the little blobs began crying in earnest, and a few others joined it. The maw turned its focus on to them, and Elyot finally got a glimpse of the blob that contained that maw. He didn't know what it was - skin or fur or scales or something else -only that his gaze kept trying to slip past it, to not see it at all.

Then three more tentacles emerged from beneath it, reaching for stalactites closer to the ledge where the enforcers stood. They grasped tightly, a new cloud of noxious gas rolled down to engulf the ledge, and the tentacle muscles contracted.

The blob was the size of a large house. It took a lot of effort to move that mass around. One of the stalactites snapped and the thing's girth started sliding back, but the tentacle quickly found another hold. Then, with a groan that rumbled the entire cavern, perhaps even the entire mountain, the thing was out of its hole, rolling up towards the enforcers.

"There's our way out!" Alextra cried. She was on her feet standing over Elyot and Keani, but she was pointing down to the floor of the cavern, to the very hole that thing had just emerged from.

There was light coming from that hole. And not the silvery light of the crystals. This was real light, the dark red glow of the setting sun.

"Are you insane?" Elyot cried. "That thing is going back down there at some point. It'll crush us for sure."

"Not if we're fast," Alextra said.

Another stalactite snapped, and the creature fell partially over its own hole again before gaining a new hold.

"That's going to keep happening," Keani said.

"We'll have to be very fast," Alextra said grimly. "It's that or wandering this maze of tunnels until we die. Or getting back up to the city and getting arrested the moment we emerge, because you know they'll be watching all the gateways, waiting for us."

"There are worse things than being arrested," Elyot said, looking at the creature that was pulling itself ever closer to the enforcers.

"And there are better things," Alextra said. "That's sunlight, direct light from the setting sun. That's a way out that isn't inside the city walls. That's freedom. And those enforcers are so occupied at the moment we stand pretty good odds of them not even knowing where we went."

Elyot looked at that patch of light, that inviting patch of light. If he followed it, he'd be in a whole other world. He had never been outside of the city before. Living inside of such high walls, he'd only seen the setting sun a handful of times in his life.

At some point, whether at Koltn Ward's order or not, the enforcers had started firing on the creature. Elyot could hear the whir of needles through the air, the soft thunks as they hit flesh somewhere deep within the maw itself. The creature made no sounds of pain, and it never stopped its slow climb up the slope.

"They aren't going to stop it," Keani said. "And after it's eaten them, what's to stop it coming for us?"

"You want to go down that hole too?" Elyot asked.

"Not really," Keani said. Then she mustered a very wavering grin. "But I really don't want to stay here."

"Further down this edge there's a sloped bit like a rock slide," Alextra said. "It'll take us to the floor of the cavern. Then we run."

If there were a quieter way to get down from the ledge, they didn't have time to find it. The three of them ran down the steep slide until the loose rock beneath them made that impossible. Alextra stayed on her feet, riding the rock slide down to the bottom then transitioning smoothly into a sprint. Keani and Elyot were not quite so agile, sliding down on the seats of their pants. Keani somersaulted forward and leaped to her feet to follow Alextra. Elyot had to wait until he had stopped sliding to get up. But he was clearly the fastest sprinter of the three, quickly making up the lost time so that they reached the edge of the hole together.

The air at the bottom of the cavern was a nearly unbreathable mix of rock-eating acid clouds, dying blob creatures, and what Elyot would have to guess was the normal funk of these creatures that spent all their time in a tangled pile of tentacles and flesh. But as bad as that was, the smell wafting up from the hole was far, far worse.

"I don't think we can do this," Elyot said, fighting the urge to gag. Alextra looked back at him, and he saw she had zipped up the collar of her cape so that it covered her face up to her cheekbones. For all he knew, she had some sort of breathing filter in there.

Keani tugged at his sleeve and then handed him a strip of cloth she had torn from the end of her own cloak. He took it and watched as she tied another over her own mouth and nose. He quickly did the same.

It didn't help much, especially not with the constant watering of his eyes that was so severe it was blurring his vision.

"Best not to hang around," Alextra said, although whether she was referring to the smell or to the creature whose entire mass was hovering just over their heads, he wasn't sure.

They couldn't see the ledge with the enforcers from where they were, but they could hear the shouting of voices followed by a weak cheer.

"Reinforcements?" Elyot guessed.

"How is that going to help them?" Keani said. "This thing can take a million needles."

"They'll have something bigger," Alextra guessed.

"Bigger, like what?" Elyot asked.

"At a guess? Plasma gun," Alextra said.

"Plasma gun?" Elyot said. "That's a ship's weapon. How would they get one down here?"

Alextra was about to answer when a sudden flash of intense light lit even the farthest corners of the cavern.

The sound of the weapon firing was surprisingly soft, just a sizzling burst of energy.

But the sound of the creature's bellow of rage nearly burst Elyot's eardrums.

"Plasma gun," Alextra said again the moment she could be heard. "The next time they fire at this thing, it's going to crush us. We need to get down this hole now."

The bulbous body over them was already quaking as it deployed its tentacles, to good effect to judge by the renewed screaming from the enforcers. The smaller blobs, the ones that were still intact, rushed to the cliff edge to catch the bodies of the falling enforcers. The bodies were spattered with the large one's tentacle acid, the enforcers either dead already or in shock. But the swarms of blobs released more acid, and the air became sickeningly thicker.

Keani tugged Elyot's sleeve again, and he saw that Alextra was already several meters down the hole. It was an easy climb, the walls of the well-like depression lined with alcoves, the alcoves filled with carefully arranged corpses. His very oldest ancestors, he assumed.

Alextra, descending with perhaps too much speed, nearly stepped on the foot of one of them. Elyot watched as the leg she had kicked away broke off at the knee and tumbled end over end, through the dying light of the sun stabbing into the well from a narrow tunnel and past it into darkness too deep for his eyes to penetrate.

With the noise of battle all around him it was no wonder he never heard the leg hit bottom, and yet he couldn't shake the feeling that the reason why was actually because the hole had no bottom.

"Elyot, come on!" Alextra called up to him. She was standing already at the mouth of the sunlit tunnel, and Keani was halfway down to her. Elyot slipped over the edge, his feet finding the first alcove. Then he looked up towards the ledge one last time.

The creature was pivoting around to one side, to avoid the fire from the plasma gun presumably. Elyot had a brief glimpse of Koltn Ward standing with his needler in his hand, his uniform smoking from a fine spray of acid Elyot guessed came from standing too close to one of the enforcers who was hit by the tentacles.

Then, as if feeling his gaze, Koltn Ward looked down and saw Elyot. He extended his arm, aiming the needler at Elyot. Elyot ducked down into the highest of the alcoves. He could hear the clatter of needles striking the stone above him, falling to the ground when they failed to penetrate.

Elyot cursed himself for being a fool. Their hope of the enforcers not knowing where they had escaped to was now gone. And it was all his fault.

He was halfway down the hole when the beast gave a bellow of rage. The bellow was followed by the sound of rock falling. A lot of rock. Nothing was falling down the hole, though, and Elyot guessed the ledge the enforcers had been standing on was now a thing of the past.

Somehow, he didn't think the monster was going to spend much time gloating over its victory. But Elyot didn't dare try climbing any faster. His arms were starting to tremble from the strain. His risk of falling was growing by the second.

"Here!" Keani cried, and Elyot realized that in his focus on not letting his hands or feet slip he had nearly climbed straight past the tunnel. He took her outstretched hand and let her help him into the tunnel.

Or, perhaps more properly, the chasm. This was no human-made space within the rock of the mountain, and it hadn't been tunneled by acid-bearing tentacles either. It was just a jagged space formed when one mass of stone settled further than another and left a gap.

The sun was nearly gone now, the last bloodred rays bathing Alextra as she stood on the ledge looking out onto the side of the mountain then up into the sky. Keani brushed past Elyot's side to stand next to her.

"We can climb up pretty easily," Keani said, tracing a route with one extended hand.

"No, not up," Alextra said. "They will have extra guards on the walls, maybe even climbing teams searching."

"For all they know, that thing killed us," Keani said. "Why would they still be looking for us?"

"Koltn Ward saw me," Elyot said. "He saw me going down the hole. He might have been killed in that rock slide, but I don't think I want to bet on it."

"Climbing teams could be anywhere then, up or down," Keani said.

"Shuttles too," Alextra said, pointing at the sky. A swarm of white dots was spilling out of the underbelly of one of the cruisers, spreading out into a formation that looked like shining knots in an invisible net.

"They'll see us no matter where we go," Keani insisted.

"The forest is closer," Alextra said. "We'd be under the cover of trees for half of the climb that way. The way to the city is nothing but bare rock."

"Maybe we should wait," Keani said.

"I don't want to wait," Elyot said. "The air is better here, but my mouth is still coated with the foul taste of that well water. It's killing my appetite, but I'm getting more than a little thirsty."

"I'm thirsty as well," Alextra said, although she seemed unbothered. "That's a lush forest. There must be a lot of water down there."

"It's not a forest," Keani said. "It's a jungle."

"Okay," Alextra agreed, dropping to a knee to examine the rocks below them more closely. Picking out a path.

"It's the Jungle of a Thousand Easy Deaths," Keani said.

Alextra looked up at Keani to see if she was serious. Then she looked at Elyot. Elyot gave a little nod.

"That's what some call it," he admitted.

"And it's a lie," Keani said darkly. "There are a lot more than a thousand ways to die down there."

"Forewarned is forearmed," Alextra said, rising back up and dusting off her palms. "Look, that's where I'm going next. I appreciate the escape route out of the burning tavern, and I wouldn't have wanted to face those tunnels alone if I could help it, but there's really no reason to keep sticking together. Not if our paths go in different directions."

Keani fumed but said nothing.

Elyot leaned past Alextra to look up and down the mountain. "I've never been out of the city before," he said. "But there's nothing up there for me anymore. There hasn't been for a long time. I guess I just needed a reason to get moving, to leave. I'll go into the jungle with you."

"Good," Alextra said. "I guess this is where we part ways, then, Keani. I do hope we meet again. I'd love to treat you to a proper cup of chai makhani."

Keani nodded. She was biting down on her lip as if afraid what would come out of her mouth if she released it.

"You're really not coming with us?" Elyot asked as Alextra started the climb down to the jungle. "I don't know what could possibly be down there that is worse than what we just faced."

"I just can't," Keani said. Her eyes were pleading with him to change his mind, but she didn't say the words out loud.

"I understand," he said. "Good luck."

"You too," she said, and they shook hands.

After climbing in the total darkness of the heart of the mountain, even the last dying rays of the sun seemed more than enough to light his way. He looked down from time to time to gauge his distance to Alextra. He guessed she was taking her time, perhaps for his sake.

Only when he saw she had reached the tops of the trees that grew closest to the mountain did he spare a glance back up towards the city.

The shuttles were flying lower now in a search formation that fortunately for them started at the city walls before working its way down. He'd be under the canopy in time.

Then he saw a flash of motion closer to him. He froze, squinting hard to make out details in what was becoming more starlight than sunset. But the sway of that cloak was a familiar motion.

Keani. She was coming down. It had taken her some time to work up the nerve, but she was coming down. If he hadn't needed both arms for climbing, he would have been thrusting a fist into the air in victory.

They had slipped past the maw at the center of the maze, a creature that had appeared in various forms in all of his nightmares as a kid. The three of them together, they were unstoppable. What could the Jungle of a Thousand Deaths possibly do to them?

3 THE JUNGLE OF A THOUSAND
EASY DEATHS

ELYOT'S ARMS and legs were trembling with the effort to keep climbing down the steep side of the mountain. Sweat from his brow pooled at the corners of his mouth. As much as he tried, he couldn't get enough breath through his nose, and when he opened his mouth, those drops of sweat would coat his tongue. The saltiness of it made him all too aware of just how thirsty he was.

The dehydration was making his muscles ache, a different kind of ache than the constant climbing. Until that day, he had no idea it was possible to be so tired that you just hurt.

His fingertips slipped over a handhold, sending scurries of pebbles raining down in mini-avalanches he could only hope weren't hitting Alextra beneath him.

She had disappeared from his sight entirely the moment she had passed the treeline. The sun was nearly gone from the sky, and he didn't know how they were going to keep moving through the jungle in the full dark of night.

He didn't know lots of things, now that he had left the city that had been his entire world since he was born.

But he was a fast learner.

The soft hum of a shuttle engine he had been tuning out started growing louder, but the way it echoed off of the rocks around him, he couldn't tell from which direction it was coming. He looked up at the purple sky and could just make out the outline of Keani almost on top of him. She saw him looking up and waved for him to get moving.

Darkness closed around him with such suddenness he was afraid he was blacking out from exhaustion. Then something brushed up his back, catching on his jacket and scratching a long welt up his bare spine.

He had reached the trees. But the tree branches weren't the soft, willowy limbs he was used to from the city parks. They had thorns. Wickedly long thorns, he amended as one slipped up his pant's leg to stab at the back of his knee.

And barbed, he amended again as a dozen bristles gouged his cheek.

If only he could see anything at all.

But if he had learned anything during his time in the catacombs under the city, it was how to climb by touch alone.

"Elyot!" Alextra hissed up at him. He paused to look down and just caught a glimpse of her pale, sweat-sheened face turned up to him. "Just drop from there. It's a soft landing."

He couldn't make out the details of her face, and he was sure she was still pretty far below him, but he decided to take her at her word. He angled his body as far as he could away from the cliff and looked down again to be sure there were no outcroppings between him and Alextra's moon-like face.

He heard something above him, a sharp hiss of alarm or pain, but he had already let go of the cliff.

The sudden escape from tension in his arms and legs filled his body with a warm, blissful glow. He had just enough time to process that this fall was taking really too long when his feet hit something like a hard mattress. His knees buckled, and he toppled forward, his outstretched hands pressing into the same almost squishy surface.

Squishy, but still gritty under his palms, like it was covered in fine sand.

Then his palms and legs began to sink into the ground.

"It's all right," Alextra told him, helping him stand up. The ground sucked at his hands, but not so much he couldn't get them free.

"I'm sinking," Elyot said, trying to lift his feet. But there was nowhere to step up to.

"Don't panic," she said, still at a whisper despite the meters between them and the treetops, and the thousands of meters more between those and the shuttles searching for them. "It's just quicksand. You'll sink to your waist, but that's it."

"Why did you tell me to drop if you knew this was here?" he asked.

"Because it really isn't a problem," she said. She was searching through the pouches on her belt. He could see her lips moving in the dim light as if she were whispering an inventory to herself.

"Keani should be coming down by now," Elyot said, staring up at the outline of the tree branches against the darkening sky.

"Oh, she came with us after all?" Alextra said, still searching through her things. "That's good."

"I think she was saying something before I dropped," he said. "Maybe she had just reached the trees."

"Lovely welcome that was, right?" Alextra said.

Elyot gave up on looking for Keani and turned his attention to his own situation. He was encased in the sand that was something between liquid and solid, pressing in on him from all sides like a compression suit, but true to Alextra's word he had stopped sinking when it had reached the level of his waist.

"I don't feel a bottom," he said. "Do you?"

"Who knows how deep this is?" Alextra said. "We stopped here because of buoyancy."

Elyot didn't quite understand what she was saying. "How do we get out?"

"You idiots!" a voice hissed above them.

"Keani?" Elyot called back, still not able to make her out.

"You're lucky I'm not Koltn Ward," she said. "I could pick you off pretty easily, stuck as you are. Fools. Why didn't you stop when I told you to?"

"I didn't hear you," Elyot said.

"I'll have us out in a moment," Alextra said calmly. She had something in her hands, metal to judge from the occasional flashes of reflected light as she manipulated it in her hands. Folded up for storage, Elyot guessed, but what was it?

"You're running out of time," Keani said. Her voice had moved further from the cliffside, and Elyot realized she was in the treetops overhead.

"We stopped sinking," Elyot said.

"That's not the danger," Keani said. There was a rustle of branches interrupted by a sharp inhalation as if from pain.

"I know how to deal with quicksand," Alextra said. She lifted whatever was in her hands up towards the trees. There was a soft pop as she fired it, then an even softer whistle before her projectile thunked home in a tree trunk.

"That isn't quicksand!" Keani said. "Elyot, grab this vine."

Elyot heard something land on the ground just out of his reach. He tried to stretch towards it, but the ground around him compressed him tighter.

"Too far," he said.

There was a whirring sound like a line retracting. Alextra's arms were fully extended over her, and she was stretching up and up, but when she started to groan, he knew she too was being hugged tighter.

"I'm too late," Keani said. "You're goners."

"What is this thing?" Elyot asked and tried to reach the vine again.

"I don't know what it's called," Keani said. "But I can tell you it's alive and it's about to eat you."

"How?" Elyot asked, looking around for a mouth part. Alextra's groans were building as the mechanism she was holding continued to try to pull her out of the… thing. "Where's the mouth?"

"No mouth," Keani said. "Just stomach and you're in it."

"It doesn't feel like anything," Elyot said. "It only squeezes when I move. Wouldn't digesting me burn like acid?"

"It will," Keani said. It sounded like she was doing something at the same time, her breath coming short. "It needs you in pieces first."

"In pieces? When it has no teeth?" Elyot asked.

"Here come the 'teeth,'" Keani said grimly.

It was too dark to see. Elyot desperately hoped that the loss of that sense was why the skittering sounded so loud in his ears.

"They'll tear you to pieces for it," Keani said. "Then it will digest you."

Elyot flailed towards the place he had heard the vine fall, but it was no good.

"I'm lowering this one slowly," Keani said, her voice directly overhead now. "It's a loop. Wrap it around you, and I'll help you pull up."

"It's not letting me go," Elyot said.

"Elyot," Alextra said between gritted teeth. "Can you reach my tanjo?"

"I think so," Elyot said. He reached out, and his fingertips just brushed her cape.

"I can't let go of this thing, or I'll lose it," she said as she tried to twist her body closer to him. "You have to get that vine around you, then take my tanjo and stab it into this creature."

"Is it even going to hurt it?" Elyot asked. Something brushed the top of his head, and he started to scream, visions of skittering things swarming all over him while he was pinned tormenting him, but it was only the vine. "I don't know how to use your tanjo," he added as he looped the vine under his arms.

Alextra stopped twisting and hung still for a moment, then gave a soft cry of pain. "It's in blade mode now," she said and twisted toward him again.

Elyot reached out again. He felt the soft wood of the tanjo handle, but only with the very tip of his longest finger.

It was hopeless. The thing that wasn't quicksand was squeezing him so tightly he could feel the blood pooling in his abdomen, unable to reach his legs. The skittering was all around him, close enough now for him to be able to see chitinous limbs reflecting the growing starlight as they kicked up the sand.

He was going to die.

He screamed something more like frustrated rage than a battle cry and touched a fingertip to the tanjo handle again.

This time it seemed to leap away from Alextra's thigh, jumping out of the sand thing to nestle in his palm. For a dangerous moment, he stared in fascination at the dark light that was its blade. He had never seen anything like it before Alextra had wielded it in the tavern.

But he forced his mind to turn from it, raising the weapon above his head.

The first of the skittering things was on him now, climbing up his jacket. He could hear the clicking of their mandibles.

Then he brought the dark blade down with all the strength he had to muster. Fear gave him more of that than he would have thought he had left after all the running and climbing.

The ground beneath him rumbled, dislodging the skittering creatures. The sudden rush of blood back into his legs was the worst pins and needles he had ever had.

But he was up in the air now, his feet dangling freely. Keani's body collided with his. She caught hold of his jacket, giving him a little shake.

"Don't drop my tanjo!" Alextra commanded. Elyot looked down and saw his nerveless fingers about to let the weapon slide from their grip.

He clutched it tightly, then gave Keani a sharp nod to let her know he was okay. Keani was hanging from a vine herself, and as he looked up, he realized she was holding the ends of the vine looped around his own body. She had jumped out of the tree to use her body weight to pull him up.

"Thanks," he said.

"Don't mention it," Keani said. "Alextra?"

"Here," Alextra called. She was sitting on a branch close to a tree trunk, using another tool to remove the projectile she had fired. The device had retracted the length of the line and rested on the branch beside her.

"You climb first," Keani said to Elyot. "We're hanging from one of the wider branches. That's going to have to be camp for the night."

"How can we camp in a tree?" he asked as he tried to climb with the tanjo in his hand.

"Throw it to me," Alextra said. Elyot was afraid he would miss, and they'd lose the weapon, but Alextra had a way of giving commands that strongly suggested that arguments were unwelcome.

He tossed it. She had to grasp a branch with one hand and swing out wide over the sand thing below to catch it, but she didn't complain about his lousy throwing.

Maybe her arms were shaking too.

"We should keep moving," Alextra said as she stowed both the tanjo and the other device.

"Not at night," Keani said. Elyot just focused on climbing the vine then getting up onto the tree branch. Keani had said it was the widest, but it wasn't all that wide.

"They're still looking for us," Alextra said. "They won't rely on just the shuttles. They'll send enforcers down here. Lots of them."

"I understand that," Keani said, "but only a fool tries to move through the jungle after dark."

"I'm not a fool," Alextra said with an edge to her voice.

"And hence you're not objecting to making camp," Keani said. She pulled herself up the vine and swung around the branch with ridiculous ease. Then she started to pull up the vine.

"Here in the tree?" Elyot asked.

"It's not ideal, but if you'll recall I did vote for not going this way," Keani said. She sawed at the sticky fibers of the vine with the knife she had taken from the tavern. At last, she had it in two pieces and passed one to Elyot. "Tie yourself to the branch with that. Tightly; you don't want to wake up back in that thing. Particularly not if you fall face-first."

"Why are we sleeping here?" Alextra asked, swinging over to their branch. "We should keep moving. These trees are close enough together."

"They are," Keani agreed, still knotting the vine around her legs. "And they're safer than the ground."

"So let's go then," Alextra said.

"Safer," Keani stressed, "doesn't mean safe. We wait until morning. Then we move through the treetops. For now, this is the safest place to be."

"With that thing down there?" Elyot asked.

"Exactly," Keani said.

Alextra still looked skeptical. Elyot pulled the ends of his vine as tightly as he could. Which still didn't seem like enough to keep him in the tree.

"Why are we trusting you?" she asked.

"Beats me," Keani said, leaning back against the trunk behind her and closing her eyes.

"You're not going to tell us how you know what you claim to know?"

"Nope," Keani said, snuggling into her cloak.

"She was right about that thing," Elyot said. When Alextra didn't respond, he added, "and you haven't explained about you either."

"Or you about you," she said.

"Me?" Elyot said, checking the knot one last time. "I'm just a kid from that city up there, lately an orphan, occasionally an employee of the tavern you helped burn down. I don't have any deeper layers."

"Everyone has deeper layers," Alextra said but pulled herself up to a higher branch before anyone could say anything further.

But she didn't leave. As eager as she was to go, and as suspicious as she was of Keani, she still settled herself on her branch and tied herself in place.

Elyot didn't know about the other two, but he didn't sleep a wink that night. He could hear the sand thing below him making a sound that was either escaping gas or a soft moan of pain from the stabbing. He could hear the skittering things moving in fits and starts. That happened often enough for him to get a sense of the ring shape of their stomping grounds around the sand creature.

He could hear the now-louder, now-softer hum of the shuttle engines, still making sweeps over the treetops and around the mountain. They weren't burning all that fuel and enforcer time on the clock on his account.

But the worst was the sound he tried desperately to chalk up to a half-dream: something massive moving through the jungle. It wasn't close, but the sound of tree trunks snapping before it made Elyot's blood turn cold.

At last, the world around him began to change from black to an ever brightening gray. He could see the branches of the tree around him, each ending in an array of leaves and needle-sharp thorns as long as his arm. But they had acquired a glistening of dew and Elyot slipped his arms out of the vine to pull a wide leaf to his mouth. It only held a few drops, but he licked up every bit of moisture before reaching for another.

Alextra landed on the branch between him and Keani, her feet in their soft boots making not a sound. She put a small disk in his hand. "Put it in your mouth and let it melt on your tongue," she said.

She turned to give another to Keani. Elyot looked at the thing nestled in his filthy palm. It didn't look like food. If he had to guess, he would have said it was some sort of battery. But Alextra saw him still regarding it and gave him an encouraging gesture.

He set it on his tongue and closed his mouth. He expected a metallic taste, but it had no taste at all. It just sat there, cold and smooth.

"Think of something you like," Alextra said. "What do you really wish you could have to eat right now? Don't speak; just think."

Elyot didn't even have to ponder. He imagined the warmth of a mug of chai makhani in his hands, the sharp smell of its spices, the oil slick surface from the melted butter.

All at once, the disk on his tongue melted, and his mouth was filled with a cloyingly sweet, oily taste that took several swallows to pass.

Elyot reached for another leaf to wash it down. "That didn't taste anything like chai makhani."

"It wasn't supposed to," Alextra said. "You just needed to get some saliva going to activate it."

"You could have warned me about the taste," Elyot said. He saw Keani grimacing as well, wiping the surface of her tongue with a leaf. He did the same.

"It's still in development," Alextra said. "But it will balance your electrolytes and get your body burning your fat stores more efficiently."

"It's not even food?" Elyot asked.

"Do you think I'm some kind of wizard?" Alextra asked.

"Yes," he and Keani said at the same time.

Alextra looked flabbergasted. "Well, I'm not. But once this kicks in you won't feel hungry, so it's close enough to food until you run out of body fat to burn."

"Thank you, Alextra," he said, and she gave him a nod that was only a little magnanimous. "Where to now?"

"Through the treetops, our guide said," Alextra said, looking to Keani.

"Where are we trying to go?" she asked, cutting her vine away with her knife.

"Where is there to go?" Alextra asked.

"Back to the city," Keani said.

"Besides that," Alextra said.

"Nowhere," Keani said. "There's nothing down here. There's no escape."

"They are still watching the cliffs for us," Elyot said, listening to the sound of shuttles flying overhead. "We can't go back the way we came."

"If we just sit here any longer they'll find us," Alextra said. "They aren't stupid. They'll work out where we must have come out of the mountain. They might be here any minute. We have to get moving."

"And just keep moving? So they can't catch us?" Elyot asked.

"That's suicide," Keani said. "They probably won't even catch us before the jungle kills us for them."

"So what then?" Alextra asked.

"Exactly," Keani said. "We have to go back."

"There's another port," Elyot said. "Another spaceport."

Now they were both looking at him. Keani was trying to signal him to stop talking, but Alextra gestured for him to continue.

"I don't know where it is," he admitted. "I saw ships landing there from the city walls once, but I'm all turned about, and even if I could figure out what part of the wall I was on, I only had the vaguest idea of the direction where I saw the ships. It was a long time ago."

"Do you know this place?" Alextra asked Keani.

Reluctantly, Keani nodded.

"And it's still active?"

She nodded again.

"Then that's the place to go, isn't it?" Alextra said.

"It's far," Keani said. "It's so far, I've never even been there."

"But you know how to find it," Alextra said.

"I know how to find it," she admitted.

"My mouth tastes like I've been sucking copper," Elyot said.

"That's just your body burning the fat," Alextra said with a dismissive wave. "Let's get moving."

Elyot mentally prepared himself for another day spent climbing, but it soon became apparent that very little climbing would be required. The trees had many wide branches that ran almost horizontal to the jungle floor, overlapping in a dense network. A few times they had to use the abundant vines to swing across gaps, but mostly it was just a matter of stepping up or down from one branch to the next.

Elyot saw no markings on the dark green wood and no sign of a worn path where they were stepping, and yet Keani seemed to know just which branches to take.

The shuttles flew ever lower over the treetops, but the foliage over their heads was more than dense enough to hide them. But by mid-morning, the hum of their engines was joined by the sounds of voices in the jungle behind them.

"Koltn Ward," Alextra said.

"Are you sure?" Elyot asked, not able to pick out that voice himself.

"Who else?" she shot back.

Then Elyot nearly collided with Keani's back. She reached behind herself to catch him until he was sure of his balance but didn't turn around.

"Why are we stopping?" Alextra asked. Then she seemed to see what Elyot was just noticing himself.

They had run out of trees.

"What's this?" he asked.

"Scar from an old burn," Keani said. "The trees haven't grown back yet."

"Can't we go around?" Alextra asked.

"It would take days," Keani said.

"But that's grass down there," Elyot pointed. "Surely that's better than jungle."

Keani turned to give him a pitying look.

Then Elyot heard it again, the massive thing knocking down trees as it moved. It was right behind them now.

"Is that thing going to eat the enforcers?" he asked.

Keani was frowning, eyes half-closed as she listened. "That's not a jungle creature."

"But I heard it last night," Elyot said.

"Last night you heard a damapom," she said.

"What's a-" Elyot began to ask, but Alextra talked over him.

"What we're hearing now is an ultra heavy class ground tank," she said. "They must have brought it down from orbit."

"It's getting closer," Keani said. "We have to cross this burn. Once we're on the other side, I know a place that tank can't go."

"So let's go," Elyot said, but she caught his arm to stop him from climbing down to the ground.

"Both of you, listen to me," she said. "Stay in the grass. Crouch low if you need to, but stay in the grass."

"Until we get to the other side?" Elyot guessed.

"Until we get to the other side," Keani agreed.

"But run," Alextra said, pulling off her cape and folding it up into an improbably small square before stuffing it into a belt pouch. "We don't want the shuttles to see us."

They all dropped to the ground, setting some unseen creature screeching away through the ferny undergrowth, but they didn't stop to investigate. They all ran flat out across the grasslands.

Just like the jungle, it was teeming with life, but life that preferred to be unseen. They were leaving a ripple of waving grasses behind them as creatures fled from their footsteps. Elyot was sure that widening wake of moving grass could be seen from the air just as easily as their clothing.

And he must have been right because the humming of shuttles deviated from its accustomed pattern. One of them was moving closer. Then two more. Then a dozen.

"Run!" Alextra shrieked and somehow managed to put on more speed. Keani was still in the lead, though, charting a path to the tree line on the far side, which was looking even farther now than before.

Then Elyot heard a sound like heavy rain. Very heavy rain, like a hail of stones.

No, boulders.

"This way!" Alextra called back to him and changed her course to head for a solitary tree in the center of the burn.

Elyot was going to protest that they were supposed to stay in the grass, but then he looked back over his shoulder.

The rain of boulders was the sound of plasma guns pounding craters into the grassland behind him. Just one ship closing in on them, but others were getting into position on opposite ends of the burn.

They were going to destroy every centimeter of it just to be sure. Hiding in the grass wasn't going to save them. He followed Alextra to the tree.

Alextra had stopped just inside the shadow of the tree, hands on her thighs as she caught her breath.

"They'll get us here too!" Elyot yelled.

She shook her head. "It's too tall. They'll save it for last," she said.

But the plasma fire was getting closer.

"Not here!" Keani bellowed as she sprinted towards them.

"We're safe here!" Alextra said, but Elyot doubted that was true even before the spiders the size of his hand started falling from the sky.

Or rather, from the tree. Elyot staggered back out of its shadow, flinging spider after spider off of his body. He brushed spastically at his own back.

"They're harmless," Keani said, plucking the last few off his shoulders and tossing them away.

"Tell her that," Elyot said, pointing to Alextra, who was screaming in a raw panic he would expect more as a response to the plasma guns.

"They're harmless!" Keani yelled at Alextra, but she didn't hear. She was slapping and clawing at herself, bending over to shake them out of her silvery hair.

She was also moving further into the shadows under the tree.

"Alextra!" Keani yelled even louder, which she had to do to be heard over the plasma fire. "They're harmless! But the tree isn't!"

Alextra stopped moving, then straightened up. She looked up into the canopy over her head, but no more spiders were falling.

"Get out of there!" Keani said.

Alextra nodded and started to run.

And immediately face-planted into the grass under the tree. It wasn't as tall there as out in the open, but it was enough to hide her from view.

"It's got her," Keani said.

"What's got her?" Elyot asked.

"The tree!"

"We have to help her!" Elyot shouted. The shuttles were almost on top of them. They didn't seem to be in any particular hurry, but only because they were being so thorough in destroying every bit of the ground beneath them.

"This isn't going to do a thing," Keani said, holding up her little knife.

"I don't have anything, but we can't just leave her behind."

He expected Keani to argue that point and knew he didn't have a counterargument and that they really should be running to save themselves at this point, but she didn't. She looked down at the knife as if wondering if it would be enough.

"Wait!" Elyot said, catching Keani's shoulder before she could plunge in under the tree. Alextra's head was just visible, forcing its way up over the tops of the grass. "It looks like something's got her."

"That's because something *does* have her," Keani said.

But then Alextra raised an arm over her head. An arm and a tanjo. She swung it down again and again.

Then she was back on her feet, waving for them to run even as she closed the gap between them.

Elyot hesitated. The shuttles on their strafing run were perilously close. It hadn't been wise for Alextra to get so close to the trunk of the tree, but if the spiders were harmless, perhaps just where he was standing was the safest place.

Then he saw something erupting out of the ground behind Alextra. At first, he thought it was an array of tentacles, but as the soil dropped from their hairy appendages, he realized they were roots. Tree roots.

But they moved. Even as he stood there frozen, they were closing in on Alextra. She paused in her full-out sprint to whirl around, both ends of her tanjo blades now, and sliced the roots that were trying to close around her.

That made the tree thing truly angry, Elyot guessed, as the ground beneath him began to quake. Tendrils of tree roots were bursting out of the soil, but he didn't stay to see how far they could reach. He ran for where he could see Keani at the treeline, pushing so hard for every bit of speed he could muster that his vision started to red out.

He didn't stop until arms closed around him and tackled him to the ground. He started to thrash, throwing fists everywhere.

"Ow! Calm down!" Keani said, letting him go. "I can't have you charging into the jungle."

"Sorry," Elyot tried to say, but his breath was so labored he doubted it was clear. He had never run like that in his life.

He hoped to never run like that again.

"They're going to hit the jungle next," Alextra said as they watched the shuttle formation advancing.

But then suddenly the firing stopped.

"Do they think they got us?" Keani asked.

The shuttles hovered for a moment, then peeled away, back up into the sky where the hovering spaceships lurked over the city.

"Koltn Ward," Alextra said. And sure enough, as the hum of the shuttle engines faded the sound of the advancing tank took over.

"He doesn't want us dead?" Keani guessed.

Alextra gave her a hard look, then gave another one to Elyot. "Is he after all three of us, do you think?"

"You think he just wants you?" Keani asked.

"I know he wants me, and he has to take me alive. You two, I'm not so sure."

"If he wants you alive, why don't you just turn yourself in before the jungle kills you?" Keani asked.

"The jungle won't kill me so long as you're here," she said.

Keani scoffed.

"You're not going to tell us who you are?" Elyot asked. "You said Koltn Ward knows."

"It's safer for you if you don't know," she said. "But the real question is: does he know who *you* are?" She looked from Elyot to Keani and back again.

"I'm not sure," Elyot said.

"Me neither," Keani said. "But if he does know who I am, I'd be a dead or alive type. And I'm guessing dead would be fine with him."

Alextra nodded then looked to Elyot.

"I don't know," he said. "I guess it depends on things. Some stuff that might have happened. I don't know."

"So we agree to keep running?" Alextra said.

"We can't," Keani said.

"Why not?" Alextra asked.

"Don't you feel that?" Keani asked, pointing at Alextra's right calf. Alextra looked down and blanched. One of the tree's roots must have wrapped around her leg before she cut herself free. It had sliced through her pants just above her boot.

"That's just a scratch," she said.

"It's awfully red," Elyot said.

"And you're already feeling the venom, aren't you?" Keani asked.

Alextra bit her lip but nodded. "I might have something…"

"It won't work," Keani said.

"How long?" Alextra asked.

"Maybe an hour before you won't be able to walk, and I'm padding that number out because you're stubborn as hell," Keani said. "Another hour after that the paralysis will reach your lungs."

"What do we do?" Elyot asked.

"I know someone who can help," Keani said. "But we need to lose this tail first."

"You have a plan for that?" Alextra asked.

"I know just the place. Come on."

The trees on this side of the burn didn't have such wide, intertwined branches as the other side, so Keani led them through the overgrowth. It looked impenetrably dense to Elyot, but Keani always managed to find a gap between the bushes, a place to stoop under the thorns, a log spanning a rain-eroded channel.

Those channels were becoming more and more numerous as the ground began to slope more steeply. Keani kept to a path that stayed level, but the ground to their left rose ever higher, to the right ever lower.

"Can a tank manage this?" Elyot asked hopefully. "When they ran tanks through the city streets they avoided the steep roads."

"This is a different kind of tank," Alextra said. He could hear how she was fighting back pain in the tightness of her voice.

"Here," Keani said, and suddenly plunged out of sight down one of the rain channels. Elyot scrambled down after her, the loose mud of the channel walls crumbling under his feet and hands. There was barely room for his shoulders at the bottom, and he couldn't see Keani. He followed her footprints around a turn in the channel, then another.

By the third turn, the mud walls around him were twice as tall as he was.

Then the muddy ground beneath him became bare rock as the channel straightened out. He could see Keani ahead of him, but not what was beyond her. The channel was too narrow for that.

"Good call," Alextra said from behind him. "They can't get that tank down here."

"They'll come on foot," Elyot said.

The channel ended in a narrow canyon with a thin stream of water sitting stagnantly in the middle. Even this canyon was too narrow for the tank, and the walls were dozens of meters high.

Keani caught them each by an arm and gestured for them to put their faces close to hers. "We're going to keep going downhill, but be as silent as you can, and don't disturb the water."

They both nodded, but Keani kept staring at Alextra until she nodded again, putting a hand over her heart in a solemn vow.

Elyot chose his steps carefully, staying as far from the water as he could, which wasn't as far as he'd like. What horror lurked under that scummy surface? It didn't look deep enough to hide anything, but if he'd learned anything from his time in the jungle, it was that appearances meant very little.

He didn't realize he had been hearing the rumble of the tank motor ever present behind them until it cut off suddenly. For a moment the jungle was in silence, but then birds resumed calling out to each other, and other creatures chittered away. It sounded like it came from another world, a world far above them.

Then he heard voices and the slamming of tank hatches. He looked back at Alextra, who had stopped walking to listen. She saw him watching her and held up seven fingers.

He had no idea how she came to that number, but he was sure she was right.

The tank might have rolled right over the mud channel they had followed, but he doubted it could cross this canyon. The enforcers might have lost their trail, but they'd find it again soon enough. They had left an abundance of footprints.

The canyon took a gentle turn, and once Elyot was around the last outcropping of rock, he saw where the canyon ended and the ground leveled out and was jungle once more.

It looked impossibly far away, and he was so tired.

The water didn't seem to get any deeper, but it did form wider puddles, and the canyon walls were as narrow as ever. Just as he wanted to break into a run and reach the cover of the trees ahead, he was forced to move ever more slowly, testing each rock before he put his weight on it because they kept tipping under him.

The voices behind them had faded away, and Elyot had assumed they were still hunting for the mud channel. Then the rock wall just over his head exploded, showering him with shards, and he knew he had assumed wrongly.

Keani spun to gape back at him, knife in hand. Alextra ran past him, balancing on the tops of rocks that jutted out of the center of the still stream with her usual effortless grace.

Elyot tried to run as well, but he couldn't bring himself to risk it.

What was in that water?

He didn't want to look behind him. Seeing how close they were to catching him or firing again wouldn't help anything. But the back of his neck prickled hotly like he could feel himself in some gun's sights.

Then there was a splash. Not a big one; no one fell into the stagnant water. Someone had just brushed a foot through it, perhaps. Such a small sound.

"Run!" Keani bellowed back to them. Then she turned and sprinted for the trees, splashing through the puddles without care. Alextra ran after her, still dancing over the tops of protruding rocks.

Elyot tried to follow her example, but he too ended up splashing into the edges of the water more than once.

Then another sound rose up behind him like water coming to a boil, followed by a sound like a hive of angry wasps waking to attack an enemy.

Then the screams began.

Elyot put his head down and forced his legs to keep moving despite the cramping. He really, really didn't want to see what was happening behind him.

The screams became more disciplined yells all but drowning out the thwip-thwip-thwip of needle guns firing. But the buzzing was louder still.

Again Keani caught him before he could charge blindly into the jungle, thrusting him against the trunk of a tree. Alextra stood against another tree, arm wrapped around her eyes as she leaned against the trunk, laboring to catch her breath.

The red of her leg wound was darkening to purplish-black.

"Your friend?" Elyot prompted, then looked past Keani, up the canyon to where the enforcers were firing in every direction. "What is that?" he asked, squinting at the black cloud that had formed around them.

"They're called guepes," she said grimly. "Sentient wasp beings. They lay their eggs in the water."

"So that's why they're mad," Elyot guessed.

"They communicate with each other by scent," she said. "They'll have marked those enforcers. The smell carries for kilometers. Every guepe that catches the scent will follow it. Those enforcers are going to die very painful deaths."

"Not Koltn Ward," Alextra said darkly. "He's going to snake his way out of this one too; just you wait."

"I stepped in the water too," Elyot said. "So did you."

"Yeah, but we didn't hang around for the adults to come get us," Keani said. "We'll burn our shoes and clothes when we get to the village just to be sure, though."

"Village?" Alextra asked, arm still over her eyes.

"My village," Keani said. "Can you walk?"

Alextra straightened up and gave a nod. Keani looked around then picked a path through the undergrowth.

"I didn't know there were any villages down here besides the prison ones for criminals classified as dangerous and beyond redemption," Elyot said as he fell into step behind her.

"There aren't," Keani said.

4 PRISONERS AND REBELS

ELYOT COULD SEE that Alextra was running out of time. He knew she knew it too, although none of them said a word as they trudged through the ever-darkening jungle. But with every minute that ticked by, her steps slowed further.

"Wait," Alextra said at last, sitting against a wet, mossy boulder to dig through one of her belt pouches.

"It won't help," Keani said again as Alextra took out a chrome capsule half the size of her thumb and squinted at some writing engraved on its side.

"It can't hurt," Elyot said. Alextra flipped open one end of the capsule and ran it along both sides of the welt on her leg. Elyot winced at the thought of touching such a foul purplish-black injury - how did that not hurt? - but Alextra didn't even flinch.

"What does that do?" he asked as she put it back in her pouch but didn't stir from the boulder.

"Slow the infection," she said. "Or so I hope."

"It's venom, and that won't help," Keani said. "We need to get to the camp. The elder can help you."

"How much further is it?" Elyot asked.

"Not far," Keani said, but she was frowning at Alextra, still leaning against the boulder with her eyes closed. Even in the faint light that reached them from the setting sun through the thick foliage Alextra's face was looking grayish white. Elyot could guess what Keani wasn't saying.

Alextra might not make it even that far.

"Lean on me while you walk," Elyot said, stepping closer to offer his arm. Alextra nodded without opening her eyes. She took out her tanjo and extended both ends until she was holding a bo staff a little taller than she was. The shimmering hologram quality to the newly formed ends glowed faintly, but not enough to be seen from a distance. She wouldn't draw attention from anyone that wasn't on top of them already.

"Okay," she said, gripping her staff in one hand then wrapping the other arm around Elyot's shoulders. He slipped his arm around her and helped her stand up.

She was heavier than she looked. A lot heavier. Did she have metal for bones or something?

Keani led the way again, glancing back often to be sure they were keeping up with her.

Alextra was still weakening, putting more and more of her weight on Elyot's shoulders. It was tiring work, made no easier by the thick undergrowth hiding any number of twisted roots or jutting rocks that seemed to lunge at Elyot's toes.

"I think I might need to take a break," he said. "Sorry."

"No need," Keani said, coming back to put an arm around Alextra from the other side. "We're here."

With some of the weight off his shoulders, Elyot found the energy to look up and around. At first he thought they were still in the impenetrable heart of the jungle, but then he saw something too boxy to be part of a tree.

A tower, just large enough for one or two people to stand atop it. It was metal with only a narrow gap visible between the roof and the sides. The sides which had notches set in them as if for guns, allowing someone up there to fire from a position of cover.

A guard tower. Only, where were the guards?

"This way," Keani said, guiding Alextra and by extension Elyot between two of those unmanned towers and into a clearing. No trees here, and little undergrowth. It was easier to see, with light from the stars and from the Commonwealth ships hovering above unfettered by foliage. There were long metallic huts reflecting the silvery light. They were all the same and had a prefabricated look to them, like they could be disassembled, moved, and reassembled in a hurry if needed. He supposed the guard towers could too.

There still wasn't any sign of people. The cabins were windowless, the doors closed. No light or sound came out of any of them. So were they empty, or just thicker walled than they appeared?

They emerged from between two huts into a large, circular open space, and Elyot could see all the huts stood in a circle, the only doors facing the inside of the circle. There was some sort of round structure in the center of everything, but he couldn't make out enough details to guess at its purpose.

Keani guided them along the curving row of huts, then stopped at a door that was identical to all the others so far as Elyot could tell. Keeping an arm around the barely conscious Alextra, she leaned forward and knocked softly on the door. Then she looked all around in a slow, methodical sweep of their surroundings.

"Are we in danger here?" Elyot asked in a whisper.

"No more than we've been since we met," she said.

That wasn't a reassuring response.

The door opened. The warm-toned light wasn't particularly bright, but to their eyes acclimated to the dark it was blinding. Elyot could see the silhouette of a figure in the doorway but couldn't even tell if it was a man or a woman.

"Keani?" the figure said. A man's voice, and not a young one.

"Jaeke," Keani said. "I'll understand if you say no, but-"

"Come in, quickly," Jaeke said, reaching out to help Elyot and Keani get Alextra up the step and over the threshold.

The moment they were inside that warm golden light, Alextra's knees buckled. Keani and Elyot struggled to keep her up off the floor.

Jaeke closed the door behind them then bustled past them. He was dressed in roughly woven clothing much like Keani's, worn and faded but not in tatters like hers. His body was all hard, corded muscle, although if Elyot had to guess he didn't think Jaeke ever ate enough to feel full. His skin was sun-damaged, especially his scalp only sparsely covered by silvery gray hairs that hovered around his head like a frizzy halo.

Despite the step up, the floor inside was still hard-packed dirt. The interior of the hut appeared to be all one room, the very back separated from the rest by a rough approximation of a curtain. Jaeke pulled it back to reveal a bed of sorts, really just a raised rectangle of packed earth covered with blankets.

"Lay her down there," Jaeke said as he turned away from the alcove to dig through a wooden cabinet. "What happened to her?"

"The spider tree caught her around the leg," Keani said. "I tried to warn her, but we were fleeing from Commonwealth soldiers at the time."

Jaeke turned around to give Keani a hard look but then went back to his searching without saying a word. Keani and Elyot helped Alextra over to the bed, her feet more dragging over the dirt than actually walking. She collapsed onto it and curled into a tight ball like a panicked insect. Elyot took the tanjo out of her nerveless fingers. He didn't know how to turn off the glowing solid hologram ends, to return it to its short club configuration. There weren't any buttons or even any markings in the smooth wood. In the end he just leaned it in the corner of the room, still in its bo staff form.

"The spider tree is quite some way from here," he said as he brought a small earthen vessel to the bedside. "You're lucky you made it here in time."

"She has Commonwealth medicine," Keani said. "I think that might have kept her moving."

"Wouldn't do a thing against the venom," Jaeke said with a click of his tongue. "But better than nothing. Help me straighten her out so I can put this poultice on the wound."

"We need new clothes as well," Keani said, indicating with a nod of her head to Elyot that he should help hold Alextra's legs straight as Jaeke dipped his fingers in the jar.

"Guepes?" Jaeke guessed as he smeared a foul-smelling, greenish-brown paste over the necrotized flesh of Alextra's leg.

"I don't think we were marked," Keani said. "But just to be on the safe side."

"You know where the stores are," Jaeke said. "Use the common fire, not any of the hut fires."

"Of course," Keani said. "We should probably get her clothes too before we go."

"No, she'll be fine," Jaeke said. He made one last pass to be sure the wound was completely covered then wiped his fingers clean on Alextra's pants leg. "This is Commonwealth tech she's wearing. Self-cleaning, self-repairing."

"It didn't repair that," Keani said, pointing at the tear in the leg.

"No, she would've told it not to," Jaeke said. "She wanted to keep an eye on the wound."

"It'll repair now?" Elyot asked.

"Or when she wakes, depending on what she told it to do," Jaeke said. "Keeping it open to the air would be better; if it repairs I'll just tear it again."

"But the guepes-" Keani started to say.

"It will have already gotten rid of any of that, trust me," Jaeke said. "You two, on the other hand, better get changed now."

"Right," Keani said, then tugged at Elyot's sleeve. "Follow me."

She opened the door but swept her gaze over the circle of dark huts before stepping outside. Elyot followed her several huts down. Keani opened the door without knocking, and the interior was dark. "Wait here," she said before disappearing inside.

Elyot waited just outside the door. He felt like he was being watched, but he saw no sign of anyone anywhere around him. He was just being paranoid, he hoped.

"Here," Keani said, thrusting a pile of clothing at him as she stepped outside. "Get changed then come over to the fire so we can burn what you're wearing now."

"What fire?" he asked.

"You'll see," she said then left him to jog over to the circular structure in the center of the camp.

Elyot shook out the pile of clothing, finding a pair of pants and sleeveless tunic as well as a short cloak and a pair of soft cloth boots.

He liked his own clothes better, but the memory of that swarm of guepes attacking the Commonwealth enforcers was still vivid in his mind. The screams from the enforcers had echoed through the canyon. He could only imagine the pain.

He quickly changed, putting his few possessions that had been in his pants pockets into the large pocket on the front of the tunic as the pants had none. The boots were comfortable enough on the ground between the huts and the center of the circle, ground worn smooth by many feet, so much constant traffic that even the tenacious jungle undergrowth couldn't grow here. He doubted they would be so comfortable on the rockier ground they had crossed since leaving the city.

As he approached the center he saw a sudden roar of flames coming to life. So some sort of gas-fueled thing, not a natural fire kindled from small bits and slowly built up with ever larger pieces of wood. When he was closer he could see Keani, her face lit up reddish orange by the flames. She was wearing almost the same thing as she'd been wearing when he met her, but this time less tattered.

He handed her his clothing and she tossed them into the fire where the last of her things were curling to ash.

"Do we have to burn my boots?" Elyot asked, reluctant to hand them over.

"Boots most of all," Keani said. "They are more likely to have been splashed then anything."

"Are they safe to burn?" he asked.

"Safe?" Keani said, rolling her eyes. She pulled the boots out of his grip and throwing them into the fire.

The chemical smell of burning plasileather was eye-wateringly unpleasant, and they both took several steps back and then upwind from the fire.

"Am I going to be mistaken for a..." Elyot searched for a word that he wasn't going to regret saying aloud. He was pretty sure they were in a prisoner camp, but then again a lot of things didn't make sense. Like the lack of guards in the towers. And the apparent lack of prisoners. "A native of this village?" he ended instead.

"No," Keani said, coming back around the fire now that the smell was dissipating to make sure all of the clothing had been consumed.

"Are you sure?"

"Very," she said. Then she kicked something Elyot couldn't see, and the flames disappeared as suddenly as they had appeared.

The darkness of the night around them closed in, and even the stars were too faint for Elyot's eyes now. All he could see were the lights from the Commonwealth ships, the fainter but faster moving lights from the shuttles flying between them.

It wasn't comforting.

"Come on," Keani said, leading the way back to Jaeke's hut. She opened the door without knocking this time, pulling Elyot inside to quickly shut the door behind them.

"How is she?" she asked.

"Better," Jaeke said. "But she'll need a day at least before you can move on."

"Can you give that to us?" Keani asked.

"Is there another choice?" Jaeke asked. "This will bring trouble, but I guess you're used to that."

"I didn't bring more trouble than we already had," Keani said.

"You've been gone awhile," he said. "I'm guessing you ran out of food."

"A week ago," Keani said.

"You didn't steal so much as that," Jaeke said.

"I found other things to eat," she said. "For a while."

"The jungle can keep you alive as readily as it can kill you," Jaeke said.

"So you've always told me," she said. "I suppose I could've lived out there forever, alone. I mean, I was doing okay. But instead I decided to climb the mountain. See the city."

"And immediately found trouble," Jaeke said. Keani didn't bother to contradict him.

"What happened here?" she asked. "It's been weeks. Why aren't the guards back on the towers?"

"No one knows," Jaeke said. "We buried the others out where no one would ever find them and came up with a story of sorts, that they'd all just left one day and never came back. But no one else has ever come to take their place. They must have been missed by now."

"If the guards are gone why are you still here?" Elyot asked.

Jaeke looked at him as if noticing him for the first time.

"He's from the city," Keani said. "His name's Elyot. And that's Alextra over there. I don't think she's from the city, but that's where we all met."

"No, not from the city," Jaeke said as if to himself, then looked up at Elyot. "You've been traveling through the jungle, yes? Can you make a guess why I don't leave my warm, safe hut?"

"You taught me how to live out there," Keani said.

"I can do it. Doesn't mean I want to. Not at my age," he said. "The Commonwealth never replaced the guards, but that doesn't mean the rest of us are free now. Are you hungry?"

"Very," Keani said. "But what do you mean about the guards?"

"Good, I added more vegetables to the soup when you were out burning your clothes, so I have enough to share," Jaeke said, leaning over the fire in the center of the hut and stirring at something in a cauldron sitting off center over the flames. "Another minute or two, I should think."

"The guards?" Keani said again.

"Well, your friends are in charge now," Jaeke said. "I don't know what they're planning, but they won't let any of us leave the camp. We're still prisoners, but this time it's not our colonizing masters keeping us here. It's our own kids and grandkids."

"But what happened?" Keani asked.

"I don't have the answers you're looking for," Jaeke said. "You'd have to ask your friends."

"They're not my friends," Keani said. "Not anymore."

"Friends or not, they probably already know you're here," Jaeke said. "They'll come looking for you. I can watch your friend until she's well. There's no reason for you to stay."

"No reason to run, either," Keani said. "Is that soup ready?"

———

ELYOT WOKE up to a rush of disorientation. When was the last time he had slept under a roof? With no windows and no natural light, he had no idea how long he'd even slept.

He was lying on a blanket near the cook fire, which was still softly glowing although the flames had died down. There was another blanket folded neatly nearby but no sign of Keani.

"She left," Jaeke said, and Elyot jumped at the sudden break in the silence. He found Jaeke sitting in a chair pulled close to the bed where Alextra still slept. Jaeke didn't look like he'd slept at all.

"Keani left?" Elyot asked, still disoriented. Jaeke didn't answer, possibly because the answer was quite apparent. "How's Alextra?"

"I need to give her a second dose of poultice, but a diluted one," Jaeke said. "Take that pot by the door and fetch me some water."

"From where?" Elyot asked as he pulled on his cloth boots.

"The well in the center of the camp," Jaeke said. "Quickly now."

Elyot grabbed the pot and opened the door to find it was still early morning, the sun rising but still behind the mountains to the east. Despite the early hour there were other people about, dressed much like he was. But none of them were his age. Instead they looked like Jaeke, possibly middle-aged or possibly far older but impossible to guess behind the mask of sun damage and the cord muscles of daily hard labor.

In the brighter dawn light he could make out more details of the circular structure in the center of the camp. The outer rim was an earthen wall of about knee height, cracked in places and showing repairs of the mud work in others. On the inside it was neatly bisected in two. One side was filled with the ashy remains of what he knew were his and Keani's clothes, fallen through the grill Keani had tossed them on the night before. The other side was filled with water. There was a metal covering over the water, but it had been folded open on one side so that the villagers could fill their pots there.

"Good morning," he said to the few that were waiting in line at the well, but none of them answered or even looked at him. So, not friendly, but not calling him out as an outsider either.

They were all wearing sleeveless tunics like his, but unlike him they also had something on their forearms. Screens, like computer screens, only they appeared to be embedded in their flesh. Elyot looked around as discreetly as he could until he was sure. Everyone had them.

Then he remembered that Keani always wore long sleeves. Was she hiding a screen on her own arm?

The woman in front of him stepped up to the well and dipped her pot into the water. As she waited for it to fill she held her arm still for long enough for Elyot to get a good look. It was a readout of numbers in five columns, the far-right column changing by the second.

The second. It was time. The readout was marking time. In seconds, then minutes, then hours.

Then days. Then years.

He looked again at the seconds. They were ticking by backwards, and as he watched it reached zero and the minute column went down by one.

What did that mean?

No use asking. People who didn't respond to a good morning weren't going to be open to personal questions. But Jaeke might.

Elyot filled his own pot then carried it carefully back to the hut. For one terrifying moment he wasn't sure which hut he had come from, but then he saw one with the door standing open and got a glimpse of Keani sitting inside. So she'd come back from wherever she had gone. He hurried his steps until he was ducking inside.

Keani was there, but she wasn't alone. She had brought six people in with her. They all sat around the fire either in chairs or on the floor, but no one was speaking.

Jaeke was waving at Elyot to bring the water to the back of the room, so he scurried past the others, none of whom looked up.

"What's going on?" Elyot asked Jaeke in a whisper as he handed over the water pot.

"Not our business," Jaeke said, pouring a bit into the poultice jar and giving it a stir with his fingers. He pulled his fingers out, watching the paste drip down with a frown, then added more water and stirred again.

Elyot leaned against the back wall, close enough to watch over Alextra but also within easy reach of her tanjo.

Keani was the only one in the hut with long sleeves. Elyot saw a screen in Jaeke's arm, numbers counting down to something Elyot could not even guess at. In the darkness of the night before he had missed seeing it entirely.

The teens gathered around Keani also had screens in their arms, but they were all blank. No numbers ticking down, just a black screen that flexed and bent when they moved their arms to reach for the bottle they were passing around to take slugs from.

The bottle was passed to Keani and Elyot watched how her sleeve moved as she reached out to take it. There was something in her sleeve on the inside that kept it from sliding up her arm, like it was attached to something. Her cloak fell back over her shoulder as she raised the bottle to drink and Elyot could see the coarse stitching that attached it to what was meant to be a sleeveless tunic like the others.

She had made her own sleeves to cover that screen. He could see why she had done it before climbing up to the city. There were people there - not Elyot personally but others - who would know such a thing would mean an escaped prisoner. But why make more sleeves when in a camp where everyone knew she had a screen? Where everyone else was a prisoner?

And when had she done it? He hadn't looked closely enough at her in the light from the fire the night before, but she had been wearing a cloak like she was now. It wouldn't have been hard to keep her arms out of sight until she could sew up the sleeves while Elyot slept.

But why?

"Talk," one of the teens said to Keani as he took the bottle from her hands. "You brought strangers here. Why?"

"We're just passing through," Keani said. "As soon as that one can walk, we're out of here. You'll never see me again."

"You said that last time," one of the girls said. "You abandoned us."

"It looks like you did just fine without me, Herlee," Keani said. "The guards are gone, and I guess you're in charge now."

"No thanks to you," one of the boys said. "And it's not just here. We took the guards' weapons and we've been freeing other camps. Every camp we get more weapons and the next one is easier."

"And the Commonwealth is just letting this happen?" Keani asked.

"So far," Herlee said.

"Why?" Keani asked.

"Who cares?" the boy scoffed.

"They must be planning something," Keani said. "They don't need to keep us contained in camps when they know the jungle can kill us. And they'll never let us escape the jungle."

"You're not in charge here, Keani," the boy said. "Not anymore. You walked away from all that."

"I was never the one in charge, Arion," Keani said. "Where's Jax?"

The six of them exchanged glances, Arion shaking his head at whatever they were silently communicating to him. Then he turned back to Keani. "He'll be free soon. Then he'll be here. And I don't think your friend back there will be up and about before then. You're in trouble."

"Right now? From the six of you?" she asked.

"No," Herlee said, as much to the others as to Keani. "That's for Jax to decide when he gets here. We're just going to make sure you're still here when he gets here."

Then the six of them filed out the door.

Jaeke was still smearing the foul paste over Alextra's leg, acting as if nothing at all had just happened a couple of meters away from him. Elyot pushed off from the wall to stand by Keani.

"What was that all about?" he asked.

"Nothing," she said, so quickly he knew it was an automatic response. He grabbed her arm and pulled at her sleeve. "Hey!" she protested but didn't fight him. Something tied on the inside snapped free and he pulled back the cloth to expose her screen. Unlike the other teens, her screen still had numbers counting down on it.

"What is this? What does it mean?" he asked.

"It's my sentence," Keani said, holding her arm out straight so he could take a good look at it.

The year column read 578.

"What did you do?" he asked, horrified.

"I was born," she said calmly, then extricated her arm so she could roll her sleeve back down and retie the cuff. "Although it looks like they added some years on account of the rebellion I wasn't even a part of. They might not be replacing the guards, but they aren't as clueless as those guys seem to think they are. The Commonwealth is going to crush them all."

"I don't understand any of this," Elyot said.

Keani took a deep breath as if collecting her thoughts. "I was born here. My parents were prisoners, but they died without completing their sentences. Whatever time they had left when they died, it's now mine. Plus a couple hundred years for the rebellion."

"But you never did anything wrong?" Elyot asked.

"None of us kids did, at least not initially. We just inherited our parents' and grandparents' time," she said. "Of course we've done some wrong since then. Some of that time is on us for stealing food and shirking work duties. But since most of us have centuries to go, that doesn't really seem to matter."

"How can that be legal?" Elyot asked.

But Keani just shrugged. "Ask the Commonwealth."

They heard a moan from the back of the room and rushed to the bedside to see Alextra's eyes starting to flutter open. Her skin was still pale, but the grayish tinge was gone.

"How're you feeling?" Elyot asked as she peered up at them.

"Not great," she said, her voice raspy. "But better."

"One more diluted dose after midday and all of the venom should be drawn out," Jaeke said. "Your own medicines will take it from there."

Alextra patted her sides and found her belt and pouches gone. She tried to sit up but Jaeke and Keani pushed her back down.

"Easy," Jaeke said. "We just took them off so you would sleep more comfortably. All of your things are right here, unharmed."

"But you pawed through them?" Alextra said, summoning an impressively imperious tone despite her obvious weakness and exhaustion.

"A little," Jaeke confessed. "Before I was a prisoner I was a doctor in the Commonwealth. I was just curious about what you had. I didn't take any of it. I recognized very little of what you're carrying. I guess things have changed while I was away."

"Perhaps not as much as you think," Alextra said, sinking back into the blankets. "Not for most people, anyway."

"No," Jaeke said. "I recognized your sigil. You're a long way from home."

But Alextra didn't answer. Sleep had already taken her.

Keani exchanged a long look with Jaeke then dragged one of the chairs out the open door to sit just outside. Elyot trailed after her.

"Are they coming back? Your friends?" Elyot asked.

"Not my friends," Keani said. "And no. Not without Jax, anyway."

"Who's Jax?" Elyot asked.

"Trouble," she said. "Jax is trouble. But Jax is also in maximum security. That won't be one of the camps those kids have taken over. No way."

"But they said he'd be here," Elyot said.

"I'll believe it when I see it," Keani said. "No, we'll be gone before anything goes down here. Alextra will be able to walk in the morning, Jaeke said. And Jaeke is never wrong."

"But where will we go?" Elyot asked.

Keani barked out a humorless laugh. "That's the real question, isn't it? You don't know anything outside of the city walls, and I've barely been out of this camp my whole life. Alextra clearly isn't from here. I don't know where we go next. But we can't stay here."

"So for now we just wait?" he said.

"We just wait," she agreed.

Elyot went back inside to find another chair then joined Keani in what he knew was really guarding the door.

The day was humid and hot, especially sitting in the sun as they were. Elyot found himself dozing through the afternoon. He occasionally woke to the soft murmur of voices, but it was always one of the older members of the prison camp speaking quietly to Keani, squeezing her shoulder as if lending her comfort before moving on.

"Everyone knows you," he said after one couple left at sunset.

"Everyone knew my parents," she said. "They were well liked. They were good people."

Just the day before Elyot would've thought that was a strange thing to say about people in prison camp meant for those deemed dangerous and beyond redemption.

But today? Today he was pretty sure no one had actually earned that label.

Elyot went inside to find Jaeke still sitting by the bed, Alextra still sleeping.

"Her color is better, isn't it?" he asked as he stood over her.

"It is," Jaeke agreed. "Her body just needed a bit of what my poultice could provide to purge itself of the venom. She'll be quite recovered in the morning."

"But shouldn't she be awake more if that's true?" Elyot asked.

"She's healing," Jaeke insisted. "Trust the process."

Elyot didn't want to argue with someone who appeared to be acquainted both with modern medicine and with whatever jungle equivalent he was currently working with. But he would feel better if Alextra were less comatose.

"Keani!" someone shouted out in the center of the camp. Through the open door Elyot saw Keani get up from the chair. She turned to lean inside the hut.

"Stay in here with Alextra," she said to Elyot. Before he could object, she was gone.

"Best stay out of it," Jaeke said. "Keani can handle herself."

He didn't know what he could do to help, unarmed as he was. But he went to the doorway all the same. He wouldn't interfere, but he wanted to know what was happening.

He saw the six teens from before standing around the circular structure at the center of the camp - half of it now a roaring bonfire - but they had another with them now. He was tall and thin, and his clothes were like everyone else's if a bit worse for wear. His olive-colored skin had a sallow tone to it, as if he hadn't been out in sunlight for quite some time. His dark hair stood high on top of his head in twisted, knotted locks in bad need of a trim or a cut or both.

"Jax," Keani said as she approached the group. Elyot knew she had the knives with her that she had stolen from the tavern, but they were nowhere in sight now. She held her hands out at her sides, palms facing slightly forward, so that Jax and the others would also see she was unarmed.

Jax raised an arm to point a finger at her in a slow, deliberate gesture meant to be observed from anywhere in the camp. "You betrayed us, Keani."

"I only betrayed you," Keani said.

"No," Jax said, then louder, "no! This isn't personal. This isn't about what happened between you and me. This is about the cause. You betrayed the cause!"

"It was never my cause, Jax," she said. "I admit there was a moment where I would've done anything for you. But then I actually thought about what it was you wanted me to do. And I betrayed you. That was totally personal. I rejected *you*."

This seemed like a very strange defense to Elyot. How could hurting his feelings help her case at all? And she was hurting him; Elyot could see it in the way his posture crumpled at her words, the way he wouldn't meet her eyes although Keani was standing toe to toe with him now, looking straight up into his face.

"No," Jax said again, his voice thick with emotion. Then he took a step back, straightening his spine and running his hands over his chaos of hair. He looked at the others gathered around him, making eye contact with Herlee the longest. She gave him a little nod as if encouraging him to continue. "A vote!" he said, raising a fist in the air. "Who here declares that Keani has betrayed our cause? No personal feelings here; this isn't about me. It's about the rebellion. Who says guilty?"

All six thrust their fists in the air with cries of "guilty!"

"And what shall the sentence be?" Jax asked. The others didn't know how to answer this. They looked at each other and shifted their weight from foot to foot uncomfortably.

But Herlee spoke clearly, her voice ringing through the center of the camp, "death."

"Death!" the other five chorused, pumping fists again.

"Jaeke?" Elyot whispered into the hut.

"Don't worry, boy," Jaeke said. "Keani can handle herself."

And indeed as if by magic both of those knives were now in Keani's hands, glowing in the light from the burning bonfire. She dropped into a low crouch then leaned forward to lunge at Jax.

But she froze. It took a moment for Elyot to realize why.

Jax had a needle gun leveled at her. He had taken enough steps back from her that she could never get to him with her knives before he could fire.

So she threw them and ran.

Jax twisted his body to dodge one, but the other sliced across his bicep, leaving a long bloody gash.

"Get her!" Jax yelled as he clamped a hand to the spurting wound. Herlee tore a strip from the end of her tunic to tie over his arm while the other five ran after Keani. She made it halfway to Jaeke's hut before they tackled her to the hard ground, knocking the wind out of her.

"I have to help her!" Elyot hissed at Jaeke. "You must have a weapon!"

"In a prison camp?" Jaeke said.

"That's not stopping them from having needle guns!" Elyot said. He looked back over his shoulder to see Keani on her knees by the bonfire, still fighting to catch her breath. Herlee put the last knot in the bandage and Jax extended his arm to aim the needle gun at Keani's bowed head.

Then Elyot was being pushed aside. At first he thought Jaeke was going out there to put an end to this craziness, but Jaeke was still standing by the bed.

The now empty bed.

Elyot ran out the door to see Alextra crossing the circle in great bounding strides, tanjo in her hands. Both of the ends were still in bo staff configuration, and when she landed behind Keani she spun it in her hands, striking Jax directly in the sternum with one end then following up with a quick strike to his wrist.

The needle gun flew from his hand to disappear in the darkness outside the range of the bonfire's light.

Jax staggered back from the blow but recovered quickly, moving forward to charge Alextra. She brought the tanjo back around. The end facing him was now a spear point, and he skidded to a quick halt when he felt that pricking at his neck just below his chin.

"You can't run," Alextra said to him. "I have you. I don't even have to stab you at this point. Just a little swipe of this very sharp spear tip and your blood will be watering this very dry ground. Try me."

Jax stood very still, hands halfway in the air. The other six started to move forward as if hoping to outflank Alextra, but he raised his hands with more urgency. "Stop! Don't do it! Just stop."

They all stopped. Elyot could see Herlee looking around for the needle gun, but he was pretty sure she was looking the wrong way. He crept in what he thought was the right direction, thankful at last for the soft cloth shoes that made his steps nearly silent.

"Keani?" Jax pleaded. His voice sounded hoarse, although there was no way that spear was pressing down on his windpipe. Not without killing him.

"Keani. Come on," Herlee said. Elyot was near where he thought the needle gun was, although he couldn't see it in the darkness. He dropped to his knees to brush his hands over the packed dirt and crabby weeds.

"Why are you calling out to her?" Alextra asked. "I'm the one who's about to execute you. And in your case, I'm pretty sure crimes were committed."

"Don't," Keani said. She sounded annoyed at herself for letting that word out, but then she got to her feet and put a hand on Alextra's forearm. "He hasn't earned execution."

"He was going to execute you. Did you earn that?" Alextra asked.

"No, but that doesn't make this right," Keani said.

Alextra frowned darkly, and Elyot hoped he never in his life had to stand there while she looked at him like that.

Then she changed the end of her tanjo back to a bo staff. She stepped back from Jax and he started to lower his hands in relief, but then the staff spun in her hands and in an eye blink he was flat on his back in the dust gasping for air much as Keani had been doing a moment before.

But she didn't stop there. She sat down on his chest, knees on his elbows. Both of the ends of the tanjo were gone now, and it was back in its short club form. But Elyot doubted that mattered to Jax when she placed it across his throat and leaned just a bit of her weight down on it.

"Alextra!" Keani cried, but Alextra ignored her.

"How did you get here so quickly?" she demanded as Jax gasped and struggled beneath her. "That's not an answer," she said after several seconds of this. "You were in max, right? How did you get here? How did you get out?"

Alextra was quite up on current events for someone who had looked to be in a coma. She must have heard everything everyone around her had said, even though she had never stirred. Maybe it really had been a healing thing.

Then his hand brushed up against something. He brought it back to grasp metal: the barrel of the needle gun. He picked it up carefully, got to his feet, and tucked it into his tunic pocket before walking closer to the fire.

"I was freed!" Jax gasped. Alextra sat back ever so slightly so he could continue speaking more easily. "The rebels. They freed me before I ever even got to the maximum-security camp. They've been intercepting communications between the camps, jamming some and spoofing others. They knew who I was and wanted me with them. They took me back to their base."

"And then?" Alextra asked.

"Then I got word that Keani was back. I had to be here. To see her."

"To kill her?" Alextra asked, raising an eyebrow.

"I wasn't going to, really," Jax said. Keani scoffed loudly.

"Don't listen to anything he says. It's all lies," she said.

"What's more probable?" Alextra asked, never taking her eyes off Jax. "That he escaped a maximum-security prison camp? Or that rebels busted him out?" Then she chanced a glance up at Keani. "That's not rhetorical. I don't know thing one about any of this, but you do. And you know him. What do you think?"

Keani looked at Jax assessingly. His eyes were clearly pleading with hers, but she was unmoved. At last she looked back to Alextra. "The rebel thing. Only probably not how he's describing it. It's more likely they hit the prison transport for its own sake, not his."

"All right," Alextra said, then leaned in on the staff briefly as if reminding Jax he was still under her control. "Now, answer me true. You know where the rebels are. You know where they're hiding. Yes?"

"Yes," he rasped. "I just escaped from there, didn't I?"

"And you can find it again?" she asked.

"Yes, absolutely," he said, nodding as enthusiastically as he could with the tanjo pressed against his throat.

"Herlee, is it?" Alextra asked. The girl nodded. "Give Keani her knives back. Both of them."

Herlee turned to the others, who quickly retrieved the knives and gave them to her. She held them out on her open palms to present them to Keani, who quickly tucked them back into her belt.

"Now listen carefully," Alextra said. "You're going to take us there and no funny business, agreed? Don't think for a minute that you and your friends will get the drop on me, because you won't. I truly hope you believe me."

"Hey, if you want to see the rebels, what's that to me?" Jax said. "I'll take you to them and good riddance to the lot of you."

Alextra gave a tight nod then swooped back up to her feet with her tanjo tucked away in one balletic move that Elyot doubted he could ever emulate. "We leave at dawn," she told the others, then waved for Keani and Elyot to walk with her back to Jaeke's hut.

"We can't trust Jax," Keani said.

"We don't, do we?" Alextra said. "He's going to insist he needs those others with us tomorrow, but that's fine. They're no match for my tanjo or your knives. Or for the needle gun Elyot has tucked in his tunic pocket."

Keani looked at Elyot in surprise then saw the bulge in his pocket. "Nice," she said. "You ever fired one?"

"No," he said. "Kind of hoping I don't have to."

"You might have to threaten with it a little," Alextra said. "First opportunity, I'll show you how it works."

"Can't you show me now?" Elyot asked, but the moment they were inside the hut he found himself once more holding a swooning Alextra in his arms.

"Perhaps a bit too soon for all that fuss," Jaeke said as he came over to help bring Alextra back to the bed.

"Perhaps," Alextra agreed as she laid back down. "I'll be fine in the morning," she said to Keani and Elyot.

"But why trust him at all?" Keani said. "I mean, why are we going to the hidden rebel base in the first place?"

"Because Koltn Ward is doubtlessly still after us. Do you have a better place to hide from the Commonwealth than in a hidden rebel base?" Alextra asked.

Then she closed her eyes and went still again. Elyot felt like continuing the discussion since clearly she could still hear them, but there wasn't much point if she couldn't respond.

He didn't know what was more worrisome, the fact that the rebel base was something the Commonwealth would gleefully bomb to a glassy crater the moment they located it, possibly with the three of them inside?

Or the word that Jax had used about leaving that place, the word Alextra and Keani hadn't seemed to have caught.

Escaped.

5 THE HIDDEN SPACEPORT

ELYOT REALLY MISSED HIS BOOTS.

Sure, today's walk through the jungle was easier going than their journey from the mountain to the comparative safety of the prison village. The ground here was drier, they didn't need to prowl through the treetops picking their way over whichever tree branches were wide enough and horizontal enough to make a sort of path, and they didn't need to battle undergrowth to make their way through. In fact, the ground beneath the trees looked almost sandy, the plants more grasslike than thorny.

And yet every step he took in those soft cloth boots, something jabbed into the bottom of one foot or the other. Sharp-edged rocks, woody thorns that stabbed deeper than the rocks, and fine nettles that he discovered still embedded in the cloth covering his ankles only after they had spread their fiery venom down through his foot.

Everyone else save for Alextra had the exact same boots, and yet no one else was flinching, let alone complaining. How tough were their feet?

At least the air was better here. It was cooler, breezier, less humid, and without the rot of vegetation he had grown so used to constantly smelling since leaving his high mountain home he had stopped even noticing it.

But having grown up within the stone walls of that city, he had a hard time placing what he was smelling now. It was familiar, but only vaguely. Like he was remembering one smell among many from a crowded marketplace he had visited many years ago as a young child.

But he liked it. It was a clean smell.

Jax with six of his gang of renegades from the prison village were leading the trio west, further away from the city, although the Commonwealth ships hovering over Elyot's hometown never seemed to get any smaller behind them when he could spot them through the treetops. Elyot was walking at the back of the group, keeping close to Alextra's side. She looked a thousand times better than she had just the night before. She didn't favor her injured leg with even the slightest of limps, and the material her pants were made of had mended themselves without any sign of the large tear that had marred them the day before.

And yet, she was definitely moving more slowly than usual. Which suited Elyot just fine. He couldn't imagine how much worse his feet would feel if he wasn't carefully choosing each step over the jungle floor.

Alextra suddenly froze, and Elyot froze too, looking up to see Jax far ahead of them through the trees. He had stopped, one fist raised in the air in signal to the others. No one moved or spoke or even looked around. So what was the danger?

Then Jax lowered his fist, turning to make eye contact with first Herlee and then Arion. Without a word between them, the two moved in forking directions ahead and to either side of Jax.

"Hey," Keani said, no more than a whisper, but still Elyot jumped. It was like she had just teleported to a spot right in front of him and Alextra, there in a flash.

"Enforcers?" Alextra asked, brushing her fingertips over the short club of her tanjo hanging at her side.

"No, another sandpit," Keani said. "Herlee and Arion are finding a way around; then we'll all go. The bugs don't really pose much of a threat when you're not trapped in the sands, but better safe than sorry."

"This doesn't seem as treacherous as the jungle nearer the city," Elyot said.

"It doesn't seem so, maybe, but it is," Keani said. "There are other things we're avoiding entirely."

"That's why our path is so serpentine, then?" Alextra asked.

Elyot said nothing. He thought they had been moving in a straight line. But then the only point of reference he had was the ships overhead, and they never seemed to change no matter where they moved on the ground.

"The guepes are more prevalent here," Keani said. "And another kind of grub, bigger than my fist, that lives in hollows in the ground. If you step on one of their hives, you'll crunch right through. Your leg will be stuck. Then they swarm you."

"You know this area then?" Alextra asked.

"Not like Jax does," Keani said.

"Are you sure about that?" Alextra asked.

"He says he does," Keani said, then heaved a sigh. "You're right. I don't know for a fact that he knows any more about this area than I do. He says we're circling the hive clusters, but I've never seen a grub hive before. I've only seen the prisoners who stumbled into them by mistake. It takes days for them to die. Long, painful days. And they always die."

"Definitely something to be avoided, then," Alextra said. "But also a handy excuse to keep people from straying off the path you want them following."

"Is he lying to us about where we're going?" Elyot asked Keani.

She sighed again. "I don't think so. He wants to find the rebels; I know that for a fact. It's all he was talking about last night after you two turned in. The more he talks, the more he comes across as some sort of hero to the rebellion. Like he has to return. Like they're waiting for him."

"And that doesn't sound like a lie?" Elyot asked.

"Oh, that part is totally a lie," Keani said. "But he wants to get back to them. That part I know is true."

"He might not be stalling, then," Alextra said. "He might just be lost."

Elyot looked to Keani to see what she thought of this assessment.

"Most of us kids wander out of the prison village all the time," Keani said. "There are tree forts built generations ago by other kids like us just outside of the guard towers. Most kids only go that far, just to prove to themselves they can. I mean, it's not like the guards don't know."

"But Jax claimed to go farther, I'm guessing," Alextra said.

"He was famous for it," Keani said. "I never had any reason to doubt him."

"Past tense?" Elyot said.

Keani looked back over her shoulder at where Jax stood conferring with one of the other renegades. "This isn't the time for that whole story. Some time when we're surrounded by four safe walls and a roof, maybe, but not here. We need to keep vigilant here."

At first, Elyot thought Alextra was demonstrating that point, her whole body tensing up as her eyes scanned the jungle around them.

Then Keani tensed up too, only she had fear in her eyes, and he knew it wasn't a game at his expense. But strain as he might, his ears picked up nothing.

Or was that the point? The jungle had suddenly gone eerily quiet.

Jax turned to look back at Keani. Elyot touched her arm and gestured behind her. She glanced back at Jax, then tugged at the front of Elyot's tunic and at Alextra's sleeve in silent command for them to walk with her.

By the time they reached Jax, they saw Herlee and Arion had also returned.

Then Elyot finally heard it. Machine sounds. Like the treads of heavy vehicles crushing everything in their path.

"We're close," Jax said in a low voice.

"What do you mean?" Alextra asked.

"Close to the rebel base," Jax said. "Those are their all-terrain vehicles. They rescued me from the prison transfer van in one of those."

"I don't think so," Alextra said with a frown.

"Well, I know so," Jax snapped.

"No, those are Commonwealth engines," she said. "My hearing is more nuanced than yours, and I've had ample time to study their unique signature." She glanced at Keani and Elyot. "It's Koltn Ward's squad for sure."

Jax's face was flushing a deep scarlet, and Elyot could swear he even saw the matted locks of his hair rising up off his scalp. When Jax blew, it was going to be loud.

Keani must have seen it too. She put a hand on Jax's forearm, just a slight touch of her fingertips with her eyes on Alextra the whole time, but it was as if she drew the anger out of him like a leach sucking away blood, only a thousand times faster.

"Both could be true," she said. "The Enforcers might not be here for us. They could be looking for the same thing we are."

"Koltn Ward," Alextra said again. Keani gave a little nod, acknowledging that his presence made that theory unlikely. Elyot understood what that name and that nod meant, but it meant nothing to Jax and his friends.

"What are you talking about?" Jax asked, but his voice was once again calm and carefully modulated not to carry through the trees around them.

"Doesn't matter," Keani said. "I hear them to the north and south but not the west."

"The entrance to the spaceport is to the west," Jax said.

"Spaceport?" Alextra asked.

"Yes," Jax said. "The spaceport. How were you not clear where we were going? This was all your idea in the first place."

"You said rebels," Alextra said.

"And they're in the spaceport," Jax said.

"This is news to me too," Keani said, then turned to stare down Jax. "Jax, if you're spinning tales, if you're lying to us, I swear by all that's holy-"

"Why would you think I'm lying?" Jax asked, raising his hands as if in surrender. "I was rescued by rebels before I could be taken to the maximum-security camp. They brought me to their hidden spaceport and kept me there until the day before yesterday. Then I left because I'd gotten word that you were back."

"Why was Keani being back so important?" Elyot asked, but no one heard him because, at the same moment, Keani was growling, "explain to me how someone hides a spaceport?!?"

Jax's face slowly turned up in a delighted grin. "You'll see. It's amazing."

Then, to Elyot's consternation, Keani grinned back at him.

"All right," she said.

Alextra started to roll her eyes but pressed a hand over them first to hide that show of annoyance. When she dropped her hand, she was all business again.

"Which way, Jax?" she asked. "And don't just say 'west.' We all know that much of it."

"What do you want me to say? The two hundred and eightieth tree beyond the boulder that looks like a Commonwealth strafe bomber? You're just going to have to follow me."

"Then lead on," Alextra said. "But step lively. Those tanks are getting closer."

Jax looked like he wanted to argue for the approaching treads to be rebel all-terrain vehicles again but thought better of it. He gestured for Herlee to lead the way down the path she had picked out circling the sandpit.

To Elyot's eye, the wide-open space they were avoiding was the same sandy ground they were all walking on. There was no border, no shoreline, nothing at all to show that one piece of ground was different from another. There were even little tufts of the same spiky grass dispersed over the sand they were avoiding.

But there were no trees there. And from time to time, he would just catch something scuttling around the far side, something that always disappeared in a thatch of grass before he could quite get a good look at it.

His only sense of where the far side of the sandpit was came when Jax and his crew visibly relaxed, fanning out to walk in an arrow-shaped configuration through the trees. Keani glanced back to make sure Alextra and Elyot were keeping up then jogged ahead to take a position just behind Jax at the point.

Alextra was moving a bit faster now, although Elyot suspected the tight line of her mouth was concealing the beginnings of pain.

Or perhaps worry. She was looking behind them a bit more frequently than seemed necessary to Elyot.

He was just looking back himself, seeing nothing out of the ordinary, when the ball of his foot came down directly on a thorn that pierced through cloth boot and flesh and he half suspected all of the way through to cloth boot again.

He didn't cry out, but even the sharp hiss of his indrawn breath had Alextra shooting him warning glances. Then she saw how he was hobbling and caught his arm to hold him up as he reached down with the other hand to pull the bloody spike out of his foot.

"They're behind us now too," Alextra said. Elyot thought she was just telling him this but then looked up to see that Keani was there too. Drawn by his hiss of pain? It hadn't seemed that loud to him.

"They're herding us?" Keani asked.

"Tell Jax that speed is of essence," Alextra said. "I really hope I'm wrong about him."

"Yeah, I've hoped that a lot myself," Keani said, then turned to run to catch up with the others.

"Can you walk?" Alextra asked. "I have some things I could give you for the wound and the pain, but it would take time we might not have."

"I can walk," Elyot said. He wasn't sure that was true, but after a few steps the pain subsided to an annoying throb. He hadn't pierced anything vital, and although he was leaving a blood trail behind them it was only a few drops with each step. Someone in a tank was unlikely to notice that.

Keani had delivered her message, but rather than moving faster Jax and the others had huddled up again, waiting for Alextra and Elyot to join them.

"Was something unclear?" Alextra asked.

"The trees start thinning out up ahead," Jax said. "We'll be easy to spot."

"But we'll be moving faster," Alextra said.

"But there'll be no cover," Jax said. "They're practically on top of us already. With no trees to hide in, we'll be easy targets."

"Hiding in the trees won't help us," Alextra said, looking up at the sparse branches far overhead. "You said we're close. You better not be wrong."

"Look, I went into and out of this place in the middle of the night," Jax said. "I didn't see much either time. But it doesn't matter. If we press on to the west, we'll reach the point where the jungle ends at the edge of a canyon. I'll know where to go once we hit that. It won't be far."

"Then let's pick up the pace," Alextra said.

"Hey, that's your call," Jax said. "We've only been going this slow on your account."

Alextra shot him a dark look then pushed past him to take the lead. It was not quite a jog, but it was a very fast walk. Keani gave Jax a smirk then fell in step beside Alextra.

Elyot had a little more trouble doing the same. He really, really missed his boots.

He could now hear that Alextra was right; the tanks were on all three sides of them now. He could even hear the snap and crunching rattle of trunks bending and breaking under those heavy treads, the canopy that had a moment before been dancing in the blue sky now ground into green mulch and churned into the sandy ground.

"Anything we should be watching for?" Alextra asked Keani as they sped through the trees. "Hives in the ground or more sandpits?"

"I'm watching," Keani said. "Maybe let me take point, though?"

Alextra seemed reluctant to fall back even half a step, but there was no arguing that this was more Keani's domain than hers. She hesitated a fraction before picking a path around a particularly thick tree trunk, and by the time she was moving due west again, Keani was just a little in front of her.

There was no sound of footsteps behind them, and Elyot glanced back, not sure if he was hoping to see Jax and the others still with them or for the opposite. But they were still there, moving through the trees if not silently then at least not so loud as the approaching vehicles.

Suddenly there was a different roar of engine noise, this directly above them.

"They found us!" Elyot said, finally seeing that what Jax had said was true. To him, it still felt like they were walking through a dense forest, but looking straight up, he saw all the gaps between the leafy branches. Anyone looking down from above could spot them.

"Not Commonwealth," Alextra said. He suspected she was using the fewest words possible. She was breathing harder than she ought to be given that they still weren't actually running.

"Are you sure?" Keani asked, trying to look up at the shadow passing over them and down at the path in front of her both at once without losing a step.

"Positive," Alextra said. "Listen."

Two more passed overhead, so low they were nearly brushing the treetops.

She was right. They weren't Commonwealth. The engines were too loud, too ragged, too sputtery to be coming from the well-maintained Commonwealth fleet.

"Rebels?" Elyot asked. "There really is a spaceport hidden in this jungle? But how?"

If Alextra answered him, he didn't hear it, not over the roar of four more shuttles streaking overhead at twice the speed of their prey.

Elyot felt hands on his shoulder pushing him aside and squawked in protest, but Jax ran past him in a dead sprint without ever looking back. The rest of his crew were sprinting as well, no care for moving silently now, not even any worry about which of the jungle's dangers they might be about to run straight into.

"Keani?" Alextra asked.

"I guess run," Keani said. "If there's any danger, they're going to hit it first, right?" She shot them both a manic grin that really wasn't winning Elyot over on this new plan.

But he didn't want to be left behind either. Finding one last reservoir of energy, he broke into a run.

The aching throb in his foot was a stabbing agony with every step, and the stitch in his side was working its way ever deeper, past his lungs to poke at his heart, when suddenly he was colliding with a body not in motion. One of Jax's crew, who caught him before he could fall down and held him until he had his balance back.

"Thanks," Elyot murmured, but the guy wasn't looking at him. He was looking ahead, the expression on his face mixing wide-eyed amazement and awe with white-lipped fear and anxiety.

Elyot looked up and felt a similar simmering pot of emotions. When he had emerged out of the cave mouth on the side of the mountain under the city, he had been amazed by the vista spread out before him. He specifically remembered it as being trees as far as the eye could see.

But below him now was nothing but sand. The canyon edge stretched as far north and south as he could see, and trees ran right up to that edge, but below there was no green. There was nothing but a yellowish-white that gleamed so brightly in the noonday sun that he couldn't look at it for more than a blink at a time.

"This doesn't make sense," Alextra was murmuring to herself. "There's no way. These ecological systems are too different, too close. The rainfall would have to change by elevation... but that makes no sense. What is going on here?"

"Alextra?" Elyot called out to her. Perhaps she hadn't noticed just how close to that edge she was standing. He could see pebbles skittering away from her feet to fall over the side to some unknown fate hundreds of meters below.

He had a sudden vision of a pile of bodies, hidden from view above. Piles the size of hills, the bottoms skeletal but the tops fresher.

"Alextra!" Keani said, catching her arm and pulling her back until she was pressed up against the trunk of a tree.

Elyot narrowed his eyes to slits against the onslaught of light then looked out over the desert again. He could see dots in the sky, the rebel shuttles with the Commonwealth shuttles in pursuit.

"Where are they going?" he asked. Then he turned to Jax. "You said we were nearly there. You never said we'd be crossing a desert first."

"We are nearly there," Jax said, exasperated. "Obviously they're leading the enemy away. If they just landed here it would no longer be a hidden spaceport, would it?"

Elyot said nothing. He knew nothing about the logistics involved.

He had never even flown on a ship before, or been to the spaceport in the city. But he was pretty sure that hiding even two shuttles and the stationary spot where they always landed had to be something a lot like impossible. Especially from an organization with the drive and resources of the Commonwealth.

Alextra was still getting her breath back. Keani handed her a canteen of water and she took a sip then passed it on to Elyot. Jax and his crew were huddled far enough away that the three of them couldn't hear what was being said.

"What do we do now?" Keani asked the two of them.

"Jax," Alextra said. "His call."

"It's too late," Jax said, stepping back from the huddle. "They're here."

The sound of the tank engines was no closer than before, and Elyot thought that Jax was stalling. The renegade really didn't know where they were going.

But the rise and fall of the engine sounds had settled into a steady drone, and there was no snapping of trunks or crashing of leafy canopies to the ground. Had they stopped moving? Why?

Then he heard a softer sound. Part of him wanted to dismiss it as his imagination, but the rest of him was too paranoid for that. It had sounded like a twig snapping somewhere close by. But he could see nothing through the layers of tree trunks around him.

Jax and his crew moved silently until they were standing with their backs together, forming a circle that bristled with a variety of knives and a few rough-hewn spears.

Elyot took the needle gun out of his tunic pocket. It felt heavier in his hand than he remembered from before. He had never fired a gun before. Was it harder than it looked? Was there some trick to it he didn't know?

Was it even loaded?

He glanced over to see Keani had her knives out as well, but Alextra's tanjo still hung at her hip in short club form. Instead, she was using her hands to signal to Keani and him to stay back.

He glanced behind him at the sheer drop down to the desert below.

It was a few meters away, but what if he lost track of it in the fight? He could end up doing the Enforcers' job for them.

"Jax, run and find the rebels," Alextra said as she moved away from the cliff, further into the trees. "I'll buy you as much time as I can. But run."

Jax looked all around them. There was still no sign of the Enforcers among the tree trunks. But that twig snap had been so close. Where were they hiding?

"Go now," Keani said. Jax didn't look back at her but gave a quick nod, putting his knives away and sprinting away to the south. He kept the cliffside on his right, but not too close.

Herlee looked at Keani, and she gave the renegade a nod. Then Herlee, too, put her knives away and ran off to the south. Arion and the others followed suit.

"What about us?" Elyot asked.

"You wait where you are," Alextra said, finally taking the tanjo from her belt. "I'll face Koltn Ward."

"Alone?" Keani asked.

"It's better that I do, yes," Alextra said.

"I'm not useless," Keani said, gesturing with her knives. Elyot looked down at the needle gun in his hands and said nothing.

"I know you're not," Alextra said. "Just stay back here while I go face him. I'll be all right. He won't hurt me."

"Why not?" Keani asked. "And how can you know that for sure?"

"Because by now, he surely knows who I am," Alextra said. "He suspected before. He pursued us without taking the time to check, pursued us without hurting us."

Elyot wasn't sure if that's how he'd characterize the last few days. Death had felt close at their heels the entire time. Not just from Koltn Ward, but mainly from him.

"But he's had the time to check now," Alextra went on. "He won't hurt me."

"But what if it isn't him this time?" Keani asked.

"It will be," Alextra said, then more loudly as if directing her words to the entire jungle around them, "I can hear his breath, the disciplined rhythm it keeps with his steps. I can practically smell the tang of his morning bowl of protein and greens in paste form. The Commonwealth Enforcer breakfast special. Such a good little soldier."

She looked back at Elyot and Keani one last time and gave them a smile she surely thought would be reassuring to them. But Elyot saw the way the curve of her lips didn't diminish the sadness that lurked at the corners of her eyes.

She didn't think she was coming back. She had enjoyed their little adventure, which apparently had never involved real danger in her mind. And now she was disappointed that it was all over.

Who was she?

Alextra passed in and out of view as she moved through the trees, and Elyot found himself taking a step closer to Keani until they were shoulder to shoulder. She still had her knives in her hands, but they were not raised so high now.

Then Alextra stopped. Whether intentionally or not, she had stopped where Elyot had a clear view of her. She started idly spinning her tanjo in one hand as if bored.

Then Koltn Ward stepped into view before her, and that spin picked up speed. The ends extended, although what form she had summoned Elyot couldn't tell.

"Captain Koltn Ward of the Empress' Enforcers of the Commonwealth of Planets of the Third Quadrant of the Kullab Galaxy," Alextra said casually. "Fourth squad," she added. "Third division."

"Alextra," Koltn Ward said. At first, Elyot found that encouraging. He couldn't have figured out Alextra's secret if he didn't even know her family name.

But then the captain went on. "Your mother is very anxious to have you home safely."

"Is she?" Alextra asked with a theatrical level of doubtfulness. She was still spinning her tanjo around her, passing it from hand to hand without slowing its momentum.

"Officially," Koltn Ward said as if allowing her this slight deviation to his original statement.

Elyot glanced over at Keani, but if she understood any more of this than he was, it didn't show on her face. Mostly she just looked like she longed to start throwing her knives at Koltn Ward's heart.

"Sir!" someone unseen in the trees called.

"Lieutenant?" Koltn Ward said, never taking his eyes off Alextra.

"We have the others," the lieutenant said. A flash of motion caught Elyot's eye, and he could just make out the back of Jax's head from between the trees. It jerked back into view then was pulled out of it again.

He was struggling. Against captors.

"How many?" Koltn Ward asked.

"Seven, sir."

Elyot's heart sank. That was all of them. That was their entire hope of rescue.

"There are two more straight on that way," Koltn Ward said, pointing directly towards Keani and Elyot. "Go fetch those."

"Yes, sir!"

"What now?" Elyot hissed at Keani.

"Run," Keani said, putting her knives away and sprinting to the south. For all the good that had done Jax and the others.

And yet it was the only direction that held any hope at all. Elyot put the gun away and followed.

They hadn't made it more than a dozen steps before the jungle in front of them suddenly came to life, underbrush shaking as if trying to ward them off.

Everything seemed to happen at once, and yet in the center of it all was Elyot's mind running with maddening slowness.

There hadn't been any underbrush here in the west.

Certainly not any underbrush with leafy arms and legs.

He stumbled back. He had some sort of plan that involved turning and running the other way, but his numb feet wouldn't execute it.

Then there was a hand gripping his arm painfully tightly, and a masked face emerged from the foliage that was attacking him.

"It's all right," a woman's voice said to him. "We're friends."

"Enforcers," Elyot squeaked out.

"We've got them surrounded," she said.

"They've got *you* surrounded," Elyot said. "They've got tanks."

"We've dealt with those, if only temporarily," she said. She started pulling him, and even though she was trying to draw him in the direction he had been going, he dug in his heels.

"Not without my friends," he said.

"They're coming," she said with real impatience now. Elyot dug his heels in again then twisted his arm out of her grasp, scrabbling and stumbling then scrabbling again until he was once more running through the trees.

Keani had broken free as well, if she had ever been caught at all, and the two of them reached Alextra's side at nearly the same moment.

Despite Alextra's words about her assured safety, Koltn Ward had his sidearm drawn and aimed at her. Elyot struggled to get his own gun free from his pocket to aim it at the captain.

"Two hands for you, I should think, lad," Koltn Ward said. He had never taken his eyes off Alextra, but Elyot knew he was talking about him and his shaking hands.

Elyot moved his left hand to support his right.

"It's all right, Elyot," Alextra said. "Captain Ward was just leaving."

Koltn Ward smirked then moved the end of his gun slightly, as if finessing his aim. But there was no mistaking the sounds of scuffling all around them. The rebels might be hard to spot when they were disguised as part of the jungle, but they weren't hard to hear when they moved about.

It sounded like the jungle itself was swallowing up the Enforcers.

And spitting up Jax and his crew, who were popping out all around Alextra's little clearing, knives in hand and looking for a target.

"Not the moment, then," Koltn Ward said, and put his weapon away. "You can't get away, and I'm in no hurry."

"Another time," Alextra agreed, her tanjo coming to a stop behind her.

"We're just letting him go?" Elyot asked, his voice screeching higher than he liked.

"The rebels will try to catch him, I'm sure," Alextra said.

"Try and fail," Elyot said. "I got away from them, after all."

"They let you go because they didn't want to hurt you," Alextra said.

The sound of gunfire echoed through the trees, close by but then further away.

Jax jogged up to Alextra. "Told you I'd find them."

"Yes, good job," Alextra said, contracting her tanjo to club form and putting it back on her belt.

Then someone else was in the clearing, a man dressed in camouflage but without the leafy branches. A black mask covered his hair and face except for just around his eyes. Judging by the crow's feet he was older, and judging from the white scar that bisected his left eyebrow, not remotely a fresh injury, he had seen a lot of action in those years.

"You're in charge?" Alextra asked. The man turned to look at her, and both of his eyebrows went up in surprise when he saw how she was dressed. The black of her leggings and tunic and even her boots was unmarred by dust or mud, and her cape was draped elegantly around her shoulders. She didn't look remotely like someone who had spent the last few days trekking through a jungle.

"You're far from home," he said. Then he turned his attention to her two companions. His gaze passed over Keani, dressed the same as Jax and his crew and looking entirely like someone who had been in this jungle since birth. His gaze was about to pass over Elyot as well, who looked much the same at the moment despite his childhood in the city.

But then he did a double-take, stepping closer as if to get a better look. Elyot fought the urge to touch his own face as if to feel out what was so captivating to this man.

"You're in charge?" Alextra asked again.

"I am," the man said, still staring at Elyot.

"Calrin," the woman who had grabbed Elyot said as she emerged from the trees. "We have to go."

"Right," Calrin said. "Their tanks are dealing with some obstacles we threw in their way, but that won't last long. We need to disappear."

"Calrin," Elyot said, but so quietly no one heard him.

"Koltn Ward?" Keani asked, loudly and urgently.

"Who?" the woman asked.

"The captain that was riding in the point tank," Calrin told her. "Captured or killed?"

"No idea," the woman said. "We got more than a few of them, but I'll have to debrief the squads and check the cam footage to know for sure if we got a captain."

"He got away," Keani said, glaring at Alextra.

"It doesn't matter," Alextra told her.

"Calrin," Elyot said again, but louder this time.

"Yes?" Calrin said, then realized who it was that was calling his name.

"Elyot," Elyot said, touching his own chest and resisting the urge to explain that these weren't really his clothes.

Calrin pulled off his black mask, tousling up his thick, snowy white hair and grinning at Elyot. "Yes, Valria's son," he said. "I thought that was you. But it's been years, and your twice the size you were when I last saw you."

"You know this guy?" Keani asked.

"I did," Elyot said. "Calrin, where's my mother?"

"Calrin, we have to go!" the woman said, more urgently now.

"Right," Calrin said to her, then made a gesture with his raised hand. The jungle around them rustled again, but this time moving as one and all in the same direction.

"Keep moving," Calrin said, giving them each a little shove as if they needed a push-start. "It's not far, and it will be safer to talk there than here."

"But my mother," Elyot insisted.

"Yes, your mother," Calrin said. "That's a long story. But the short version is, she's alive. And I just might be able to get you to her. But not if we don't get safely underground first. Come on!"

And yet again Elyot found himself sprinting through the woods, but this time the pain in his foot didn't slow him down.

This time, nothing could.

6 SECRETS AND LIES

THE REBELS MOVED SWIFTLY through the jungle, charting a path through fallen trees and sinkholes that spoke of deep familiarity with the terrain. The camouflage they wore meant they were each covered in leafy branches, but despite their speed and the occasional leap over a rotting log, the only sound they made was little more than a whisper of wind through the undergrowth.

Keani and Jax and the rest of the kids from the prison village were just as adept at moving swiftly and silently, if less familiar with the specific terrain here. And Alextra's ethereal grace was only slightly diminished by the injuries she was still recovering from.

Compared to all that, Elyot felt like he was crashing through the undergrowth with all the quiet subtlety of one of the Commonwealth enforcer tanks. He was wearing the same cloth boots as the Jax's crew, but somehow his footsteps still slapped loudly as he stumbled more than ran through the trees.

The rebels were leading them on a path more or less parallel to the cliff-side, although they were keeping under the cover of the trees. Elyot could hear the sound of Commonwealth shuttles, but they weren't close by.

Then the rumble of the tanks that had been at such a constant, low pitch he had stopped really hearing it suddenly roared back to full life. The rebel in front of Elyot stopped and looked back. It was Calrin, but he wasn't looking back at Elyot. Elyot looked back over his own shoulder but saw nothing behind him through the overlapping trees.

"Calrin?" one of the other rebels asked.

"Get them to the cliff-side," Calrin said.

"But the shuttles—"

"Aren't as close as those tanks," Calrin said. "Get these kids moving faster." The rebel nodded and started whispering into some sort of wrist communicator. Calrin turned his attention to Elyot. "Double time, boy. We're nearly there."

Elyot nodded and scrambled around a massive tree trunk and over a tangle of fallen limbs, no longer concerned with the amount of noise he was making. No one pursuing them was going to hear anything over the sounds of their own tanks now, anyway.

The trees grew sparser, the ground more grassy as they approached the cliff-side. A hot, dry wind blew into his face, carrying with it a very different aroma from the thick vegetation smell he had been breathing constantly since leaving the city that had been his only home since birth.

Elyot climbed around another half-fallen tree and emerged in an open clearing where another blast of hot air hit him. It blew through his hair, drying the sweat from his brow in an instant. But the wind was full of particles of sand that abraded the skin of his face and coated the back of his already parched throat.

He closed his eyes and turned his face away until the wind died back down, but when he started to move forward again, a hand gripped his shoulder, restraining him. He blinked the sand from his eyes until he could see all the rebels standing still as statues, wrapping their arms around his companions as if to lend them the cover of their own camouflage.

Then Elyot heard the erratic rattling of the rebel shuttle engines as they came from behind him, passing overhead and nosing down hard to plunge along the cliff-side. Six Commonwealth shuttles followed, their own finely tuned engines almost silent in comparison. Three dove after the two rebel shuttles, the others splitting apart in a three-pronged formation out over the desert.

They were still in view when Calrin wove a hand in the air, and everyone started moving again.

"But those shuttles can still see us," Elyot said, fighting the urge to cling to the trunk of the last tree.

"Our shuttles aren't going to be able to give us a better opportunity," Calrin said. "This base is burnt for us for sure now. But we have to get inside before we can evacuate."

"Inside where?" Elyot asked.

Then he saw one of the rebels leap over the side of the cliff, branches of his camouflage fluttering in the air before he plunged out of view.

And then Alextra jumped after him.

"It's all right," Calrin told him, and Elyot realized his mouth was hanging open in horror and disbelief. He shut his mouth, biting down on his lip for good measure. Keani was at the edge now, but she stopped to look back and wave at him before stepping over the edge to plunge down into... what?

"Our turn," Calrin said, and Elyot followed him over the sun-baked grass of the clearing to the cliff's edge. The wind picked up again, and he lifted an arm to protect his eyes from the blowing sand.

When he lowered his arm, he found himself standing on a bare outcropping of rock, the desert spread out on all sides below him.

Far below him.

A wave of vertigo rocked him, but then he heard Keani calling his name.

"It's just like the mountain," she said to him.

He wanted to argue that point. The mountain had been steep, sure, but this cliff seemed to curve in on itself. It wasn't the same at all.

"Elyot, just look at me," Keani said. He realized he had shut his eyes against the glare of the noonday sun reflecting up off the sand. He opened them and looked around until he finally saw Keani waving up at him. She was below him, standing on a ledge that was barely wider than her shoulders. "Just jump down to me."

"It looks worse than it is," Calrin said from behind him. "That ledge is angled towards the cliff wall. If you do stumble, you'll fall towards safety. But I don't think you'll stumble."

"Elyot, the shuttles are coming back," Keani said.

"Back up a bit," Elyot said to her. "I don't want to fall into you and take us both over the edge."

He expected her to argue, but she just nodded and took several steps back. Without looking behind her, which made his stomach flutter in alarm. He took a deep breath, made sure he wasn't about to bite down on his own lip or anything if he landed hard, then stepped over the edge.

The rock he landed on was like a concave dish, as if smoothed by countless feet, making the same landing. The ledge was narrow, but unlike on the outcropping above, he no longer felt like he was being thrust out into nothingness. The sand was just as far below, but easier to put out of his mind.

Keani was waving him to follow, and he realized Calrin was still standing above. He kept one hand on the surprisingly cold stone under the shadow of the clifftop and walked along the ledge.

This he could do. It was just like walking along the tops of walls and over rooftops back in the city. The sands below were no more a pressing concern than the views of the jungle below from his mountaintop home.

The ledge ran more or less level, although it made three blind hairpin turns around outcroppings of rock. He could usually see Keani in front of him, but the others were too far ahead.

Then he slipped around one last stony protrusion and the ledge became a sort of natural staircase up to a long, low cave. He had to duck to get inside, but thankfully, once inside the cool darkness, there was room enough to stand.

"Keani?" he called. After the blinding whiteness of the desert, the sudden darkness was disorienting. Worse, the walls were too far away for him to reach. He shuffled forward, once again wishing he had his own boots back, with their reinforced toes.

"This way," Keani said, and he felt her hand brush against his. "There's another couple of turns, but then you'll see the light."

At first it was only like the blackness became more of a grayness, one where any details of the world around him were still obscure. Then he could see Keani's silhouette in front of him. That silhouette gained definition as they continued walking, but even rising up on tiptoes to look over her head, he saw nothing like a light source.

"Keani, anyone still ahead of you?" Calrin asked from behind Elyot.

"Not that I can see," she said. "The cave takes a turn. Are we going back out?"

"No, stop here," Calrin said.

Elyot could see nothing different about where they were standing. Keani also gave up, looking around with a careless shrug.

The fact that Calrin as well looked stumped about what to do next was not particularly comforting.

"Okay, it's here," he said, running his hands over the stone wall of the cave. "Somewhere around here," he amended, fingers still probing the wall.

"You don't know how to get in?" Keani asked.

"I don't usually leave the bridge," he said.

"You came out for Elyot?" Keani guessed.

"No," Calrin said. "I had no idea Elyot was out there. It was the tanks. Tanks in the jungle, and not on one of the Commonwealth transport roads. Very unusual. Ah, here we go." He stepped back from the wall. At first nothing seemed to be happening, but then Elyot realized he could see the satisfied grin on Calrin's face more clearly than before. Where was that light coming from?

Then Calrin took a step into the stone wall. Into, and then through it.

"Come on," Keani said, catching at Elyot's sleeve before following Calrin to pass ghost-like through the wall.

Elyot plunged after. The uneven stone floor became smooth and level, and he could finally see where the light was coming from.

The cave was now a squared-off tunnel, still entirely of stone but no longer naturally formed. Lights were set into the ceiling so that the circles of illumination they cast down onto the floor just overlapped at the edges.

"This way," Calrin said, and lead the way at a pace that was more jog than walk. Elyot looked back down the endless tunnel behind him, but all he could see was light after light until the tunnel was no more than a point in the distance. Where did it go?

"Elyot! Come on!" Keani hissed back to him. If the tunnel ran endlessly on in a straight line like it appeared to, there was little chance he would lose his way. And yet, having just walked through a solid wall of stone, there could be all sorts of cross passages he wasn't seeing.

He ran until he caught up, just in time to see Calrin once more step through a wall and disappear. But the tunnel had better light than the cave, and he could see more details here. The wall itself still looked like ordinary rock, even now that he knew it wasn't, but at the moment Calrin had passed through it, the entire thing had shimmered. It wasn't like a flicker of light, more like a pool of water disturbed by a tiny pebble, sending ripples out but quickly settling back to stillness.

"Have you ever seen anything like this?" Keani asked, reaching out a hand to touch the wall. Her fingertips just brushed the surface, sending out more ripples.

"Never," Elyot said. "We have holograms, or they do in the richer parts of the city, but they're nothing like this. Not that I've seen, anyway," he finished lamely. He had spent his entire life within the high mountain walls of the largest city on the planet, but until this moment it had never occurred to him that he hadn't seen much more of anything than Keani had, and she had been raised by prisoners in a labor camp.

"I bet Alextra has," Keani said, but there was no bitterness to her tone. No, it was full of wonder, as if the mere thought of what Alextra had seen in her lifetime delighted her.

"Let's go," Elyot said. He didn't want to lose Calrin, but he didn't want to go first either. He wanted another chance at seeing what exactly happened when someone walked through the wall.

Keani nodded, then plunged through, but even when he was watching closely, it was all over too quickly for him to see it all. He supposed that made sense. If the effects lasted more than a second, it would be useless as camouflage.

Elyot stepped through to find himself in what looked like a storage room. There were shelving racks all around him, loaded with sealed containers of various sizes. The light was only a little brighter than in the tunnel behind him, and was coming from the far end of the room. He stepped out from between the shelves to see that the light was streaming in from an open door.

He turned to look at the wall behind him. It still appeared to be stone. He leaned into the space between two shelves to touch a spot on the wall as far as he could reach from the camouflaged doorway. It felt like stone, cold and slightly damp.

But the other three walls were a dull gray metal broken up into sections about an arm's reach in size. He could see where the sections were clamped together. He walked away from the stone wall, past the rows of shelves, to the far wall to get a better look. Yes, he could see it now. Each arm's-wide section had two anchors that fit into the stone floor. He gave the wall a testing push, but it was solid.

"Elyot!" Keani called from the doorway. He could barely see more than the outline of her head; the lights in the corridor behind her were too bright compared to the dim storage room he was standing in.

"This whole thing comes apart?" he asked her as he headed towards the doorway.

"The prison camp structures do too," Keani told him. "This looks like more solid material, though. I wonder where they got it?"

"Stolen," Calrin said from where he was standing, arms crossed in the middle of the corridor, waiting for them to catch up. "From the Commonwealth." Then he turned on his heel and resumed his fast walk.

"How big is this place?" Elyot asked as he fell into step beside him.

"It's our second largest post," Calrin said. "Nearly two hundred fighters are stationed here."

"And the Commonwealth has never suspected?" Elyot asked.

"We've been careful," Calrin said. "But it's over now. We're already preparing to move operations."

"Move operations?" Keani asked. "You mean take this all apart and load it up on trucks?"

"Shuttles mainly," Calrin said. "And I don't think we'll be able to take all of it. Time isn't on our side."

They were still walking down the same corridor, but they had passed many cross corridors. They were moving too quickly to get more than a glimpse down any of them, but Elyot saw people bustling about, dodging around hover loaders filled to nearly the tipping point with containers of supplies, stacks of weapons, and pieces of equipment.

"We came at a bad time?" Elyot asked hopefully. Calrin didn't answer, but the look he shot Elyot said enough.

The rebels were packing up and leaving because Elyot and his friends had inadvertently led trouble right to their door.

"My mother—" Elyot started to say, but Calrin raised his hand to interrupt him. They had reached the end of the corridor and were now in the back of a long room. There was enough room for a row of work-stations, then a few steps down to another row, and then another. Every workstation faced the open space where the opposite wall of the room should be.

And that open space looked down over a massive hangar space filled with shuttles, fighter ships, surveillance drones, and other kinds of craft he could only guess the purposes of.

The moment they had stepped inside, four people had jumped up from their workstations to rush towards Calrin. Calrin pulled the first aside to have a whispered conversation out of the doorway, and the other three fell in behind to wait their turn.

"Look, there's Alextra," Keani said, pointing to the far end of the room. Jax and the others were at the very edge, leaning over a railing to peer down into the hangar below, but Alextra was back a bit, talking with one of the rebel women. Then she saw the two of them and raised a hand in greeting. She said something else to the woman, then strode up the stairs until she reached Keani and Elyot.

"What's going on?" Elyot asked.

"It's as we feared," Alextra said. "We brought trouble with us, and now this spaceport has to be abandoned."

"But how was this our fault?" Keani asked. "Those Commonwealth shuttles were already chasing the rebels all over the sky. That's nothing to do with us."

"That's not the problem," Alextra said. "The rebels have put a subprogram in the Commonwealth shuttle systems. The rebel shuttles disappear from their scopes, and the spaceport is not detectable by them at all."

"How is that possible?" Elyot asked.

"It was done from the flagship," Alextra said with a shrug. "A spy installed this subprogram there, and all the shuttles in this system get their updates from there. No one has found it in routine checks, at least not yet. The rebels here were safe so long as they were careful. Their pilots made a convincing show of losing their tails through skillful flying, even though they would've been visible if the Commonwealth scopes weren't actively hiding them."

"So they could be seen by someone just looking out a window? And no one has done that in how long?" Elyot asked.

"Yes, they could be seen by someone in a shuttle looking out an unenhanced window, one not connected to the scopes. But all functional windows, such as for pilots or gunners, are enhanced. They're meant to aid in seeing targets, but that makes them vulnerable to this sort of spoofing."

"Okay," Elyot said, letting a thousand followup questions go for the moment. "But what's that got to do with us?"

"The tanks," Keani guessed.

"Exactly," Alextra said. "Someone in a tank saw something. The tanks also have enhanced windows, of course, but the subprogram doesn't affect tank systems."

"They saw the shuttles, then? They weren't close enough to see the hideout," Elyot said.

"Maybe they didn't see anything," Alextra said with a shrug. "But they might have, and the rebels can't take that chance. And once they revealed themselves to rescue us, it really was all over. The Commonwealth will scour this entire area. So they're moving this whole post to another location, and in a hurry."

"How is that going to be hidden?"

"It's not," Calrin said, suddenly standing over the three of them with no one else clamoring for his attention. "We'll be leaving here in full view, conducting a series of demolition raids and nuisance missions, and hopefully keeping the Commonwealth so busy, a few key transport shuttles can sneak away."

"The shuttles are incoming, sir," someone called.

"Thank you, Dex," Calrin said over his shoulder.

Elyot caught hold of Calrin's sleeve before he could turn away. "My mother?"

"Your mother is on the Commonwealth flagship," Calrin said, then put his hand over Elyot's own. "She was a spy, but she was caught."

"Killed?" Elyot choked out.

"No, at least not yet," Calrin said. "There are conflicting reports about what happened and when. She may have been disciplined for some completely unrelated offense and put in the brig for a short time. Or she might have been caught spying and is being detained for that."

"That carries a death sentence," Alextra said, "after a short investigation and even shorter trial."

"We're aware," Calrin said. But now that his attention was focused on Alextra, the matter of Elyot's mother seemed to fade from his mind. He just tapped a fingertip on his lips repeatedly, lost in thought.

Thought that was interrupted by Jax marching up to them, taking the steps two at a time.

"Don't listen to anything those three tell you!" he said.

"Jax, wasn't it?" Calrin asked with a frown.

"That's right," Jax said.

"Do you have an explanation for your behavior?" Calrin asked.

"I brought back recruits," Jax said, gesturing at the other prison camp kids clustered behind him.

"You weren't asked to go fetch recruits," Calrin said. "You were asked to stay put until we could move you to one of the other posts where we could use you. We don't break in newbies here, this close to the capital. You were told."

"I waited," Jax said sullenly. "I waited as long as I could, but nothing was happening and no one was telling me anything."

"You were told to wait," Calrin said. "Repeatedly."

"I don't want to wait; I want to fight!" Jax said.

"We have no use for a soldier who won't follow orders," Calrin said, then looked past Jax to his friends. "And if this lot follows your lead, it's probably best if all of you slip away like you did last time."

Jax's face flushed red, but he avoided meeting the inquisitive gaze of any of his companions. His jaw kept clenching and unclenching as he churned through possible responses without coming up with anything. It was only when Calrin started to turn his attention away from the group of them and back to Alextra that he finally found the words.

"You can't trust her," he said, stabbing a finger at Alextra. "That enforcer captain had her in his grasp and he let her go. She's clearly one of them."

"Captain Koltn Ward was following protocol," Alextra said as if answering a query from Calrin and not an accusation from Jax. "He intended to detain me through nonlethal means, and was exhibiting an abundance of caution to avoid doing me even a minor injury, but I assure you he was not letting me go."

"No, I could see that," Calrin said. "You were using that to buy time for the rest of your companions to escape."

"Attempting to," Alextra said. "Of course I was hoping to still evade capture myself."

"I want to ask you why," Calrin said, "but I would want a complete answer, and now isn't the time."

Alextra gave him a tight nod. "Is there anything I can do to help?" she asked.

Calrin raised a single eyebrow. "Are you siding with us? Openly?"

"That might not be wise," Alextra said. "Or indeed helpful to you. But I have skills that could be of use to you more covertly."

"What are you two talking about?" Elyot asked.

"Nuisance missions," Alextra said, still looking only at Calrin. "Like you said before."

"Interesting," Calrin said and started to lapse back into lip-tapping thought, but instead gave himself a little shake. "I have to see to some things here first. And I'm already late for a meeting with the other rebel leaders. We'll talk again in a few hours. In the meantime, I'm going to have Dex take you to the pilot ready room. If you need to eat or sleep or shower and get a change of clothes, Dex will take care of you. Take advantage of it while we can still offer it; this spaceport will be little more than a windy cave by nightfall."

"But my mother—" Elyot started to say.

"Is exactly what we'll be discussing when I see you next," Calrin said, walking backwards away from them. "Your mother, and nuisance missions," he said, pointing first at Elyot and then at Alextra. Then he turned and left the room through a smaller door off to the side of the top deck.

"This way," Dex said, waving for them to follow him back the way they'd come.

The pilot ready room was one doorway back down the corridor. One side of the room was rows of chairs facing a holographic display currently showing all the Commonwealth ships hovering over the city. The other side of the room was more casual, with tables and chairs and a kitchenette along one wall.

"Showers are through there on the left," Dex told them, pointing down a short hallway opposite the door on the other side of the room. "And bunks are on the right. You can crash on any of them; they aren't assigned. Eat anything you find in the cabinets. It saves us packing it up and moving it. Does anyone want a change of clothes?"

"Yes, please," Elyot said. "Anything is better than what I'm wearing. Do you have proper boots?"

"Like mine?" Dex asked, turning a foot back and forth so that Elyot could admire his brightly polished ankle-high boot. There would be no slipping with the treads on those heavy soles, and no thorn could pierce that thick leather. They were nicer than anything he had ever owned.

"Perfect," Elyot said.

"I'll find a couple of sizes so you can see which fit best," Dex said. "How about the rest of you?"

"We're good," Jax said. The others just nodded, a few shooting Elyot dirty looks, apparently for slandering his borrowed wardrobe, which was identical to theirs.

"Come with me, then," Dex said, and Elyot followed him down the short hallway and to the right. This room was a barracks with about a dozen bunks surrounded by rows of lockers. Dex started opening locker doors at random, tossing out anything that looked like it might fit Elyot.

When they were done, Elyot was wearing black pants of a thick but stretchy fabric that didn't bind up or get tight when he moved. The pants had several large pockets on the outside and even tiny pockets hidden on the inside, perhaps for sneaking computer disks with infiltrating subprograms onto Commonwealth flagships. His shirt fit close to his body but like the pants didn't get tight when he moved, and the olive green vest he wore over it gave him still more pockets. He dispersed his few possessions among the pockets, tucking the needle gun into a side pocket on his pants that was designed for just such a purpose.

And the boots were, indeed, perfection.

When he finally came back out into the ready room, he found Keani and Alextra sitting apart from the others, heads close together as they talked.

"Everything all right?" Elyot asked as he pulled up a chair to sit with them.

"Just waiting for Calrin to make his appearance," Alextra said. "Dex said it might be a while. He's in a remote conference with the leaders at the other rebel posts."

"Are you hungry?" Keani asked, pushing various foil-wrapped packages across the table towards him. "That meat and gravy thing is pretty good. I had three myself."

"I'll try that," Elyot said. The only label on the package was a pictogram that didn't exactly give him a clear idea as to the contents, just a line drawing of a bowl emitting steam. But Keani gave him a little nod when he touched one, and when he pulled open the tab, the contents instantly self-heated to a steaming warmth.

"It's a shame we led the tanks here," Keani said with a sigh. "Imagine if we had gotten here unseen. We could've joined them and just lived here, all hidden away."

"We'd have to join the rebellion to stay here, right? Sign on to be soldiers?" Elyot asked around a mouthful of actually quite good chipped meat in brown sauce.

"Soldiers or spies or something that makes a contribution," Keani said. "But that's true everywhere. Wherever we go, we're going to have to find something to do if we want food and shelter."

"There are worse jobs," Elyot agreed. "But we can still join, right? I mean, they're moving this post, but there are others. And this one will just be in a different place. They'll still need recruits."

"Is that what you want to do?" Alextra asked. He suspected she was using a lot of care to keep her voice inflectionless.

"I guess so," Elyot said. "I mean, my mother is one of them. It feels like I belong here."

"But you weren't here," Alextra said. "Maybe that was deliberate, on your mother's part."

"I was just a kid when she disappeared," Elyot said. "I'm not a kid anymore."

"Fair enough," Alextra said. "What about you, Keani?"

"Me?" Keani said. "I never made any plans at all. I mean, escaping from the prison camp wasn't even really a plan. It just sort of happened. After Jax and his friends started all the trouble, it seemed wisest to stay out of sight until it all cooled back down."

"But you came to the city," Alextra said.

"I was curious," Keani admitted.

"And now?"

"I don't know," Keani said. "I'm not going to be in a hurry to turn my back on food and shelter unless what's asked in return is really bad, I'll tell you that."

"I get that," Alextra said.

"But what about you?" Elyot asked her. "What do you intend to do next?"

She was about to answer when two people came into the room, both in flight suits. The man headed straight for the kitchenette and started digging through cupboards, but the woman's eyes scanned the room until she saw Elyot, Alextra and Keani all looking at her. Then she gave a little nod and walked over to their table.

"Hey," she said, pulling up a chair. She was keeping her voice low, as if she didn't necessarily want Jax and the others to hear. "I'm Laera. Back there is my copilot, Wayde."

"Elyot, Keani and Alextra," Elyot said, pointing at himself and then his two companions with his spoon before going back to scraping the last of the gravy off the sides of the container.

"Calrin told me who you were," Laera said.

"What else did Calrin tell you?" Alextra asked. Laera looked her over carefully as if checking aspects of her appearance off a mental checklist. "That's mostly classified," she said. Then she looked up as Wayde approached, a food packet in each hand with a steaming drink balanced on top. He hooked a foot around the leg of a chair and maneuvered it into position, sitting beside Laera and setting a packet with its still-balanced drink in front of each of them.

"Hey," he said to the three of them, also keeping his voice low.

"What's going on?" Elyot asked.

"We're eating," Wayde said, pulling the tab off his food packet and releasing a cloud of steam along with the odor of about a dozen spices.

"We only have a short turnaround between missions," Laera said. "When we get the word, we'll be heading out again. No sleep for us."

"You were on one of those shuttles we saw," Alextra guessed. "You flew over us with those Commonwealth ships on your tail."

"We lost the tail," Laera said.

"We always do," Wayde said.

"Until the day we don't," Laera said with a sharp look.

"Never happen," Wayde said, ignoring her deepening frown.

"Don't tempt fate," Laera said to him before turning her attention to her own food. "But he's not wrong. Our little rebellion never would've lasted this long if we weren't twice as good as any Commonwealth pilot. We have to be."

"This is a remote world," Alextra said. "These pilots are not exactly the Commonwealth's best."

Elyot frowned at her. Why did she sound defensive about the Commonwealth all of a sudden?

"I suppose that's true," Laera said around a large mouthful of food.

"You don't understand," Alextra said. "The minute your rebellion becomes more than a nuisance, the minute the Commonwealth chooses to actually respond, you'll be done. You'll all be gone, and it won't even take a full minute."

"I suppose that's true," Laera said again with a shrug.

"Hey, captain," Wayde said to her. "Tell her to stow the helpless commentary. It's putting me off my digestion."

"Your digestion will be the least of your problems," Alextra started to say, but Keani quickly talked over her.

"Elyot, tell us about your mother," she said.

"My mother? I wouldn't know where to start. She's been gone so long, and she never told me about any of this," he said.

"Your mother is a hero of the resistance," Laera said without looking up from her food.

"You know her?" Elyot asked.

Laera nodded, but it was Wayde who spoke. "We're the ones who flew her up to the flagship." Laera shot him a hard glare, and he quickly amended, "I mean, I wasn't a copilot yet, but I was on the shuttle crew. A valuable member of the crew," he said, giving Laera a look like he was daring her to contradict him.

"You manned the door," she allowed.

"That was part of getting her on board without being detected," he said.

"True enough," Laera said, then leaned forward to speak to the other three. "You can't blame Wayde for bragging up his part in that mission. The rebellion hasn't matched that success since. We get spies on board from time to time, but they get burned within days. But your mother, she's been up there for years. She's the one who inserted the subprogram into the Commonwealth shuttle nav systems. And she's surely the reason they've never found that subprogram."

"Surely? You don't know what she's been doing?" Elyot asked.

"It's hard for her to get messages out," Laera said.

"Calrin said she was caught," Elyot said. Laera and Wayde traded a long look.

"That's what the uppity-ups seem to think," Laera said.

"You don't think they're right?" Alextra asked.

"I don't like the source of that intel," Laera said, wrinkling her nose. "Never trusted that guy."

"I never liked him either," Wayde said. "But I don't see what he would gain by lying about Valria."

"I'm just saying, we should be doing more to find out what's really going on," Laera said. "Especially now that they're bound to dig out that subprogram."

"Why would they do that?" Elyot asked.

"The tanks saw things the shuttles didn't," Keani guessed. "They'll figure that out soon if they haven't already, and they won't stop digging until they find out why."

"But if they didn't know about that before now, why is my mother in trouble?" Elyot asked.

"She's been undercover far longer than anyone else we've inserted," Wayde said.

"That we know about," Laera said. "It's not like the identities of all of our intelligence operatives are common knowledge to shuttle pilots."

Just then, the door to the room banged open and Calrin came in, looking flustered and harried. "Good, you're all still together. That makes this easier."

"Are we going to rescue my mother?" Elyot asked.

"Not until we find out why Koltn Ward didn't kill your friend there," Jax said from the far side of the room.

"You aren't going anywhere," Calrin said to Jax, and gave him a cold glare until he slowly hunched back down into his seat to stare sullenly at his food.

"I can explain," Alextra said calmly.

"No need," Calrin said. "At least, not to me. I'm hoping you'll explain it to your friends on the ride up."

Elyot expected her to say that they weren't really friends, but she didn't. And then he finally actually heard the end of that sentence. "Ride up to where?" he asked, hardly daring to hope.

"Laera, are you and Wayde prepared for another flight?" Calrin asked the pilot. Wayde sat forward in his chair, clearly longing to declare his total preparedness.

But Laera responded more sedately. "We're always ready, sir. Is this another dogfight?"

"Nope. Blockade run," Calrin said. "I need you to get these three up to the flagship."

"That doesn't sound like a nuisance mission to me," Alextra said.

"No, it's a little more significant than that. But don't worry. We're not selling you out," he said. "I have someone up on that flagship who is anxious to meet you."

Elyot wanted to ask if this person was his mother, but having been cut off every other time he tried to mention her, he held his tongue. But the warm glow in Calrin's eyes answered his question, anyway.

He was going to see his mother again. He wouldn't be alone anymore.

"Just the three of them are going up?" Jax asked.

"Just the three of them," Calrin said. "I have jobs for the rest of you if you want them. But I'm warning you, it's no easy life here. If you choose to stay, you will work and work hard. I don't have any place for a wanna-be hero who can't be troubled to carry heavy loads when carrying heavy loads is required."

Elyot expected another one of Jax's outbursts, and indeed Jax's silence had a sullen quality to it. But he looked to each of his comrades in turn, and when they all gave him the nod, he said, "we'll do it, sir. Just point to what you want carried and where you want it carried to."

"Excellent," Calrin said, and sounded genuinely pleased. "I'm sorry I don't have another moment to spare you all, but I have a spaceport to vacate. Laera, I'm counting on you to get these three up to the flagship without getting caught."

"Never been caught yet," Wayde said, and Laera shot him a quick glare.

"You can count on us, sir," she said. Then she and Wayde stood up and started gathering the remains of their quick meal. Elyot piled up the empty foil containers and was about to bring them to the trash when he saw Jax standing uncertainly a few meters away.

"Keani?" he said.

"Not now, Jax," Keani said.

"We might not see each other again," he said.

"That was true the last time, too," she said. Then she turned her back on him and strode out of the room. Alextra gave Jax a cold look, then followed.

"I'm sure you'll see her again," Elyot said. He didn't know why he said it. He had no way of knowing if it was true, and no reason to want Jax to feel better about anything. But he said it anyway.

Then he followed Laera and Wayde out of the room, jogging to keep up as they hustled to the flight deck and their waiting shuttle.

He was going up to those Commonwealth ships, the ones that had been mutely oppressing him for so many years.

He was going into space.

7 RUNNING THE BLOCKADE

THE INTERIOR of the shuttle was far snugger than Elyot would have expected. There was barely room enough for him to stand, and Alextra had to stoop to keep her head from hitting the bulkheads. Keani had an easier time. Perhaps the people who had built this ship had been scaling it to someone more her size.

The interior had a stale people smell to it, like too many people had sweated inside this enclosed space and not enough cleaning had been done between missions. There was also a sweet smell, but Elyot was pretty sure that was from whatever sort of puddle he stepped in as he came inside the door. Someone's spilled drink, mostly dehydrated now.

Then Keani, the last one up the ramp, closed the door behind her, and the inside of the shuttle immediately felt too close and too stuffy. Elyot had never been claustrophobic in his life, but he really hated the feeling of being inside a tin can, unable to let himself out.

Then a vent beside his head started blasting him with cool, metallic-smelling air. Not great, but better than the hot, close alternative.

He moved further inside to get out of Keani's way. There wasn't much to see inside the shuttle. It was almost like someone had gutted whatever had been built inside originally to allow for this open space. For hauling people or cargo, he supposed.

Laera and Wayde sat in chairs that were set lower than the main floor inside of little half-spheres of space completely surrounded by panels and displays. The chairs could pivot in any direction, and the two of them were whirling about as they hit this switch or adjusted that setting in preparation of launch.

Everything behind those cockpit chairs was cold, unadorned bulkheads and the inside curvature of the hull. Elyot feared they would be sitting on the floor, and started looking around for any sort of handhold. He had no idea what flying was even going to be like, but he had seen the way the shuttles that flew over his head had banked and turned, sharply and at great speed. He could only imagine what it was going to be like riding inside of one when they maneuvered like that.

But Alextra seemed quite at home inside the ship. She pounded the side of her fist at what seemed to Elyot to be random spots on the inside of the hull, but then little squares of metal dropped down to hang horizontally.

Seats. She had made seats appear.

"Buckle in," she said, taking the seat closest behind Laera. Elyot sat across from her, behind Wayde. Keani pounded her own seat open and sat down next to Alextra.

"You've been on a shuttle before," Keani said to Alextra.

"Never this model," Alextra said. "But yes."

"Is that part of what Calrin wanted you to tell us?" Elyot asked.

"Probably, but let's hold on to that thought for now," Laera said as she and Wayde locked their chairs in a forward position. Some of their taller displays folded down, and one continuous display appeared behind them, stretching from a point beside Alextra all the way around the front of the shuttle to a point beside Elyot.

Then that screen flickered to life, and Elyot saw the opening of the spaceport with the brightly lit desert beyond.

"What's the plan?" Alextra asked as she leaned over Laera's shoulder as far as her seat's restraints would allow her to. Elyot was still fussing with his own belts, trying to work out what went where.

"We're going up to the flagship. We have a contact inside that will give us permission to dock. Then we'll meet in the hangar and make the exchange," Laera said.

"Exchange?" Elyot asked.

"You three are meeting the contact, and the contact is giving us some intel to bring back to Calrin," Wayde explained.

"Who's the contact?" Elyot asked.

"We'll see when we get there," Wayde assured him.

"The flagship is on the far side of the moon," Alextra said.

"That's correct," Laera said.

"There are a thousand shuttles on patrol between us and the flag-ship," Alextra said.

"Don't worry about it," Wayde said with a little wave. "Laera is the best blockade runner in the rebellion. She and I have done this dozens of times."

"You don't have clearance codes or anything?" Alextra asked.

"Nope," Laera said, touching her ear piece briefly as if listening to something the rest of them couldn't hear. Then she gave Wayde a nod, and the shuttle lifted up off the ground.

Elyot's stomach protested this strange new motion at once. He didn't like it. It felt too out of his control.

But nowhere near as out of control as what Laera was still explaining.

"We have to avoid the patrols. It's tricky. They don't stick to any sort of pattern, and their equipment is better than ours. But we'll be fine. Trust me," Laera said.

"If Calrin trusts you, that's good enough for me," Alextra said. But when she sat back in her seat, she started adjusting the tightness of her restraints.

Elyot copied her motions. Apparently, this was going to be a bumpy ride.

The shuttle hovered as it slowly advanced along the flight deck. But then they ran out of flight deck and were hovering over the desert sands far, far below. They seemed to hang there forever, although Elyot was sure it was only a second or two.

Then he was blasted back and to his left. His seat had no arm to it, no side at all. He grasped his own restraints and held them tight, trying to keep his buttocks centered on his seat. He could only occasionally catch a glimpse through the front screen as they climbed up into the sky. Then they hit a cloud and there was nothing to see but a fog of whitish-gray.

"Wayde, five o'clock," Laera said, her voice almost lost in the roar of the wind past the hull of the ship.

"I see them," he said, already shifting in his chair to touch a different control panel. They rolled to one side and now Elyot's feet were flying up in front of him. He was being pulled forward against his restraints, and he was really worried they weren't tight enough. If he slipped out through the bottom, he was going to fall on Alextra and Keani. He could see them across from him, smashed back against the hull behind them, looking up at him as he kicked his feet ineffectually.

"Don't worry, Elyot. We'll be out of the atmosphere soon," Alextra told him.

Then the shuttle rolled all the way around. For a moment everything felt upside down, then they were back to that tilt only now the other way. Elyot was pressed back into his seat and Keani's feet were swinging wildly in the center of the shuttle. Only Alextra remained completely calm, her feet folded together and tucked neatly beneath her seat.

How did she do that?

Then they leveled out again but blasted forward, and Elyot once more had to fight to keep from sliding to the left.

He hated flying.

Then, all at once, everything just stopped. The roar of the wind was gone, and nothing was pulling him in any particular direction.

Quite the opposite, in fact. He felt like he was floating in water. His feet buoyed up in front of him, but when he bent them back down, they obeyed.

He looked through the front screen but saw nothing but black.

"We stopped?" he asked, breathless.

"We're still moving, we just stopped accelerating," Alextra told him.

"We evaded that patrol before they even saw us," Wayde said, turning in his seat far enough for even Elyot to see him grinning. "The rest of the trip shouldn't be anywhere near as eventful."

"But we'll be keeping our eyes peeled all the same," Laera said pointedly, and Wayde spun his chair back around to pay attention to his screens.

"This is the moment, then," Keani said to Alextra. "This is when you explain what's been going on with you?"

"Of course," Alextra said. "But first, how much do either of you know about the Commonwealth and Adghal's place in it?"

"Not much," Elyot admitted. "They showed up here a few years ago and just told us they were in charge. They said we're a colony of their government, and we couldn't really fight back. We had little technology, no space flight at all. They picked our current governor for us. He's basically their puppet. And my mother was part of the resistance ever since the real candidate lost that election."

"I was born on Adghal, but in a prison camp filled with prisoners from other parts of the Commonwealth," Keani said. "I know I'm not really from here, but I don't know where I'm from. Not really. My parents never talked about it. But from some things that Jaeke told me, I gather they were from another colonized, low-technology planet like Adghal."

"But what do you know about the Commonwealth specifically?" Alextra pressed. They both just gave her blank looks and shrugged. "I mean, do you know who rules the Commonwealth?"

"I thought the Commonwealth *was* who rules," Elyot said, confused by the question.

"There's an empress," Laera said from the cockpit. "She rules."

"Just one woman?" Keani asked. "No emperor or advisers or anything?"

"There are advisers, of course, but the final say on everything, absolutely everything, is hers," Alextra said.

"What does the empress have to do with you?" Keani asked. "Are you one of her bodyguards or something?"

"A daughter," Elyot said at almost the same time. Although given her proficiency with fighting and her unique weapon, Keani's guess made more sense.

But Alextra looked to him before nodding.

"Doesn't that make you a princess?" Keani asked.

"No wonder everyone has been trying to find you," Elyot said.

"That's not for my own sake, I promise you. I'm a very minor princess," she said.

"What does that even mean?" Keani asked.

"The empress has seventy-seven daughters," Alextra said. "In fact, I've only met her once, briefly, when my cohort of sisters turned sixteen. It was a state event."

"How could you only meet her once? You were her baby," Keani said.

"That's a little different when you're dealing with my mother," Alextra said with a sigh. "For generations, the rule of the Commonwealth passed down from father to son. But then the family stagnated. Fewer children were born each time. When my mother was a little girl, her father took ill. The officials in the Commonwealth scoured every corner of every planet in our dominion for even the most distant relative to pass the emperorship on to. But there were none. And so, when my grandfather died, my mother became the first empress of the Commonwealth."

"Isn't that a good thing?" Keani asked, but Elyot could tell by her voice she was thinking the same thing as he was. From the look on Alextra's face, it clearly had not been a good thing.

"She swore there would never again be an emperor. And so she produced her own daughters, with her the only genetic parent. She had her scientists recombine her own DNA into the eleven most perfect daughters, and they were implanted in surrogates and born precisely on her own eighteenth birthday."

"Eleven at once?" Elyot said.

"Eleven surrogates gave birth," Alextra said. "And then four years later, eleven more. And so on."

"How far down the line are you?" Elyot asked. She had called herself a minor princess, after all.

"I was part of the sixth generation. I descend from what's considered the fifth of the original eleven genetic templates," Alextra said.

"That sounds so cold," Keani said, hugging herself.

"Oh, wait!" Elyot said, suddenly remembering. "Koltn Ward said something about this when he met you. Because of your name? I don't remember exactly."

"No, you have it," Alextra said. "Every name given to a princess becomes unusable in the rest of the Commonwealth. It is unique to the princess."

"Seventy-seven names no one can use?" Elyot said.

"You said you had it first, so it was okay," Keani remembered.

"It's a legal gray area," Alextra said. "Most parents choose to rename their children, anyway. Just to be on the safe side. The empress is capricious, but never to be trifled with."

"So Koltn Ward thinks he's trying to get a runaway home?" Elyot asked.

"I don't know exactly what he thinks," Alextra said. "But I suppose technically I am a runaway. I was meant to be attending a prestigious university in a far quadrant from the home world. But that was a lie. I sent another girl in my place. I suppose she's been caught by now, if Koltn Ward reported me the moment he saw me."

"Why are you here?" Elyot asked.

"I wanted to learn what the Commonwealth was really like. I was pretty sure my princess education was not entirely truthful, and I wanted to see for myself what was true," Alextra said.

"That's the only reason?" Elyot asked. It didn't seem like enough, considering how much trouble Koltn Ward was going through to bring her home again.

"I did learn something upsetting just before I decided to leave," Alextra admitted. "Well, it wasn't something I stumbled across, it was something I dug up. But it never made sense to me why my mother had seventy-seven heirs. Even the first eleven was excessive, but seventy-seven?"

"What does she need them all for?" Elyot asked, but he was pretty sure he didn't want to know the answer.

"She thinks having living copies of herself gives her power," Alextra said. "In which case, my real question was, why stop at seventy-seven?"

"I suppose they get hard to manage," Keani said. "Are you the only one who's run away?"

"So far," Alextra said. "I couldn't persuade any of the others to even listen to me."

"What did you find out?" Elyot asked.

"Everything changes in four years. Everything," Alextra said. Elyot supposed it was only surprising it took this far into the story for her to finally sound bitter. "My youngest cohort of sisters is fourteen now. When they reach the age of eighteen, everyone's education is going to be considered complete. It doesn't matter who we are or what we're studying or how far along we are. We'll all be called home again."

"And then what?" Keani asked.

"Then we'll be imprisoned in the palace," Alextra said. "I've seen the designs. She's having a tower built to house us all. We'll be walled into individual cells. We'll never see each other again. We'll never see anyone again. We'll just all be in one place, amplifying my mother's power."

"Until she dies?" Elyot guessed.

"She has the best scientists in the known universe working for her," Alextra said. "She can live for centuries. *Centuries*."

"So why are you here, then?" Keani asked. "Why aren't you stopping her?"

For a minute, it looked like Alextra was going to start to cry. Keani looked just as alarmed at this prospect as Elyot felt.

But then Laera interrupted, saying, "we're coming around the moon now, if you want your first look at the flagship."

Alextra immediately leaned over Laera's shoulder to look. Elyot suspected this was more about getting out of the conversation than anything else, but that was fine with him.

Half of the front screen was the silver curve of the moon's surface turning slowly below them. Then something else came into view. Elyot's mouth went dry when he saw the Commonwealth ship emerging from behind the moon, just as dominating as the other ships hovering over his home city for so many years.

Then he realized what he was looking at wasn't a ship. It was just a part of a ship. A jutting protrusion, maybe the command deck or something, but whatever it was, it alone was the size of the ships he was used to gawking at the immensity of.

But the rest of the ship just kept emerging into view below it. It went on and on, spreading wider and deeper. He couldn't wrap his head around the size of the thing.

"That's a flagship," he said to himself.

"That's the flagship they send out to conquer minor worlds," Alextra told him. "The ones we use to defend ourselves from other world systems at our own level are quite a bit larger."

"Being big just means it's easier for us to be ignored," Laera assured them. But then she gulped. "Sorry. It's just, I'm an Adghal girl myself. I've learned how to fly Commonwealth tech, and I know more about the rest of the universe than most, but that thing never fails to make me feel like a teeny-tiny bug."

"It's meant to," Alextra said.

"I'm sending the security codes now," Wayde said as he worked at one of his control panels.

"Roger that," Laera said. She sounded calm, but her hands gripping the yoke were white-knuckled. Elyot leaned closer to the screen. He could see little dots everywhere, like gnats attracted to a light source.

Then he realized they were shuttles. They were all Commonwealth shuttles on Commonwealth business, moving to and from and just generally around the flagship.

"How do you spot patrols in all that?" he asked.

"Mostly at this point we don't need to," Laera told him. "If our codes are good and up-to-date, once we get an acknowledgment from flagship security, we'll be green-lit on all Commonwealth scopes."

"*If* they're good?" Elyot asked.

"If they aren't good, we just run away," Wayde said with a grin.

"That's the plan?" Keani asked, her voice almost cracking.

Wayde touched his ear piece then spun back around in his chair to look at his control panel. "We're good," he said.

"I can see us green-lit on the scopes," Laera confirmed with relief in her voice.

"We're being directed to dock in hangar AHH467," he said.

"AHH467," Laera said, tapping at something on a panel to her left. Then the shuttle made an adjustment, just a gentle change in momentum that changed the direction they were heading. Their head-on view of the flagship shifted down ever so slightly.

"Who's telling us where to dock?" Elyot asked.

"Our contact," Laera told him. "Whoever it is. It might be your mother, but like I said, we haven't had contact with her in a while. But we have other people implanted in the crew."

"We never know who we're meeting until we're face to face," Wayde said. "Not even then, frankly, unless it's someone we recognize."

"Everyone implanted in the crew has a fake identity as a Commonwealth citizen," Laera said. "It's safer for everybody if we don't know any more names than we need to."

"But we're here to find my mother, right?" Elyot asked. He couldn't see another reason why Calrin would send the three of them up in a shuttle to the flagship.

"Hopefully," Laera said. Then she turned her attention back to her flying. The shuttle was very close to the hull of the flagship now. Elyot watched window after window pass beside them, interrupted at regular intervals by the bulging protrusions of heavy cannons. There were no windows on the cannons that he could see, and even the other windows had prominent metal shutters above and below them. They were all open now, but he was sure a single command could seal the entire ship tight in the blink of an eye.

He saw figures passing by the windows, all in Commonwealth uniforms, but every window he could see through only showed him another featureless hallway.

"Preparing to dock," Laera said, and the shuttle shuddered as she banked it a hard left. Then that hovering feeling hit Elyot's stomach again as they slowly advanced inside the open doors of the dock. The flying itself wasn't so bad, but whatever engines handled this hovering motion were really not his favorites.

They passed the open heavy duty doors of the dock, then landed on a flight deck so tiny Elyot doubted more than two more shuttles could ever be parked there. As it was, theirs was the only shuttle in that space. Elyot could just see some sort of observing room jutting out of the wall to their right, but no one was moving behind those windows.

The shuttle settled to the ground, and then it was like someone's hand smashed down on them from above.

Gravity was back. He had been so engrossed in Alextra's story, he had never even noticed it had been gone. But his feet were back on the floor, and the others were already unbuckling and standing up.

"Where to now?" Alextra asked. "It doesn't look like anybody is even here."

"We're on an unused flight deck," Laera said. "Either we meet our contact here, or we find them elsewhere."

"We just have to get into the command room over there first and access a computer," Wayde said, pointing to what Elyot had just been looking at. Then he got out of his chair well and brushed past Elyot's knees to get to the ramp in back.

"We can breathe out there, right?" Elyot asked in a rush when he saw that Wayde was about to open the hatch.

"Sure. There's a force field over the dock opening," Wayde said. "They only close the blast doors when they're under the sort of attack where someone is going to try to board."

"This ship is huge, but it's also technically under-crewed," Laera told him. "There's a lot of open space. A lot of empty rooms or corridors for us spies to do our work in."

"*Why* did you come here?" Keani asked Alextra as Wayde and Laera watched the ramp slowly lower down.

"It wasn't where I was intending to go," Alextra admitted. "I was almost caught at the spaceport back on the home world. I got away by jumping on the first ship I could find that was departing for anywhere at all. But it's not like it mattered. What's happening here is happening everywhere. One place is as good as any other."

"How many planets are being colonized right now? Do you have any idea?" Elyot asked.

Alextra shook her head sorrowfully. "No one knows, except perhaps my mother the empress. And I'm not sure she's really counting."

"Sucks, doesn't it?" Wayde said with a wry grin. "If we're going to be conquered and subjugated, it'd be nice for it to at least mean something to the victor."

"We'll figure out a way to stop it," Laera said, then ducked under the bulkhead to descend the ramp, turning to head towards the command room.

Alextra, Keani and Elyot trailed behind with Wayde. Alextra kept her hand close to her tanjo, and Keani was fidgeting with her knives. Elyot thought about taking out his needle gun, but he still didn't really know how to use it. And neither Laera nor Wayde even seemed to be armed.

Elyot held his breath as Laera pushed open the hatch into the command room, but there was no one inside. She waited for them all to step through, then shut the hatch behind them. The clang echoed ominously.

"Right," Wayde said as he sat down at the nearest computer terminal. He cracked his knuckles loudly, then started typing on the keyboard.

"No password?" Alextra asked.

"I have an admin one that always works," Wayde said, but in a muted tone. He was focused on his work now, whatever it was. He typed and tabbed through screens faster than Elyot could follow.

"Check the detention cells first," Laera said as she peered through the tiny window built at eye level in the hatch. She was keeping watch over the shuttle, Elyot realized.

"I'm checking that second," Wayde informed her. "I have an inbox to check first. No message from our contact. Okay, detention cells…"

"You think that's where my mother is?" Elyot guessed.

"It's possible," Laera said.

"No, nothing on her. Not under Valria Taelor or under Islae Jaro," Wayde said.

"That's her Commonwealth identity," Laera explained to Elyot. "Islae Jaro is a Lieutenant Commander on this ship. She's worked her way up from Ensign."

"Since she left me?" Elyot asked.

Laera gave him a sympathetic look, but that wasn't what he meant.

She had only been gone for a few years. He didn't know much about the Commonwealth, but he knew that was a lot of ranks to rise through in such a short time.

She must be really good at her job. But that meant being really good at the Commonwealth military job that she was only doing so that she could operate as a spy for the rebellion.

But if she was good at *that* job, wouldn't she have made it back home by now?

It was all too confusing.

Then suddenly, Wayde sat back in his chair, hands raised up and hovering in midair. The look on his face was almost like he was offended for some reason.

"What's going on?" Laera asked him, trying to look at him and out the little window at the same time.

"I've been locked out," Wayde said. He still looked offended, but then he switched to angry determination and bent over the keyboard again. The keys clacked loudly as he typed. "I was just running an inquiry on Islae Jaro, trying to get a current location. If she's not in the brig or... worse—which she isn't!—then she *must* be our contact. I mean, someone gave us our docking instructions. But no one is responding to any of my messages on any of the dead drop boards."

Then he pounded on the keyboard with both of his hands, all ten fingers at once. Elyot was pretty sure that wasn't typing anything. He pounded twice, then sat back in his chair with a huff.

"Definitely locked out," he said. Then he gestured at the computer as if it were a coworker he was having a beef with. "In my defense, I'm not a computer guy. I'm a pilot."

"Copilot," Laera said automatically.

"I know how to put in a password and use it like any other user. I don't know what to do when it turns on me like this," he grumbled.

Alextra sucked in a breath. "We run," she said.

"He probably just hit a wrong key," Laera said, but Alextra was shaking her head too emphatically.

"No, we run," she said, then caught Laera's hand before she could open the hatch. "Not that way."

"The shuttle is that way," Laera said.

"It's a trap," Elyot guessed. "Someone lured us here and then went silent. Has to be a trap."

"Right," Laera said, and turned towards the other door.

But they were too late. The door opened with a bang. The light from the corridor beyond was blinding. Elyot fell back, blinking against the silvery whiteness that seared his eyeballs. When he could finally see again, it was to find them all surrounded by Commonwealth security officers.

And they were outnumbered two to one.

There was a lot of shouting and confusion, and even more pushing as they were herded out of the tight space inside the command room, down the narrow corridor beyond and then into a larger but more normally lit corridor.

"Just cooperate," Laera hissed to the others. "Play for time."

Alextra looked like she wanted to argue with this, but Wayde, who was closest to her, whispered something to her, too low for Elyot to hear. But Alextra nodded, and stopped struggling against the two guards who had her by the elbows.

They reached the end of the wider corridor, then stopped suddenly, for no reason that Elyot could see. The security officers then lined them up and pushed them down onto their knees. Elyot felt something wrap itself around his wrists, then snug painfully tight, and realized he had been cuffed.

One officer walked past all of them, not looking at any of their faces, just checking that they were all cuffed and on their knees. Then he turned and gave someone else a hand signal.

"What now?" he asked. Could they execute him as a spy? He had never actually done anything?

But the Commonwealth was all about guilt by association. And he was very guilty in his associations.

Boot heels rang loudly from somewhere out of sight, a single person striding purposefully towards them. Then she came into view. She was taller than most of the other officers, her uniform navy while theirs were black. She had a lot more insignia on her uniform as well, not that he knew what any of it meant.

But all of that faded away the moment Elyot got a good look at her face.

"Lieutenant Commander Jaro," Laera said dryly. "It's been a long time."

"It has," Elyot's mother agreed. But then she tapped the insignia on her breast. "But it's Commander Jaro now."

She didn't seem to have noticed Elyot there at all. Somehow, calling out to her didn't seem like the right thing to do just then. He really hoped this was all just her acting the part. Once she got them away from the other Commonwealth security officers, that was the time to try talking to her.

"Another promotion?" Laera was saying. "Congratulations."

"Yes, it's been a big change," Jaro said. She looked Laera over, then took a step and examined Keani for a long moment. Then she glanced back at Laera again to say, "there have been a few big changes, actually. But I'm sure you'll catch up soon enough."

"I don't want to trouble you if you're busy here," Laera said airily. "We can get out of your hair and be on our way."

"Is that meant to be amusing?" Jaro asked, now looking down at Wayde. But she passed him over quickly to look at Alextra.

She frowned, and Elyot watched as uncertainty turned to suspicion, then confusion. She looked like she was about to ask either Alextra or possibly Laera a question. But in the end, she just shook her head and took another step to her left.

And was face to face with Elyot.

He bit down on his lip hard, desperate not to say anything, but just as desperate to say *something*.

But she only just glanced at him, her eyes moving on as quickly as they fell on him. Even Wayde had gotten more of an examination than that.

She turned his back on him, and he could see her hands folded behind her. They clutched each other tightly, the thumb of one rubbing at the palm of the other as if in thought.

Then she looked up at the officer who Elyot had assumed was in charge before.

"Lieutenant Ternce," she said to get his attention.

"Yes, commander?" he said, snapping to attention. But he relaxed again almost at once, and Elyot sensed that the two of them had worked together for some time, despite the formality of their speech with each other. "To the brig? Or straight to the nearest airlock?" he asked with a subtle sneer.

"Airlock? No. Not without a trial," Jaro said with marked sarcasm.

Elyot leaned forward ever so slightly. He didn't know exactly what he thought he could do, but sitting on his knees and playing for time wasn't it. But Laera hissed a warning sound at him even before the guards behind him pulled him back into the line.

"Brig, then," the lieutenant said, and started to raise a hand to direct the other guards.

"No, Ternce. Not just yet. This doesn't seem like the usual riffraff from the surface to me. I think I'll bring them directly to the admiral myself," Jaro said.

"The admiral?" Ternce stammered.

"One of them meets a description I've been given. A need to know thing," Jaro said.

"I thought I knew all your need to knows?" Ternce said.

"Oh, sure, but not your whole squad, lieutenant," she said with a laugh that sounded discordant to Elyot's ears. That wasn't the way his mother laughed at all. All high and shrill like that?

And yet Ternce didn't seem to find anything unusual in it as he laughed along good-naturedly. Then he made another hand signal and the guards behind Elyot dragged him back to his feet by his armpits.

It wasn't comfortable at all, being picked up that way. And it wasn't easy to walk with his hands cuffed behind his back, not at the pace the guards were setting for them.

But Elyot barely noticed any of that. All he could think was, what were the odds the admiral was also a rebel spy? Could one of them have worked their way so far up the ranks?

Or was his mother no longer a spy?

What if she was a traitor?

But what really made him feel sick to his stomach was that she hadn't seemed to recognize him at all. And he didn't know if that was going to make whatever happened next better or worse.

Was she going to find a way to protect him?

Or was she disappointed in him now that she had caught him spying on the group that had her current loyalties?

Would she push him out of an airlock, even knowing who he was?

He wished he could say for sure that she wouldn't. But he really didn't know.

And as immense as the Commonwealth flagship was, he didn't have long to figure it out before they got to this admiral. Then his fate would be decided.

Whatever that would be.

8   THE PERILOUS ESCAPE

ELYOT HAD SPENT the last several years sleeping under the open sky, staring up at the Commonwealth ships that never stopped hovering over his city. They had just hung there, massive, brighter than the stars. It was like he had still sensed them there, so close, even as he slept.

Now he was inside the Commonwealth flagship, a battle cruiser that dwarfed all of those ships put together. More than that, he stood on the command bridge of that flagship. He had never been inside a larger space in his life. Not the hidden spaceport hangar where the rebellion hid their shuttles from the Commonwealth patrols. Not the cavern deep under his city where that nameless monster lurked with its thousands of tunnelling offspring. Not even the stadium at the heart of his city, built to contain multitudes.

He couldn't even see to the far side of the space under the curving dome of the screen that displayed the star field around them, and yet every person under that dome was working towards just one goal.

Controlling that flagship. And through it, dominating his world.

His arms ached from having his hands shackled behind him, and his mouth tasted like metal, blood from when he had bitten his lip one of the many times he had stumbled. He was also terribly thirsty. The air in the ship was even drier than it had been at the edge of the desert.

Was it only a few hours since he had stood there? And only a few more since he had been in the jungle itself, where the air had been far less dry, but far more thick with smells.

The guards around him and his friends steered them up to the highest of a serious of tiered decks. Crew members glanced up from their workstations as they marched by. A few of them whispered together after they had passed, but stopped quickly under the hard gaze of their commanding officers.

Elyot stumbled yet again on the last fight of stairs. The guards at his elbows yanked him aggressively back to his feet, but he could already taste fresh blood in his mouth. He had bitten his lip again. But he didn't have time to worry about it before he was pushed down to his knees again. They were all lined up, but the only face Elyot could see was Wayde beside him.

Wayde wasn't grinning. And even though he tried to give Elyot an encouraging nod, Elyot could see the panic in the copilot's eyes.

"Commander Jaro reporting, Admiral," he heard the woman who was once his mother say. He didn't know who she was now. She hadn't given him more than the slightest of glances, but there was no way she couldn't have recognized him. He was her only son. She must know.

But it didn't seem to matter to her. At all.

"Prisoners, Commander Jaro?" the admiral said, sounding amused. Elyot couldn't quite get a good look at him. As much as they were on the tallest deck of the bridge, the admiral was standing on a higher platform. Only the very top of his balding head was visible from where Elyot was on his knees.

"Yes, sir," Jaro said. "You asked to see any spies we apprehended. This crew flew in on phony security credentials. Their shuttle looked like it was stolen, then stripped, but my people are still searching for its ID number to verify that."

"The rebels buff those off," the admiral said.

"Yes, sir. Just being thorough," Jaro said. "Sir, these don't look like fighters to me, though. I would say smugglers, and not very good ones at that. The shuttle was in very bad shape. I doubt it's combat-worthy. And most of these prisoners are little more than kids."

The bald head moved a little, but if he could even actually see any of them, the admiral didn't give them more than a glance.

"Shall I have them returned to the surface for incarceration by the local government?" she asked, and even took half a step back. As if she was that sure the admiral would say yes.

"No, not just yet," the admiral said. "Not that I doubt you, but there is a reason I'm holding all prisoners for personal inspection."

"They're here now," Jaro said, gesturing to them all on their knees behind her.

"Yes, but my agent is not," the admiral said. "It's all very annoying, commander, more for me than for you, I promise you. But please take them all to the brig and process them. Once my agent arrives and I've debriefed him, I will let you know what has been decided in regards to their fate."

"Yes, sir," Jaro said. Her voice sounded tight, like she was clenching her jaw. But she just snapped a salute, then signalled for Ternce to have his crew pull them all back to their feet again.

And once more they were walking, awkwardly with their hands bound behind them, back off the bridge and through the endless maze of the flagship corridors.

But it wasn't hard to tell when they reached the brig. They had to pass a double set of doors, like an airlock, the door behind them closing before the door ahead of them buzzed open. There were more Commonwealth Enforcers here, many of them standing guard in various doorways. And all of them were armed.

Every corridor they passed seemed to go on forever, lined on both sides with prison cells sealed off with force fields.

There'd be no reason to leave a force field up on an empty cell, would there? And yet Elyot didn't see a single cell that wasn't sealed behind a soft glowing field of energy.

They reached a sort of command hub where four corridors met with a control station in the middle. Elyot watched as his mother spoke in a voice too low for him to overhear to one of the guards inside of that control station. The man nodded, then saluted sharply.

Elyot's mother spun on her heel, then marched back the way she had come. She passed so close to Elyot that, if his hands hadn't been bound, he could've reached out to catch her sleeve.

But she never so much as looked at him.

Elyot watched as one by one his friends were searched. They took Alextra's tanjo and Keani's knives, as well as the needle gun Elyot had completely forgotten was lurking in his pocket. But they found nothing on either Laera or Wayde.

Then they were all led down the same corridor and put into individual cells. Elyot was afraid the force field would block out any light or sound from the corridor, leaving him clueless as to what was going on. But after removing his cuffs and shoving him towards the bed that was built into the far wall, he could hear the two guards walking away, back down the corridor. And when he turned, he could see Alextra looking just as confused as he felt standing in the cell opposite his. The field gave everything an electric blue tinge, but he could see clearly all the same.

He looked around his cell. He wasn't sure what he had expected prison to look like. Perhaps more like Keani's prison camp, all built by hand from scraps or bits of the jungle. But of course that wouldn't be the case up in space, on a ship.

But it felt like a lot of space for one person. He could walk ten paces along the length of it, turn and pace ten steps back. From the bed to the force field was only five, but that still felt ample.

And there was a bed. He hadn't had a bed in years. The mattress looked thin, and the "blanket" was really a plastic-feeling layer that was part of the mattress, unremovable. He would have to wiggle into it from the top, then wiggle back out of it again when he woke up. He couldn't pull it free to use it to escape, somehow.

But it would probably keep him warm at night. If he was still here at night.

Although he might need to duck his head under the edge of it to sleep at all, as bright as it was in the room. The walls, floor and ceiling were all featureless white plastic with no joins or gaps. He ran his fingers over it. It felt just as smooth and cool as it looked. But it reflected the light like crazy.

Everything not only looked sterile, it smelled sterile too. No hint of any kind of cleaner he knew of, but no hint of any people smells either. He couldn't remember the last time he couldn't smell people smells.

Well, he smelled them coming off of his own body. He had done a lot of nervous sweating since that shower back on Adghal. Which felt like it had been a million years ago.

He walked back to the force field, looking as far up and down the corridor as he could. There were no signs of any guards, but he couldn't see all the way to that control station. And he was pretty sure the guards there could see all the way down all the corridors. And there were probably also cameras everywhere. Even in the cells.

Escape didn't feel remotely possible.

"Why would they put us all together like this?" Alextra asked.

"Because they're not remotely worried about what we'll do?" Keani said. She sounded absolutely miserable. Elyot moved to the far left of his cell door and could just see Keani standing next to her own force field in the cell next to Alextra's. She was opening and closing her hands, looking down at them as if the absence of her knives wounded her very soul.

"What happens now?" Elyot wondered aloud.

It had been a rhetorical question, but Laera, who sounded like she was in the cell to Elyot's left, answered all the same. "That depends on how much they know about the three of you. If Jaro convinces them you are all harmless, you can expect to be sent back down to a work camp on the surface to serve out your time."

"Oh, goody," Keani grumbled.

"That's not good news," Alextra said, as if she hadn't caught Keani's tone at all. "If they bring us down there, they'll notice what's going on in those camps. Jax and the others will be in even more danger than they are now. And it could make things a lot worse for Jaeke and the other prisoners."

"What's the alternative?" Elyot asked.

"That they decide you, like Wayde and I, are rebels," Laera said.

"They already know who we are. Our fates are already sealed. But we'll do all we can to convince the enforcers that you aren't involved," Wayde said grimly.

"If they even bother to question us," Laera said. "We'll do all we can, but it might not be much. I don't want to give you all any false hopes."

"It's the airlock for rebels, then?" Alextra asked flatly.

"We knew that when we came," Laera said. "It's always a risk, but one we're prepared to take."

"But it's not one they should have to face," Wayde grumbled. "They're just kids."

"I don't think that's how it's going to go down," Laera said. "Valria is going to get us out of here."

"Are you deluded?" Wayde asked.

"She's already working to get us out of here. Didn't you hear her? She tried to get us back down to the surface in the first place. That's why she brought us to the admiral first and not straight to the brig," Laera said.

"No way," Wayde said. "She was following orders. That's what she does now. Things got too hot for her as an undercover agent, so she's going native. She's not one of us anymore, Laera. You have to face that fact."

"I know Valria. She would never betray the cause," Laera said firmly. "Never."

Elyot wished he was so sure. But at this point, he wasn't even sure she was still his mother. It was like some sort of alien was running around, wearing her face.

She didn't know him at all.

"Alextra won't be going down to the prison camp, anyway," Keani said. "They'll figure out who you are for sure, won't they?"

"I don't see how they don't know already," Alextra said. "They took my tanjo."

"Does it have your name on it, or is it encoded to your DNA or something?" Wayde asked.

"Wait, didn't Koltn Ward say it was forbidden for anyone to even touch it?" Keani asked.

"The tanjo is the ceremonial weapon of the Imperial Guard," Alextra told them. Now she was the one looking down at her hands, missing her weapon. "Only the elite of the guards are allowed to train with it, to carry it. And only the empress's personal retinue can ever carry it outside of the palace. They only do so when protecting her wherever she goes."

"So you stole it?" Elyot guessed.

"I trained for years in its use under the guidance of my personal bodyguard," Alextra said. "When I decided to leave, she was the only soul I told. And she gifted me her own weapon, to protect me on my journey. But such a gift was forbidden. So I guess you could say yes, I stole it."

"These enforcers don't seem to know what it means," Keani said.

"No," Alextra agreed.

"But Koltn Ward did at once," Elyot said.

"Yes," Alextra said. "Isn't that strange? I wonder why. I wonder who Koltn Ward really is."

"All the enforcers at the tavern knew him well," Elyot said. "I had never seen him before, I don't think. But if he was new to Adghal, I don't think they would've treated him the same way."

"Yes, they were all very friendly," Alextra said.

"He seems very disciplined. Focused. Like someone who spends their days off preparing to work again," Keani said.

"Maybe he's been here for years, but he never left the Enforcer compound in the city until that night," Elyot said. "Most of the patrols are in full armor with face shields. I could've encountered him at a hundred checkpoints and not recognized him later."

"I suppose he came out that night because he was already looking for Alextra?" Keani said.

"I'm afraid I have to agree," Alextra said with a sigh. "All our troubles, you two can go ahead and lay them at my feet."

"You came out here because you wanted to fix things, right?" Elyot said. "You came out here to help us."

"I certainly learned shortly after arriving here that the process of colonizing an unwilling populace is needlessly brutal, and the conditions in the prison camps are inhumane," Alextra said. "As much as I can help, I swear I will."

They all fell silent at the sound of boots returning. It was Ternce, returning with six guards.

"Prisoners, turn, face the far wall and put your hands behind you,"

Ternce ordered. Elyot turned away from the force field and put his hands behind him. He heard two of the guards walking up behind him, then felt the cuffs closing over his wrists once more.

"Where are we going?" he asked, but no one answered his question. Again he was pulled around by his elbows, pushed at an aggressive pace out of his cell and back down the long corridor towards the control station. Alextra and Keani were ahead of him, but no one was behind him.

Laera and Wayde were being left behind in their cells. But why?

They didn't stop at the control station, just continued on past the double set of doors, back out into the flagship's main corridors. Their guards were the only Commonwealth enforcers in sight outside of the brig. No one else was armed or wearing body armor, only simple military uniforms designed for support crew, not combat.

These Commonwealth officers bustled anxiously up and down the corridors. Everyone seemed in a nervous hurry, but they all carefully pressed closer to the walls to make way for the enforcers marching their trio of prisoners down the center of the hall.

None of them made eye contact with Elyot. Not that he thought any of them would help him. But he still felt a little tickle of hope. Laera and Wayde had said there were other rebels embedded in the crew on the flagship. Somewhere, someone might see them who would want to help save them.

But he doubted the odds of crossing paths with them by chance were anything other than infinitesimally small.

The guards brought them to another closed set of doors, and Ternce knocked loudly. The doors parted, and the guards hustled them all inside.

"Very good, Lieutenant. You may leave them in our care. Wait outside," Elyot heard the admiral say.

"Yes, sir," Ternce said, although he sounded a little startled by the order. The guards filed back out the doors, and Elyot found himself standing between Alextra and Keani at the foot of a very long table. All of them still had their hands cuffed behind them, but no one was standing anywhere near them. They were all clustered at the far end of that immense table.

The man seated at the head had to be the admiral. Elyot recognized the dark skin of his bald head. The face beneath was all harsh angles, frowning fiercely. Standing just behind his left shoulder was Elyot's mother, looking as stern as ever, but not at him.

And sitting at the table to the admiral's right hand was Koltn Ward.

"That's her," Koltn Ward said at once. "I'm sure of it."

"I can certainly see why you think so," the admiral conceded, but grudgingly. "She looks the part, and the enforcers took a tanjo off of her. But why would she come here, of all places?"

"Why would she leave the palace at all?" Koltn Ward said with a shrug. "It's all a mystery."

"You could just ask her," Elyot's mother said.

"We could do that, and then spend days sifting through the lies," Koltn Ward said. The admiral gave him a look that Elyot couldn't interpret, but said nothing.

"What do you suggest, then?" Jaro asked. "We can't verify her DNA. We know it won't bring up a match. And if we even suspect she is who you say she is, even trying to look at her DNA would be a death sentence for all of us."

"My orders are to bring her home," Koltn Ward said. "I will see that done." Then he seemed to remember that he was not the highest ranking person in the room. In fact, he was the lowest. But he only looked at the admiral when he said, "with your permission, of course, sir."

"Far be it from me to stand in your way," the admiral said.

"Yes, go ahead and let him take me away," Alextra said with a little toss of her head. "I'll only escape again, like I have before. This man is not remotely good enough to keep me prisoner."

Koltn Ward flushed a deep shade of scarlet, and the admiral covered his mouth with his hand as if to hide a smile.

But Elyot was in agony. He could tell that Alextra was doing something behind her back, but he couldn't tell what. He desperately wanted to turn his head to see, but the very last thing he wanted to do was draw attention to her. And yet all eyes were on her, anyway. What could she possibly be doing? And why not wait until someone else was the center of attention?

"From reviewing all the situation reports, I think she might have a point, sir," Jaro said. "Perhaps the captain should have some backup in his mission to bring her home? I have a few officers I can recommend."

"My own officers will suit just fine, thank you, Commander," Koltn Ward said drily.

"I'm glad to hear that. I'm shorthanded enough on this ship as it is," the admiral grumbled. "So, what about the other two?"

"They mean nothing to me," Koltn Ward said dismissively.

"We have a file on the girl, sir," Jaro said, leaning down to place something on the table in front of the admiral. Elyot was too far away to see what it was, but the admiral studied it for some time before he spoke.

"Escaped prisoner, then?" he said, glancing back over his shoulder at Jaro.

"That makes sense," Koltn Ward said, almost to himself. But then he looked up at the admiral. "That situation is out of hand, from what I've seen. You need to send enforcers to lock those camps down, sir."

"Because I have so many to spare?" the admiral said to him with a raised eyebrow.

"I can send for more squads from the capital, sir," Koltn Ward offered.

"You have that kind of pull?" Jaro asked skeptically.

"I have that kind of pull," he told her.

"That would be excellent, Captain Ward. Thank you," the admiral said to him. Then he turned to Jaro again. "Once the prison camps are secured, she can go back down and serve out the rest of her sentence. Plus, whatever more gets tacked on for an escape like this. I assume it's all covered in the punishment algorithm."

"I'll have my crew look into it," Jaro said. "I'm sure there are categories assigned for all of it. We'll have it downloaded to her personal counter as soon as we've run the numbers, sir."

"Excellent," the admiral said. "Now, what about the third one, the boy?"

Elyot's heart started pounding. Whatever Alextra had been doing, she wasn't doing it anymore. And nothing had changed. Had she just been fidgeting?

But fidgeting meant nervousness, and Alextra was never nervous.

"He's a different case entirely," Jaro said. "We have no record of him."

"What, at all?" the admiral asked, twisting in his chair to look up at her.

"None at all. We have no idea who he is or where he's from," she said.

Elyot sucked uncertainly at his already bitten lip. He had no idea what was going on here. None of it made sense. It seemed like the safest thing was to remain silent.

But he knew they knew who he was. They had to. They had taken his identcard when they'd taken the needle gun.

Then the admiral said, "didn't we confiscate an identcard?"

"Yes, sir, but it was fake," Jaro said. "And not a very good one. Unless you think this boy looks like an Izbella Scout?"

Koltn Ward sucked in a breath as if the name offended him deeply.

"No, clearly not," the admiral said with a scowl.

But Elyot was more confused than ever. He knew his identcard wasn't fake. He had been using it almost daily for years.

"We can send him down to the local governor's police force," Jaro said. "They might be able to identify him for us. Local knowledge and all."

"He's definitely local," Koltn Ward put in, to Elyot's surprise. He doubted that Koltn Ward was trying to help him out, and yet that's kind of how it sounded.

"Of course he's local," the admiral said. "*All* of our problems are local." He sat back in his chair for a long moment, quietly stewing. Then he sat up again, reaching for a tablet and scrawling something on the screen. "He turned up here in the company of two rebel pilots. We know exactly who they are and what they've been up to. Guilt by association, eh?"

"Sir?" Jaro asked, reaching for the tablet. But he was still scrawling on it.

"He can be executed with the two of them. I don't see any reason to wait for a formal identification."

"Sir?" Jaro said again. She sounded a little off, like she kept losing track of the conversation or something. Her hand still hovered there, waiting for the tablet. But when he finally finished writing and shoved it towards her, she fumbled to grasp it, as if her hands had gone numb.

"Shall I call the guards back, sir?" Koltn Ward asked as he got up from the table.

"Hmm?" the admiral said, distracted from his puzzled staring at Jaro and her strange reaction.

"To bring the boy and the prison camp girl back to the brig," Koltn Ward said. "Alextra, I can escort directly to my private shuttle myself."

"Oh. Yes. Of course. Please," the admiral said, gesturing towards the door.

Elyot twisted at his cuffs uselessly. He wanted his hands free, even though he had no idea what he could do even then. Even if no one in the room was armed—and he really doubted that Koltn Ward was unarmed, even now—and they were three on three, they were nothing like equally matched.

And even if they somehow got the upper-hand, they were still in the heart of the enemy's flagship. With an entire squad of armed enforcers waiting for them just outside the door.

And yet, doing nothing was just intolerable. Elyot struggled harder.

Keani nudged up against him, catching his eye, then shaking her head at him. But she couldn't even whisper to him, because Koltn Ward was already close enough to hear.

Then he was close enough to reach out for Alextra. He must have been intending to catch her arm, to start to guide her out of the room before sending the enforcers in for Elyot and Keani.

But he never quite touched her. Faster than Elyot's eyes could see, Alextra spun. Her head swooped low as her foot swept high, catching Koltn Ward hard in the jaw.

He fell forward on his knees, his eyes startled and wide.

Then Alextra stepped back as he fell facedown onto the floor.

She looked up at the admiral and Commander Jaro at the far end of the table. Then a slow grin spread across her face as she settled back into a fighting stance.

Only then did she raise her hands.

Her unbound hands.

The admiral jumped to his feet. He must have intended to shout for his guards, but his voice strangled on the first consonant. Then he, too, was falling to the ground.

And Commander Jaro was left standing, also in a battle stance, one hand cocked back after delivering the chop to the back of his neck that had knocked him out.

"Mom?" Elyot gasped, feeling a little bit strangled himself.

"Elyot," she said with a curt nod.

Elyot was more confused than ever. It was like she thought he was just another fellow rebel fighter. Did she *still* not recognize him?

"Elyot," Alextra said, not helping his confusion at all. Now everyone was just saying his name? He turned towards her, then completely failed to catch the needle gun she tossed up to him. It bounced off his chest and fell to the floor.

"Alextra, I'm still cuffed," he told her. It didn't seem like he'd have to point that out.

"I'm not," Keani said, giving him a wild grin. Then she launched herself up onto the table and jogged across the top of it to the far end, where she stooped and swiped up something from in front of the admiral's unmoving head, then something from where Koltn Ward had just been sitting.

She turned back around, hands high, brandishing a new pair of knives. Elyot had his doubts how good steak knives would be as throwing weapons, but Keani was so obviously elated to have them he didn't dare say a word against them.

"Here," Alextra said, and Elyot felt the cuffs around his wrists fall away. He rubbed his wrists briefly with his hands still behind his back. He hadn't realized how numb his extremities had gone.

Then Alextra was shoving that needle gun into his chest again, and he brought his hands forward, numb as they were, to take it.

"Ready?" she said to him.

"I..." he stammered.

"We don't have time here," his mother said as she and Keani made their way down the length of the room. Keani jumped down from the end of the table, still grinning like crazy. "I didn't hit the admiral hard enough for him to be out for more than another minute or two."

"You're trying to protect your cover identity?" Alextra asked her.

"I might still need it," his mother said. "My work here is not done."

Alextra took a second to think this over, then gave a curt nod. "He'll likely not have a very good memory of the last few seconds before you knocked him out. He'll believe anything you tell him. And Koltn Ward will be in no position to contradict you."

"So I'm hoping, but none of that matters if we don't get out of here now," Elyot's mother said.

"There are seven enforcers outside that door," Keani said. But she was clutching her knives with an eagerness that just made Elyot's stomach go all queasy.

"Which is why we're taking this back door," his mother said, and waved her arm in front of a bare wall.

That opened up into a secret tunnel.

"That works," Keani said, and plunged into the darkness. Alextra gave Koltn Ward one last look, then followed.

Elyot was about to go after them when his mother caught hold of his shoulder and pulled him into a bone-crushing hug.

"It's good to see you, son," she said. He couldn't say a thing, because she was squeezing all the air out of his lungs. But she didn't even seem to notice. "I never thought I'd live to see this day. It is *so good* to see you." Then her whole tone changed, and she was back in commander mode. "Now, move! Time is short!"

Elyot slipped into the dark crawlspace, made all the darker when his mother came in behind him, then closed the wall back up.

Elyot could feel himself grinning. He only hoped it looked a little less manic than Keani's grin did. But even if it did, he didn't care.

He finally had his mother back.

9 PLAYERS IN THE LONG GAME

ELYOT FOLLOWED close behind his mother as she led him, Alextra and Keani through a maze of narrow passageways that snaked through the walls of the Commonwealth flagship. It was so dark all he could see of her was a grayish outline, even though she was so close he could reach out and touch her if he tried. The passage was so narrow his shoulders were constantly brushing up against the walls. Their feet stirred up clouds of dust so thick it coated the back of his tongue, and he struggled not to sneeze.

Sneezing would be really bad. Because he could hear people talking and moving around in the rooms they were passing between. And if he could hear them, they could hear him. He walked as softly as he could, both to keep his boots from making any sound and to try to keep from throwing up any more dust. But his mother's fast pace made that difficult.

Suddenly she disappeared from the passage ahead of him. He strained to see where she went in the blackness, then saw a rustle of motion at the level of the floor. She was climbing down a ladder to a lower level. Another step, and he would've fallen down the shaft right on top of her. He squatted at the edge of the opening and felt around for the rungs before lowering himself into the even tighter space and climbing down after her.

He heard Keani scuffle to a stop, then saw her start down the ladder after him. But he could only assume that Alextra was still behind her. Even if Keani hadn't been blocking his view, Alextra moved without a sound, and she had drawn a hood up over her silver-blonde hair. Dressed all in black, she was invisible in these dark passages.

Elyot's foot tried to step down onto nothingness, and he gripped the rung in his hands more tightly to keep from falling. There were no more rungs. There wasn't even any more passage. It was just a fall into an open space.

"Go ahead and let go, Elyot. It's not far," his mother said from below him. He lowered his foot again, then the other one, then let go of the ladder and dropped. Despite what his mother said, it was several meters to the bottom, and he landed awkwardly. But before he could even recover, his mother grabbed a hold of him and pulled him out of the way.

Keani landed where he had just been with far more grace than he had managed. Then she stepped back and a blacker patch of darkness dropped after her. Alextra.

"We're between storage rooms now, so it's safer to talk," his mother told them. "Then we'll be passing through the brig area. The walls there are reinforced. No one will be able to hear us."

"That's where we're going? Back to the brig?" Elyot asked.

"Yes. You're going to need those pilots to get back home," she told him, then started leading the way again, down another narrow passage between two rooms.

"Are you coming with us?" Alextra asked her.

"To the brig, yes. Off the flagship? No," she said as they walked. "I'm too needed here."

"Is that why you left?" Elyot asked. He wanted to add "without saying goodbye", but bit it back at the last moment.

"I never intended to leave, Elyot," she told him sadly.

"What happened?" Alextra asked.

"Oh, that's a long story," his mother said. "And we're nearly to the brig now. But I'll give you the short version. I've been a part of the rebellion since the very beginning, since the very day the Commonwealth ships appeared in our skies and their leaders started making demands. At first, I was part of a political group that was lobbying our leaders to stand up to the Commonwealth, to fight in any way we could. But they refused to listen to us. And then our puppet leader was put in charge over us, and any hope of a political solution was gone."

"I understand there was never any open warfare when the ships arrived," Alextra said.

"We had nothing to fight ships with. What could we do? It took years to figure out how to fight back," Elyot's mother said. "But even after my political group dissolved, I still wasn't a fighter."

"You were a spy," Keani guessed.

"That's right. I worked in the Commonwealth headquarters in the city. That was where I was first Islae Jaro, native of Adghal but collaborator with the Commonwealth military. I had to keep my real identity secret to protect Elyot," she said.

"I never even knew you had another name," Elyot said. If he had, maybe he could've figured out what had happened to her, that day she never came back from work.

"No, it wasn't safe for you to know," she said. "I passed information from the Commonwealth military to the fighting rebellion that was just forming out in the wilds. I was intending to do that forever. It was how I could help the cause and still come home every night to Elyot."

"Until the day you didn't," Elyot said.

"I was nearly caught in the act of spying," she said. "I would've been executed for that. But my commanding officer was suspicious. He hadn't seen me copying his files, but he had found me in his office when I shouldn't have been there. He was fond of me, though. That's what saved me. As good as I was at spying for the rebellion, I was equally good at my work for him."

"But if he let you go, why didn't you come home?" Elyot asked.

"After he listened to my flimsy excuse for being in his secured office, he decided to test me. To test my loyalty. He offered me a position on the flagship. A promotion. Valria Taelor would say no, of course. She couldn't be apart from her son. But Islae Jaro would jump on it. It was too big of an opportunity."

"If you had turned him down, do you think he would've fired you?" Keani asked.

"I feared he would do more than that. He'd be watching me more closely, whether he kept me in his employ or not. He'd be watching Elyot. I would be burned as a spy, useless, but even worse I might be executed for what I had done. And Elyot might be in danger."

"You left me all alone," Elyot said. "I had no one to look out for me."

"I'm sorry about that," she said. "I had hoped when I accepted the job that I would be allowed to stay a few days to arrange for your care, but I was sent to the flagship that very minute. Then I hoped I could come back on my time off, but that was forbidden. I was stuck there, on the far side of the moon, and I had no way of finding out how you were doing."

"Mama Scotti looked out for me, as much as she could," Elyot said. "She's dead now, though. She died a few days ago." He rubbed at his head, trying to remember how many days it had been. It felt like just a few, but then it felt like an eternity.

"I'm sorry to hear that," his mother said. "But you've found your place in the rebellion now. They'll look out for you. And you have friends."

"I guess so," Elyot said. He was annoyed that she wasn't asking more, about what his life had been like all the years she had been gone. But maybe she knew already, or suspected. She didn't want to hear him say it all out loud, how he slept on the roof of a building and ate whatever food he could get his hands on. He couldn't really blame her for that, especially as they only had a few moments together. It would be impossible to say everything he wanted to say.

And he knew that her job was important. Everyone he had met in the rebellion had been telling him different versions of that. The fate of their entire world rested on her being where she was, right beside the flagship admiral. The rebellion needed the intelligence that only she had access to.

His own personal happiness was such a small thing beside that. He knew it. But still he wished things were different. He wished his mother was different.

Suddenly, she stopped, motioning for the rest of them to gather close around her. It was tight in that space, but Keani knelt down so Alextra could see over her, and Elyot was tucked close against his mother's side.

She still smelled the same. He had forgotten that smell. Mom smell. Like vanilla-scented soap.

"All right, the control station hub is just under this panel," his mother told them, whispering now. "I can't be seen here. I can't use my rank to get the pilots out. So you three will have to storm the control station and overpower the guards."

"Right," Keani said, and Elyot could see the blades of those steak knives reflecting what little light there was inside the passageway.

"I have Koltn Ward's gun," Elyot said, digging it out of his pocket to hold it at the ready. "But what about you, Alextra?"

"I'll be fine," she said. "In fact, let me go first. If it's possible to take the guards down without making a ruckus, I think that's the best plan."

"I agree," his mother said. "From what I've seen so far, I'd say you trained in fighting with the Imperial Guard."

"Yes," Alextra said. "My personal bodyguard was also my mentor. In so many things."

"Interesting. I wish we had more time to talk," his mother said. "But, alas, we don't. Get down there, take out the guards, and let me know when it's safe for me to join you."

"Will do," Alextra said. She and Keani changed places as Elyot's mother opened the panel.

They were directly over the control station. Only two guards were in view, one in the center of the control station and the other just outside of it, looking at a tablet in her hands and talking with the guard below them. She turned her back to them to look down one of the corridors, still talking in a low murmur. The guard below them was engrossed in whatever he was doing at his workstation.

Alextra made eye contact with Elyot and gave him a little nod. He gave her a thumbs up, then lowered his pistol to aim it at the guard with the tablet.

Then Alextra dropped down to the floor below, landing soundlessly behind the closest guard. He didn't look up from what he was doing or even pause in his typing. Alextra incapacitated him with a blow to the back of his neck. He crumpled and fell without so much as a whimper.

The only other guard in the room was still talking, but the instant she started to turn—no doubt wondering why the first guard had stopped responding to her words—Elyot squeezed the trigger of Koltn Ward's gun, sending a burst of needles into her chest. She looked down at them in almost comical surprise, the tablet dropping nervelessly from her fingers. Then she too was on the floor.

Keani jumped through the opening the minute Elyot's gun stopped firing, knives in hand. She ran from corridor to corridor, but found no other guards lurking nearby.

"We're clear," Alextra hissed up to Elyot and his mother.

"Let's go," his mother said, then jumped down into the control station. Elyot put the gun away. Unlike the others, he needed his hands to get through the open panel and then to catch his balance when he landed below.

"Two more needle guns," Keani said, tucking the steak knives into her belt then picking up both the dropped weapons. Elyot's mother kicked the unconscious body of the first guard out of the way then started tapping at the same workstation he had just been using.

"I need my tanjo," Alextra said.

"I know," Elyot's mother said. "Pilots first, then gear. Then we disappear."

"Back to the shuttle?" Elyot asked.

"That shuttle has been impounded and is almost certainly under guard," she told him. Then she looked up from the screen just long enough to give him an encouraging smile. "Don't worry. We'll figure something out."

"The pilots are down this way," Alextra said. Elyot didn't know how she could tell that. Every corridor looked the same from here, and running back through darkened hidden passageways had thrown off his mental map from when they were here before.

"I can open the force fields from here," his mother said. "Go lead them back this way. Quickly."

Alextra nodded, then she and Keani ran down the corridor.

"I want to stay with you," Elyot said to his mother.

"That's impossible," she told him, still typing away at the workstation.

"I'm not much use down on the surface. I don't really know how to fight," he said.

"You did just fine a second ago," she told him.

Elyot looked over at the guard he had shot. Her whole body was numb from the nerve agent that tipped every needle that had struck her, but her eyes were still alert. She was watching him. Her mouth hung slackly open, a thin dribble of drool slowly descending towards the front of her uniform. But her eyes were watching him, and silently telling him that the minute she could move again, she was going to come after him.

"I want to be up here with you," Elyot said. "There must be something I can do up here to help."

"Not without a cover identity, which you don't have," she said.

"I could get one," he said, although he had no idea how that would even work.

"Not from here, you couldn't," she said firmly. "You have to be seen arriving with other recruits. And you have to already have relationships with those recruits. It takes a long time to create that kind of legend."

"I have to be legendary?" Elyot asked, confused.

"No, a legend is a fake person you're pretending to be. Like Islae Jaro. There was no such person before I became her."

"Okay, so I don't have an alter ego, but can't I stay, anyway? I could lurk in the empty parts of the ship, travel through your hidden passages," he said.

"Those aren't secret passages. They're utility access passages," she told him. "They are usually empty, but not always. And the other parts of this ship, the uncrewed parts, are the same. Usually empty, but not always. It's not safe for you to stay there."

She stopped tapping at the screen then looked up at him. "Go signal

Alextra and Keani that the force fields are coming down. Then wave them to hurry back."

Elyot ran to the end of the corridor and pointed towards the side of the corridor where Laera and Wayde's cells were. Alextra nodded, and she and Keani took their places. From where he was, Elyot couldn't see the fields come down, but he did see Alextra and Keani yank Laera and Wayde out into the corridor before they went back up again.

Then he waved for them to hurry back.

"The panel behind you is about to open," his mother told him, and he spun on his heel to see a panel opening in the side of the control station console. An endless carousel of identical black boxes was rushing by. Then the carousel stopped, and the box that was positioned in front of the panel lifted up invitingly towards him. "Take it," his mother said.

Elyot lifted the box out then set it on the floor to open the lid. Inside was Alextra's tanjo, Keani's proper knives, and the needle gun he had brought with him from Adghal. Now he had two guns, just like Keani.

"Tanjo," Alextra called out to him. She was still running up the corridor, but she had her hand out in front of her. He picked up the tanjo and tossed it to her, and she caught it neatly, separating the two components then locking them down in their usual locations on the outside of her thighs.

"I'm not throwing your knives," Elyot said to Keani.

"I've got them," she said. She handed one of her needle guns to Laera and the other to Wayde, then bent to take up her knives, adding them to the steak knives already tucked in her belt.

"I have a spare gun if you want it," Elyot offered. He held it up to her. She frowned as she looked at it resting there on his palm, but in the end she took it.

"You never know," she said.

"Valria!" Laera said as she and Wayde finally reached the control station and recognized their rescuer. "I knew you hadn't flipped on us."

"Never," Elyot's mother said with a grin. "Laera, this is for you." She reached into her pocket and pulled out a small drive. Laera took it, shoving it deeply into her own pocket.

"That's the intel?" Elyot guessed.

"The patrol rotations for the next fourteen days, the latest equipment acquisitions due to arrive from the Commonwealth home world, and the most recent roster of personnel stationed on and around Adghal," his mother said to Laera.

"That's a big haul," Laera said as Wayde gave a low whistle of admiration. "This could be a game changer for us."

"I don't think so," Elyot's mother said. "They are bringing in more reinforcements and a lot more equipment. Things are about to get very hard for the rebellion. And that's on top of losing the space port. That's a blow that's going to be very hard to recover from."

"You know about that?" Elyot asked.

"Enforcers found it just a few hours ago," she told him. "The last of the rebels were gone before they got there, but the reports indicate they just missed them. I don't know where you're going to hide shuttles now."

"We have another port," Laera said, but in a low voice, as if she wasn't sure if she should even be saying that out loud.

"Hey!" someone shouted, and before Elyot could even figure out which direction that voice was coming from, the air was suddenly filled with needles. He ducked behind the control station, Keani pressed up beside him. Alextra had her tanjo already in her hands, whirling it with blinding speed and sending the needles more or less back the way they had come.

"We've got company," she said.

"No kidding?" Elyot said. He and Keani both had their guns in their hands, but the constant onslaught of needles didn't let up enough for either of them to even peek around the console to line up a shot. Or see anything at all. "How many?"

"More than a dozen," Alextra said, still spinning her tanjo. "We have to get out of here."

"Can we get back up there from here?" Elyot wondered. He looked up at the open panel above them. He thought he could reach it, maybe, if he got on tip-toe on the top of the console.

But he would be exposed to needle fire the entire time. That wasn't going to work.

"There's another way out back the way you came," his mother said.

"I'll cover you all," Alextra said, taking a step forward then another, the tanjo in her hands never slowing. Laera and Wayde had taken cover in the side corridors, but now they moved out into the room, crouching low. Most of the console was between them and the guards making their way up the corridor that Alextra was facing; that helped. Then they were behind the protective shield of Alextra's spinning tanjo.

They turned to run down the corridor they had just come up a minute before. There was no sign of any guards down that corridor yet, but they kept their needle guns at the ready.

"You two, go," Alextra said as she took another step closer to the advancing guards. The needles she was sending back to them were keeping them pinned close to the walls, but none of them stopped firing even for a second.

"Mom?" Elyot called. She had still been inside the control station when the needles had filled the air. He thought she had ducked down in time, but now he wasn't sure.

"I'm fine. Go on and run behind Alextra now," he heard her say. She didn't sound like she was injured.

Elyot and Keani exchanged a nod, then at the same moment they sprinted away from the control station, ducking around opposite sides of the blur of the spinning tanjo.

Then they were in the clear. No needle was going to hit them with Alextra there providing cover.

Laera and Wayde had reached the end of the corridor. The dead end of the corridor. They were standing there uncertainly, heads leaning in towards each other as they discussed what to do.

Then Elyot was shoved aside as his mother passed between him and Keani, sprinting down to the end of the corridor. He and Keani followed. He looked back over his shoulder to see Alextra taking deliberate steps backward now, making her way back towards them.

"There must be another access passage at the end of the hall," Keani guessed.

Elyot just nodded. But inside, his thoughts were in turmoil. Had those guards chasing them just seen his mother running to the end of the corridor to help two prisoners escape?

Because if so, her cover was definitely blown.

And she could come back to Adghal with him. She would have to.

But then he looked behind one more time and realized that he couldn't make out more than the rough shapes of guards through the dark blur of the spinning tanjo. He doubted they had seen her well enough to be certain of it. His mother would still be able to talk her way out of trouble. She was going to stay.

Without him.

He reached the end of the hall and followed Keani into the open access passage. Alextra came behind, looking to make sure that everyone was clear before she abruptly snapped her tanjo in two pieces and stowed them before shutting the access door behind her.

"That's not going to even slow them down," Elyot said.

"Yeah, that's why we're running," Keani said.

But running in the dark in such a confined space was almost impossible. Elyot's shoulders kept hitting the walls to either side. His thoughts were in a constant panic, remembering how he had failed to see the ladder going down before. His mother had known it was there. But if it had been him in the lead, he would've fallen the whole way down before he'd even realized what was happening.

But his mother was in the lead again, and she knew these passageways well. They made a dozen different turns, circling around in a way he was sure was meant to confuse the enforcers who must have followed them into the walls. Then they went down another, longer ladder. His arms were aching from the effort before he finally reached the bottom of that.

They were in a sort of room. He thought it was totally enclosed, but everything was a lighter shade of gray, so light must be coming in from somewhere. They had stopped running, so Elyot leaned back against a wall, hands on his knees, and took advantage of the brief rest to get his breath back.

"Where are we?" Wayde asked. Elyot could just make out his face shining in the darkness.

"Just off one of the tertiary flight decks," his mother said. "Your shuttle is out there, impounded. The inspection teams have already combed over it, but it is still under guard."

"How many people could there possibly be?" Keani asked. "The flight deck wasn't very large."

"It's not where you left it," Elyot's mother said. "It was moved for the convenience of the inspection team."

"Tertiary, you said, so not the biggest?" Elyot said hopefully.

"Not the biggest," she agreed, but grimly. "The alpha flight decks have about five hundred shuttles apiece, and every shift is fully crewed. The beta flight decks are about half that size, but still crewed round the clock."

"And the tertiary?" Elyot asked, his mouth dry.

"The number varies, as they are not kept to full capacity like the alphas and betas. This one has a little under a hundred shuttles."

"But how many guards?" Keani asked.

"We don't need to worry about the whole flight deck," his mother said. Elyot wasn't reassured by the way she had just dodged the question. "Your shuttle is just outside this panel. It's separate from the rest of the flight deck since it's impounded. If we're lucky, you can all sneak on board without the guards even noticing. Then I can remove the impound protocol, and you can be on your way."

"And if we're not lucky?" Elyot asked.

"Doesn't matter. The only way out is through," Wayde told him, and raised his needle gun to a ready position.

"I can't go out there with you," Elyot's mother said. "I'll be inside the control tower. Once I see you all are safely inside, I'll release you."

"Got it. Thank you, Valria," Laera said. Then she patted her pocket, or rather the contents hidden inside. "For everything."

"Mom?" Elyot said.

His mother gave him another crushing hug. "You have to go with your friends now. I'll be all right. Don't worry about me. I'm just happy I got to see you, even for such a short time."

"Me, too," Elyot said.

But then she was gone. He didn't even see how she got out of the darkened room. It was like the shadows just swallowed her up.

"The handle to open the panel door is just here," Alextra said. Elyot couldn't see her at all, not even an outline. He guessed her hood was still up. "Everyone ready?"

"Ready," they all mumbled, more or less together.

Then the door opened with a quiet snap, sliding to one side with a soft hiss. And they could see their shuttle, sitting alone on a patch of flight deck that was painted with wide stripes of an alarming shade of yellow.

Alextra's arm was across the doorway, preventing any of them from leaving the room. But even after visually sweeping the area several times, there was no sign of any guard.

"Let's go," Keani hissed impatiently. Alextra dropped her arm then crept out of the relative safety of the dark room, out onto the exposed flight deck.

"It's clear," Wayde said, and he and Laera jogged to the lowered ramp of the shuttle.

"There might be someone inside," Elyot whispered, but they didn't seem to hear him.

Then a very familiar voice shouted, "halt!"

And Koltn Ward emerged from behind a low wall of shipping containers. He had six guards with them, and they all had long guns trained on Elyot and his friends.

"Run!" Laera shouted back over her shoulder. She and Wayde had quickened their jog into a sprint, but Alextra stood uncertainly only a few steps outside of the room.

And Elyot realized that he and Keani were still inside.

"We should run," he said to her. She nodded, but didn't move. He tugged at her sleeve then ran towards the shuttle. To his relief, she only hesitated for a bare fraction of a second before following him.

But Alextra was still not moving. Without a word between them, Elyot and Keani moved apart. It was like they both had the same plan: to grab Alextra by the arms and drag her with them towards the shuttle.

But before they had quite touched her, the air was suddenly full of enemy fire. But this wasn't needles tipped with paralytics. Not this time.

It was laser fire. Elyot had never seen it before, but he'd heard rumors. The Commonwealth used needle guns on the people of

Adghal because they wanted to take everyone alive. They wanted to subdue, not kill.

But they were using lasers now. And lasers were always fatal.

"How dare you!" Alextra boomed at Koltn Ward. The cold look of anger on her face chilled Elyot's blood, but Koltn Ward just laughed.

"They aren't trying to hit us. They just want us to stop," Keani said to Elyot. He realized it was true. The lasers left visible streaks through the air, a frightening thing to see all around you. It made you feel trapped.

But they weren't hitting anything. And that had to be deliberate.

"Alextra, run!" Elyot said as he and Keani caught hold of her arms.

But she didn't move. And it was like she was an iron statue, one with a substantial base hidden below the level of the ground. Not only could they not budge her, they both stumbled back from trying.

He had just regained his footing when he was blasted back again, but this time what struck him was a wave of intense heat and a boom so loud it felt like it burst his eardrums.

He was sprawled out on the flight deck. So was Keani. But she wasn't looking at him. She was looking at the smoking remains of their shuttle.

It had just exploded.

Elyot struggled to his feet. Alextra was still just standing there, like nothing around her could ever touch her. The edges of her cloak were on fire, but she didn't notice. Her eyes never left Koltn Ward.

But beyond her, Elyot saw Laera and Wayde lying motionless on the ground. He and Keani both braved the waves of acrid smoke and merciless heat to get to the two pilots.

Luckily, they were starting to stir as he and Keani reached their sides. But they were both bleeding heavily from head wounds, and their entire front halves were scorched. Their flight suits were barely holding together.

"Come on!" Alextra shouted at them, as if they had been the ones just standing there the whole time. Then she had her tanjo in her hands. Both ends were blades now as she spun it up, then launched behind the scanty cover of the shipping containers.

But Elyot and Keani had their hands full helping the half-blind, wounded pilots stumble free of the blast zone. They all collapsed together close to the wall, unable to go any farther.

"Your mom is going to help us, right?" Keani asked.

But Elyot couldn't answer. He didn't know. How important was her cover, really?

"Come on," Alextra called again as she marched out of the thick, black smoke towards the four of them. Her tanjo was in staff configuration, and she was using it more like a walking stick. She had some fresh cuts to her face, but at least her cloak was no longer on fire.

Then she emerged fully from the haze, and they realized she wasn't alone. She had Koltn Ward with her, dragging him by an arm. He looked dazed, but was conscious enough to walk where she lead him.

"Where to?" Keani pleaded. "Even if we steal a shuttle, how are we going to fly it? These two are going to need patching up first, and we don't have the time."

"Lucky for us, we have another pilot," Alextra said. "Come on, there are other shuttles beyond those shipping containers. We'll take the first one. Help those two run, if you can."

"You know how to fly?" Elyot asked. That probably shouldn't be surprising. At this point, he was willing to bet that Alextra could do pretty much everything.

But she actually shook her head at him. Then she pushed Koltn Ward to walk in front of her towards the undamaged shuttle.

"I don't, but he does," she said. "He's going to get us back to Adghal whether he wants to or not. That I promise you."

As intense as the flight up to the flagship had been, somehow Elyot suspected his second trip in a shuttle was going to be even worse. But they couldn't stay where they were.

He pulled Laera back to her feet then followed Alextra and Keani as quickly as he could.

10 THE RACE ACROSS THE DESERT

THE TERTIARY FLIGHT deck on the Commonwealth flagship was large enough to contain a hundred shuttles. That was room enough for them all to be docked away from the active take-off and landing area. And the space was as tall as it was wide. When Elyot had first gotten a glimpse of it out of the panel in the wall he and his friends had emerged from, the entire space had felt inconceivably immense.

Now, it felt far too small. The smoke and heat from the explosion of just one shuttle filled the air, too dense to avoid. Elyot's lungs burned from the heat of the air, and he needed the oxygen to keep moving. His eyes stung and watered from the smoke, so intensely he could barely see the world around him. It was all a patchwork of distorted, watery images through the tears in his eyes.

But worst of all was the smell, burning electricity and melting metal and plastic, clinging foully to the inside of his mouth. There was no getting away from it.

Then hands were reaching out to him, to pull him and the limping Laera he was half-carrying up the ramp and into the belly of an intact shuttle. He stumbled at the top of the ramp, not able to see where the floor leveled off. Then the ramp closed up behind him, and everything was blessed silence. No cacophony of alarms, shouting voices, and the roar of the fire.

That lasted for a second, then the ventilation system inside the shuttle kicked into high gear, taking the last of the smoke and the smell away.

"We have to get out of here," Elyot said. He still couldn't see, but when he tried to wipe the tears from his eyes, he realized there were particles there, caught in the moisture, and he had just scratched the surface of both his eyes.

Now they were really burning.

"Koltn Ward is going to get us out of here," Alextra said from somewhere ahead of him.

"I can fly. I can fly," Laera was murmuring over and over. Elyot squinted at her. He knew head wounds tended to bleed heavily, even minor ones, but somehow he didn't think even when they cleaned all that blood away, she was going to be able to see well enough to get them out of there. For one thing, her pupils were two different sizes.

"How's Wayde?" he asked.

"I got him here, but he's out now," Keani said. Then he felt her hands on his face. Startled, he tried to pull away, but she held him fast. Then he felt cool, wonderful relief dripping into his eyes.

"Thank you," he said.

"Thank Alextra, but later," she said. "Give it a minute, then let me know if you think you need more. I've done mine three times, but I think I'm good now."

He realized he had been hearing the sound of voices arguing from the front of the shuttle for the last minute or so, but didn't really pay attention until he heard the soft thwip-thwip-thwip of a needle gun.

Followed by Koltn Ward's bellow of pain and defiance.

"I've got this," Keani told Elyot. She had an entire pouch of Alextra's medicines and was looking over Laera even as she said it. He knew she had been close with a former Commonwealth doctor back in the prison camp she had grown up in. He didn't know how much Jaeke had ever taught her, but it was surely more than Elyot knew. So he just nodded and pulled himself step by step through a narrow hallway between two rooms until he reached the cockpit.

Koltn Ward was clutching his knee and glaring up at Alextra. Alextra was still holding the needle gun she had just shot him with, but not in a threatening way. It looked like she had totally forgotten she was even still holding it. But Elyot wasn't fooled. And he didn't think Koltn Ward was either.

"Fly," Alextra said.

Koltn Ward clutched his knee, his breath in painful hisses, but still shook his head in stubborn refusal.

"You fly or I do," she said with a sigh. "And if I crash and kill myself along with the rest of you, it will all be on your head."

Elyot wanted to point out a problem with her logic, but to his surprise, Koltn Ward actually turned a grayish sort of pale at her words. Like having her death be on his head was somehow worse than his own death would be.

He let go of his knee, shoved his now-paralyzed leg under the control panel, then started touching buttons. Seconds later, they were hovering over the flight deck.

Elyot expected his stomach to revolt at this like it had before, but it didn't. Either Koltn Ward was a better pilot than Laera, or this was a better shuttle.

He looked around at the gleaming leather of the pilot seats, then back at the two rooms he had passed without a glance before. A fully stocked galley on the one side and three bunks with a toilet inside a closet on the other.

He would bet it was the shuttle.

"You're never going to get away, you know. This is all completely pointless," Koltn Ward growled, but Alextra just shrugged as she sank into the copilot's chair.

"Not that I want to agree with him, but just where *are* we going?" Elyot asked. "The one spaceport we kind of know how to find, we know for sure is abandoned now."

"I'm not going to try flying straight back to the rebellion. Not with this guy on board," Alextra said, pointing vaguely at Koltn Ward with the needle gun. "Anywhere he can set us down on the surface will work. Then we walk. It's better that way."

"But what Laera has is time sensitive, remember?" Elyot said.

"We'll walk fast," she said.

Elyot went to the back of the shuttle to see how Keani was doing. She had Wayde and Laera both in chairs rather than on the floor, sitting inside a sort of booth on either side of a table whose surface was a computerized screen. The screen was blankly gray, but had a quality of light to it, like it was ready to fire up at a touch.

"Koltn Ward is going to land us somewhere, and then we're going to walk," he told Keani. She was using a handheld instrument the size of a fork to close up the wound in Laera's forehead. He was relieved to see Laera's pupils were the same size again, although she was still pale under all the blood.

"How far?" Keani asked, looking from one of her patients to the other.

"No idea. Depends on where we go down and where everyone else is now," Elyot said.

"We know how to find them," Laera said, but she sounded like someone talking in their sleep, not really there.

"We have to get that intelligence to Calrin as soon as possible, right?" Elyot said.

"I'm just not sure how far these two are going to be able to walk," Keani said. "I can patch them up, but Alextra doesn't really have anything that will give them any of their energy back. That takes food and rest."

"I think there's food," Elyot said, and went back to the galley. He opened a few cupboards and started to pull things down, but then crossed the central hallway to where the bunks were. He pulled the cases off of the pillows, then went back to the galley to fill them with freeze-dried food and bottles of water.

"I know you're lying to me," he heard Alextra say to Koltn Ward. He could tell she was exasperated just by the way she was talking louder than before. "You can land this shuttle anywhere. I know you can."

"Well, you know wrong," Koltn Ward said to her. "I need space. Lots and lots of space."

"You didn't need a lot of space to take off," Elyot said from the galley doorway. "You hovered up off the flight deck and then, boom. We were gone."

"The flagship controls handled that," Koltn Ward said. It sounded reasonable. It sounded like the truth. But the smug look on Koltn Ward's face made Elyot feel like he was lying.

"This is the latest model of shuttle," Alextra said. "I know it has all the automated systems. Including hover-controlled landing."

"Then you do it," Koltn Ward said, lifting his hands up away from any of the controls and even sliding his seat back. That last was a little awkward, as he was still effectively paralyzed from the right hip down. But his point was clear.

"It's going to be a few hours before we get there. Is that time enough for you to figure it out?" Elyot asked Alextra hopefully.

"Flight is complicated," she said, shaking her head sadly. "I'm afraid, privileged as my upbringing was, my education was still woefully limited. Especially when it comes to practical skills. I learned a lot from my bodyguard, sure, but only what she could teach me in the confines of my rooms in the imperial palace. Until I came out here, I had never even seen the cockpit of a shuttle before."

"So that's a no?" Koltn Ward asked, hands still in the air.

"You said we could walk from anywhere," Elyot reminded her.

"Get some rest while we can," she told him. "It's going to be the longest walk he can contrive for us, clearly."

Elyot handed her one of the meal packs, then carried the three bulging pillow cases to the back of the shuttle. He handed a meal to Laera, and she pulled the tab and peeled back the cover. Wayde had been napping sitting up, but he opened his eyes the minute the smell of her meatballs and sauce drifted across the table to him.

They all ate. Then Elyot and Keani helped Laera and Wayde get into two of the bunks. Elyot let Keani have the third, then slipped into the smaller seat in the corner of the cockpit behind the two pilot chairs. He reclined it as far as it would go, then crossed his arms and dropped off to sleep.

He woke to the bright warmth of the sun on his face. The shuttle was bouncing gently beneath him, and he sat up to see they were once more in atmosphere.

"He got past the patrols?" Elyot asked in a sleepy voice.

Alextra looked back at him, then grinned. "Did you realize this is his personal shuttle? He has clearance to go anywhere at anytime. No one even questioned us."

"His personal ship? Is that a good thing?" he asked, scratching at his head. Then he leaned forward to look out the viewscreen. There was nothing there but sand from horizon to horizon. "Seriously? I know he said he needed a wide open space, but come on."

"It's fine," Alextra assured him. "And I'm not just saying that because I so very much look forward to parting company with Captain Ward."

"My mom risked a lot to get that intelligence to us," he said.

"I know. Can you wake the others and tell them to buckle in?" she asked. Then she gave him a significant look. She didn't indicate Koltn Ward in any way, but he still knew what she meant.

She was expecting him to try something.

Elyot got up from his chair and went to each of the bunks, waking the others. Keani looked like she'd really rather keep sleeping, but was otherwise fine.

But Laera and Wayde were both groggy, and were slow and clumsy getting out of the bunks. He had to take them by the arm one at a time to get them to the back and buckled into the seats at the table. Then he and Keani went back to the cockpit to get into the smaller seats behind the pilots.

There was still nothing to see but sand and sky. Just how far away from everything were they?

"Anywhere around here should be fine, surely?" Alextra said to Koltn Ward. He looked like he was going to say something sarcastic back, or just blandly keep stalling, but Keani spoke first.

"See that bright light there?" she asked, pointing at the horizon on the viewscreen. "Those are the burning sands. We have to avoid those. Anything else is fine, but avoid those."

"But that's where it's flattest," Koltn Ward said, changing their heading until the burning sands were directly in front of them.

"Just put us down. It doesn't matter where," Alextra said. She had the needle gun in her hand again. When she was sure Koltn Ward wasn't looking, she shot Keani a look of deep irritation.

"I guess I know where we're landing," Elyot murmured.

They flew level for another minute or two, but then the nose dropped suddenly and they were in a dive. Elyot was buckled into his seat, but he gripped those straps as if his life depending on it.

All he could see out the viewscreen was sand rushing up at them.

That, and Alextra sitting calmly in her seat.

At the last possible second, Koltn Ward pulled the nose back up and they hit the ground. The impact was intense enough for Elyot to fear he had cracked some of his clenched teeth. But at least they had stopped moving.

"Everyone all right in the back?" Keani called down the hall. Laera and Wayde both shouted something unintelligible that didn't sound like panic.

"Sorry," Koltn Ward said, clearly not sorry at all.

"I expected nothing else from you," Alextra said.

Elyot unbuckled and got up from his seat, but the minute he had stepped into the hallway to follow Keani to the back, he once again heard the thwip-thwip-thwip of a needle gun.

"What happened?" he asked, turning back to see Alextra standing over a now-inert Koltn Ward. She had shot him in the chest, just under the base of his throat. He didn't have the ability to even cry out in pain now.

"He was trying to trigger the emergency beacon," she said. "Not that it matters. They can trace this ship without it. They can trace Koltn Ward's body, for that matter."

"So we're not taking him with us?" Elyot asked.

"No, definitely not. There is a suspension cocoon on this shuttle somewhere, to be used when adrift outside of hyperspace. He'll be fine until they find him. Which won't be long, so we should really get moving."

Elyot went to the back of the shuttle to see Keani already had the ramp down and was pushing a hovering cart off the end of it, out over the sand. It was designed to load and unload supplies and armaments from the shuttle, but it would fit two injured pilots and three pillow-cases of food just as well.

"Where's Koltn Ward?" Keani asked when Alextra came down the ramp alone.

"He's staying behind," Alextra said. "Do we have everything?"

"Everything but a direction," Elyot said. "We wore out our guides getting them out of the shuttle," he added, pointing to the two pilots who were drifting in and out of consciousness, but more out than in.

"We won't need them until we're much closer," Alextra said. "I know which way the city is."

"You have a map?" Elyot asked.

She shook her head, but then she pointed. He followed her finger to see a smudge of gray over the horizon. The ships hovering over his home city.

The hovering cart left no mark on the sand, but the same couldn't be said for the other three. Alextra sent Keani and Elyot on ahead with orders to make as fast a time as they could. Then she ran off in an entirely different direction, towards the setting sun.

A few hours later, she caught up with them. She was dragging something behind her, a wide thing like a rake, with many long strips of cloth tied to the ends of it. She swept it back and forth behind her, obscuring the trail of their footprints. But once she reached them, she let it drop and left it behind.

"They can see us from the sky anyway," she said. "That was more to keep Koltn Ward from following us."

"You shot him with a needle gun, then shoved him inside a suspension cocoon," Keani said.

"Like that's stopped him before," Elyot said. But then something else caught his attention, and he immediately stopped walking. "What's that sound?" he whispered to the others.

They all stood still in complete silence, listening. Faintly, so faint he almost thought he was imagining it, was the sound of music. A low, sonorous humming. But was it voices or some sort of stringed instrument?

"It's the singing dunes," Keani told them, but there was a sense of wonder in her voice.

"But it's night," Alextra said, sounding confused.

"Well, they're always there," Keani said, also confused.

"It's a known phenomenon, for sand dunes to make sounds like music," Alextra explained. "But it requires a certain size and steepness to the dune, and it only happens when the temperature is very high, and the winds are erratic."

"You don't think it's hot enough?" Elyot asked. He was drenched in sweat himself, despite the lack of pounding solar heat. The ground was still radiating the heat it had absorbed all day.

"It's plenty hot, but not as hot as it will be during the day," Alextra said.

Elyot didn't like the sound of that at all.

"All I know is the singing dunes of Adghal are famous," Keani said. "And they sing all the time."

"Who am I to argue?" Alextra said.

"What about the burning sands?" Elyot asked. "That's what you were pointing out before."

"I'm curious about that myself," Alextra said.

"At night, when it's cooler, it will be like a sea of glass," Keani said. "Or so I've heard."

"But by day, burning liquid glass," Alextra guessed. "And Koltn Ward made sure we were surrounded by it when he crashed the shuttle. We'll have to get as far as we can tonight, then rest during the day."

"Where?" Elyot asked, raising his hands and gesturing at the nothingness all around them.

"I was watching as we flew in," Alextra said. "I saw something that might have been an oasis between the city and where we crashed. I hope we can find it before the sun comes up."

They started walking again, but another thought struck Elyot's mind.

"Famous to who?" he asked Keani.

"What's that?" she said.

"The singing dunes of Adghal are famous, you said. But famous to who? No one else knew this planet existed before the Commonwealth came, and no one else can visit now since we're always on the verge of open war," he said. "So who knows about the singing dunes of Adghal?"

She frowned. This had clearly never occurred to her before. "All I know is that they're famous."

"I wouldn't discount it," Alextra put in. "The prison camp is made up of people from a lot of different planets. They know what other people are talking about, not on Adghal. It's not inconceivable that word got out about the singing dunes. Although famous might be a stretch."

They pressed on under the light of the moon, always listening for the sound of approaching shuttles. But the only sounds were their own footsteps and the low reverberations from the dunes.

The sky to the east was turning a lighter shade of gray when they reached the edge of the first sea of glass. They could see the far side, the sand there piled up in low mounds.

"We can make it," Keani said. "That's a thirty-minute walk, but the sun will barely be up then. It won't be hot enough to melt the glass yet."

"We have to try, because the oasis I'm looking for is definitely on that side of this sea, and it would take too long to go around it," Alextra said. She looked to the left and to the right. For as far as Elyot could see, there was nothing but glass glowing in the light from the stars. She had to be right.

They pushed the hover cart over the glass. The cart hovered off the ground, but it still had to be pushed, and that took work. The weight of two grown people and three bags of food, plus the weight of the cart itself, wasn't nothing. Two of them would push it at a time, with the third resting as they walked beside.

But as the sun gained on them, its first rays jutting red into the sky before they were even halfway to the far side of the sea of glass, Alextra started helping Keani and Elyot push it along.

The sun rose higher, fully over the horizon now. No stars were visible, and the whole sky had a drenched, wash-out look to its particular shade of blue. And still the shore taunted them, so far away. Without a word, they all quickened their pace.

Then they were running, running and pushing the cart. The air was baking hot, but not just from the sun.

It was like the sea of glass below them was waking up. It was generating its own intense heat.

And it was turning to liquid. It clung like heavy sludge to their boots, slowing them down just when they really had to hurry.

"Run ahead," Alextra said, taking a position at the back of the cart with both of her hands on the supports. "My boots will last longer than yours. You need to run."

Elyot looked down. His new boots were starting to smolder. But Keani's were smoking.

They ran.

By the time they were finally stumbling over the mounds of sand, which turned out to be outstretches of dunes that rose twice their own height, both of their feet were burning hot. Elyot reached the top of the dune, rolled down the far side, then sat on the ground to tug at his boots.

"No, don't do that," Keani hissed at him. He could tell she was speaking through tears of pain. But she forced herself to sit up and pull a bottle of water out of a pocket. She carefully poured the water over the soles of her shoes until they stopped smoking. "We can't get home barefoot. Not here."

"Right," Elyot said, and took the bottle from her to douse his own feet. It took the edge off, but it wasn't enough. He knew he had blisters, not from walking but from burning. But if he took off his boots to look, he would never get them on again.

"Alextra," Keani said, then crawled back up the dune they had just rolled down. But before she reached the top, they saw Alextra appear over the ridge. She gave the cart one last shove, and it glided down the far side, much more smoothly than either Keani or Elyot had done it.

But Alextra just face-planted where she was, on top of a mound of hot sand.

"I'm up!" Wayde said from where the cart had come to a rest some distance away from the bottom of the dune. Elyot figured he was just raving in a dream, only vaguely aware of his surroundings. But then he saw Wayde roll off the cart, landing on his feet to jog back to where they were.

"You look better," Keani said.

"Feel better. Not great, but better," he said. "I'll go get Alextra and bring her down to the cart. I think if you help Laera sit up and give her some water, she can take a turn walking too."

"I'll do that," Keani said, pushing herself to her feet with a wince.

"Where's Alextra's medical kit?" Elyot asked as he, too, stood up.

"I still have it," Keani said. Then realized what he really meant and dug inside of it. She popped something in her mouth, then tossed the container to Elyot. He took one of the little pills himself.

It didn't instantly help. He kind of hoped it would.

"It's not far," Alextra murmured as she went past them, leaning on Wayde's arm. Her boots looked as pristine as ever. If anything, like she had just given them a fresh polish.

But her face was flushed red, and her hair was limp and dry. Elyot wasn't sure if she had never broken a sweat, or if it had evaporated as soon as it had appeared on her skin, but given that she looked like she had been partially mummified since he had last seen her moments before, he'd go with the latter.

"The cart must have a protective field of some kind," she mumbled. "The heat from those sands was incredible. But you're okay."

"I'm okay," Wayde assured her. Alextra reached into one of the pillowcases and retrieved another bottle of water, but only took a few sparing sips.

"You should get more than that," Elyot said, still worried about the weird puffy yet dry look to her skin.

"No, we're going to need this if we don't find my oasis," she said. But she took one more sip, then said, "not that I'm not totally sure we'll find it. Because I am."

"Sure," Elyot agreed. But his heart sank.

"There are two more seas ahead of us. I can see the heat shimmer off their surface on the horizon," Keani said, pointing.

"If we try to pass between them, will the super-heated air stifle us? Even if we're not on the glass?" Elyot worried.

"No, that's my landmark," Alextra said. "We are going straight up to that isthmus between them, but we don't have to cross it. I saw that oasis right there."

"Or between two other seas of glass," Keani said glumly.

"No, it's there. I'm very sure," Alextra said.

Elyot didn't want to argue. They all had to keep their spirits up if they were going to keep going, especially on their ruined feet. But he was pretty sure if there was an oasis closer than those two seas, there'd be some sign of it they could see. And there was nothing.

"Laera, you good to walk?" Wayde asked. Laera was sitting up and touching the wound on her head with tentative fingertips, but she gave him a tired nod.

"Keani, you and Elyot ride on the cart," Alextra said. "Laera can walk while Wayde and I push you. It's not far. Once we're there and under cover, it will be safe enough to take off your boots and I can tend to your feet."

Elyot didn't like the idea of being deadweight, but given how painful the few steps to reach the cart were, he knew if he tried to walk the whole way he'd only slow them down. And time was definitely their enemy here. Every minute, the sun was higher, and the desert was hotter. They had to get out of the sun as soon as possible.

Keani climbed onto the cart beside him, and the two of them sat back to back, unwilling to sleep while the others worked. But it was a dozy feeling, riding along on the smooth force bubble that kept the cart aloft. The dunes were singing louder than ever, three distinct notes making a chord that rolled on forever. Elyot had to fight to keep his eyes open.

Then suddenly the warmth of the sun was gone from his face and he opened his eyes to see the cart floating into a canyon cut deep into the ground. There was almost no sand here, nothing but smooth rock. Rock that had probably been smoothed over centuries by windstorms. They were lucky to find this place open. The last storm must have blown it clean.

Alextra led them through the little canyon to the mouth of a dry, cool cave. They only went deep enough inside to be sure that the afternoon sun wouldn't reach them later in the day. Then they all just sprawled out on the surprisingly comfortable rock and fell into a deep, well-deserved sleep.

Elyot wasn't sure what woke him up this time. Some change in sound? No, the dunes were still humming the same chord endlessly. The air in the cave was warmer, but still pleasantly cool.

He sat up and took a few sips of water from the bottle he still had in his tunic pocket. Then he noticed a row of bottles lined up beside the cart. Droplets of water glistened on their sides. Those weren't the fresh bottles. He could still see the outline of those inside the pillowcases. These were the empties they had kept on the cart, full now.

Only then did he notice he wasn't wearing his boots, and that his feet felt better. His boots were standing together nearby, waiting for him. His socks looked like they had been washed and wrung out before being draped over the tops of his boots to dry.

He crossed his legs to look at the bottom of his feet. He had fallen asleep before examining his blisters, but there was nothing there now. He wondered how bad it had been. It was probably better he didn't know.

He looked around the cave and saw Keani nearby, also barefoot, with her shoes and socks arranged beside her. Then he saw Laera and Wayde, positioned closer to the opening of the cave as if they had been sentries before succumbing to sleep.

But there was no sign of Alextra.

Elyot pulled on his shoes and socks, then took a greedier drink from his water bottle. Where she was now, she had found a source of fresh water somewhere. They might have to ration during that night's walk again, but as long as they were in the cave, he could drink as much as he liked.

After one last drink, he tucked the empty bottle into his tunic pocket, picked up one of the refilled bottles, then got up to look for Alextra. He followed the wall of the cave away from the canyon, deeper into the twilit darkness. Several meters in, the two sides of the cave formed a narrow passage that ran between two irregular rock faces, then took a sudden hairpin turn, then another back again. After the third, he saw sunlight ahead of him. The passage had straightened out and was heading straight out into daylight.

There was still no sign of Alextra, but now he could hear something besides the dunes. He could hear water, a trickle like from a fountain. But also birds. Birds, singing in the middle of the desert.

The sunlight up ahead was too bright to make out details beyond it until he was out in it. As he stepped out of the cave, he shaded his eyes from the midday sun and looked around. He was in an almond-shaped canyon, open to the sky above, but enclosed on every side. The rock was too smooth and too steep for him to climb, and it was a good twenty meters to reach the surface.

And there were trees. Not like any trees he had ever seen, with tall, bare trunks that reached up high overhead before spreading wide, flat leaves that danced and speckled the sunlight. He took a few steps further in, under their cover, so he could stop shading his eyes from the sun. It was pleasantly cool the very instant that the sun was no longer on him.

There was grass below as well, a scrubby, harsh sort of grass, but lushly green. He didn't see anything that looked like food. No fruits or berries or nuts or anything. But it was still nice, to be surrounded by living things. And, unlike in the jungle, nothing here seemed eager to kill him.

Occasionally, the wind above would pick up some of the sand, but it never fell down into the canyon where Elyot was. It always kept blowing in hypnotic patterns, spinning on to the far side of the canyon. Like it had no desire to go down there.

Or like it couldn't. If there was something like the force fields that had closed off the cells in the flagship brig. He saw no hint of that electric blue effect. The sky above was still that washed-out shade of blue that was more hazy white than anything. But he was pretty sure he was right. And that was probably why the canyon they had entered from was clear of sand as well.

It was protected. But it had let them in.

"Alextra?" he called as he went further in. He found the fountain in the center of the cave, a little spigot that shot up only a few centimeters into the air but filled a basin all around it. He dipped the empty bottle inside it until it was full, then capped it and put it back in his pocket.

"Alextra?" he called again, more loudly this time.

"Elyot? Over here," she called back. She was on the far side of the eye-shaped space. He strolled over to her, enjoying the garden and just not having feet that were in agony.

He found her crouched beside a white boulder, examining something on the underside of a protrusion. The rock looked out of place, not like the other rock in the area. Elyot supposed it had been added to bring another element to the garden.

The trees and plants and birds were strange enough, but the fountain made it clear that someone had built this place. So the rock wasn't exactly strange. Except the whole thing was strange. Who would build a garden all the way out here, a garden with no house beside it or anything?

"You saw all this from the shuttle?" Elyot said as he sat down on the grass and took another drink of water, still cool from the fountain.

"No, I saw a shimmer," she said, pointing up at the sky.

"So it *is* a force field. I thought so," Elyot said.

"The eye-shape of the construct is also distinctive," she told him.

"Distinctive of what?" he asked.

But she didn't answer his question. Instead, she touched that rock again, brushing off the undersurface. "Take a look at this."

Elyot took another drink, then crawled over to look at the rock. It was dark under there, and it was hard to angle his head in a way where he could see into that shadow without simultaneously being blinded by the sun overhead. But he was pretty sure what he was looking at was writing.

"An inscription?" he said. Then he, too, was running his fingers over it. It felt like it would be easier to feel out the letters and read that way than trying to look at them. But they were too smooth in too many places. He got nothing.

"Guys?" they heard Keani call. Then there was a splash, a loud one.

"Over here!" they called together. Keani jogged into view. Her entire head down to the shoulders was soaking wet.

Elyot should've done that. He was tempted to go do it now, but he was too curious about the writing.

"Take a look at this," Alextra said to her, and Elyot scootched back so Keani could peer at the markings.

"What is it?" she asked.

"Some kind of inscription, from whoever made this garden. That's what I think," Elyot said. "But who makes a garden like this, out in the middle of nowhere where no one can enjoy it?"

"Good question," Keani said as she slicked the wet hair back out of her eyes.

"It's not actually a garden, per se," Alextra said. "The whole thing is a logo. The eye that contains the blue waters of the garden, the underground cave, then the canyon beyond that hooks around like a decoration under the eye. It's a logo."

"A logo of what?" Keani asked.

"And I'm still stuck on why out here, where no one can see it," Elyot said. "Before the Commonwealth came, we had a few flying machines, but not many. And I don't think anyone was risking them flying over this desert."

"No, in fact, it's meant to be seen from space," Alextra said, and pointed up to the sky.

"By who?" Elyot asked. But he could tell Alextra was getting excited now. Her eyes were gleaming.

"I wasn't sure. When I saw it from the shuttle, I was sure I was imagining it," she babbled.

"And you brought us this way across the desert, anyway?" Keani demanded.

But Alextra didn't seem to hear her. She just kept babbling. "But it *is* what I think it is, and you have no idea what that means."

"No. We don't," Elyot agreed. He hoped pointedly.

"It means the Commonwealth have no legal right to colonize you," Alextra said. She leaned forward, grabbing Elyot's hand in her left and Keani's hand in her right. She squeezed them both too tightly.

"How can it mean that?" Keani asked suspiciously.

"Because this isn't a naturally formed world," she told them. "Your world was formed by one of the larger corporations inside the Union of Free Worlds. It is totally illegal for them to be here now. And once we tell the Union, they will absolutely be forced to leave."

Apparently, Keani was gaping at Alextra just as mind-numbed as

Elyot felt. Because Alextra gave an exasperated sigh, then squeezed their hands again.

"Just get me back to a communications center, and I'll take care of the rest. You're all going to be free. No war necessary. Adghal will be free."

11 THE FINAL SHOWDOWN

EVERYTHING about the world of Adghal felt different to Elyot now that he knew his planet wasn't a natural formation. It had been created by people, for people reasons. And then just forgotten about. For centuries.

He had no idea how his ancestors had even ended up there. And then somehow forgot everything about the rest of the universe, including how to build ships to get back there.

It almost made sense. Given enough time, anything could be forgotten. Hadn't he himself walked the winding catacombs underneath his home city? Hadn't he seen for himself how their customs had changed over time, deeper down the catacombs taking him further into the past, to a people whose ways were almost inexplicable to him?

That he could understand.

But the fact that all of that had taken place within the lifespan of a single corporation? *That* boggled his mind.

And yet Alextra insisted that the corporation that had crafted his world to someone's unique specifications still existed. It was far away in a different part of the universe, far beyond the reach of the Commonwealth, in a region of space called the Union of Free Worlds, but it existed.

And Alextra knew how to contact them. All they had to do was get her to the right kind of communications equipment.

The only problem was the rebellion didn't have it. Laera and Wayde, the rebel pilots that were currently trapped in the middle of the Adghal desert with Elyot and his friends, were very sure about that.

But they thought the governor of Adghal might.

And the Commonwealth surely did.

But all of that was still kilometers away when the sun finally set and they could continue their race across the desert.

And everything felt different, now that Elyot knew what he knew. It kind of made him love his home world in a way he never had before.

The low, humming song of the dunes was their constant accompaniment as they crossed the desert. The water from the fountain was sweet, almost citrusy, and more refreshing than the plain water they kept as backup. And the stars in the sky above them seemed closer here than they ever had in the city. Perhaps the lack of Commonwealth ships hovering low overhead made them seem brighter.

Not that they needed the starlight to see by. The moon was nearly full and shined with such a silver intensity it lit up the desert around them in sharper detail than the hazy sun had by day.

But even by night, the seas of glass were warmer than the sands around them. They skirted as many of them as they could, but they still had to cross five of them before the rising sun once more forced them to find cover.

Luckily by that time they had reached the edge of the desert. Not that Elyot had any idea how they were going to get back up to the top of the cliff. And even if they did, the jungle still lurked there, waiting for them. But Laera and Wayde brought them to a cave, little more than a hole in the rock, but it was out of the sun.

Once more, exhausted from a long night of running, they all collapsed on the cave floor and fell promptly to sleep.

Elyot woke in a panic to the sound of a shuttle landing, but realized at once this was the rough-sounding engine of a rebellion shuttle, not the whisper-soft smoothness of a highly tuned Commonwealth machine. And Laera and Wayde were already emerging from the cave, waving at someone in the cockpit.

It was still day, but it was late in the afternoon. The last of the fountain water was gone, and Elyot was all too aware of how much his body stank after too many days in the same clothes with no shower. He hoped wherever this shuttle was taking them, it would have the same amenities he had so briefly enjoyed at the hidden spaceport.

"Bring the food, but leave the cart. We won't need that," Laera told them as she came back into the cave to find the three of them awake and on their feet.

"Where are we going?" Elyot asked.

"They are going to drop us off at the main headquarters," she said. "Like, literally. They can't land there, and depending on the patrols they might drop us quite a ways away. I'm sorry, it might mean more walking."

"We can handle it," Keani said, and Alextra nodded.

They climbed into the back of the shuttle. Like Laera and Wayde's ride, this one's interior had been entirely stripped down to the bulkheads and the minimal number of seats. At least this time, Elyot knew how to make his seat drop out of the wall. He buckled himself in.

"Calrin will be there?" he asked Laera as she buckled in beside him.

"Definitely," she said. "Plus some of the other rebel leaders, the ones that don't usually leave the city. The outpost we're going to is at the base of the mountain, but has tunnels that go up to the city. The shuttle can't land there because there's no port, but there are a small number of ground vehicles."

"It's more of a political meeting place than a military stronghold," Wayde said. "But that's where Calrin told us to go."

"I just hope we're not too late," Elyot said. He was worried. They had never seen a shuttle pass overhead, but somehow he just knew that Koltn Ward was no longer in the suspension cocoon inside the crashed remains of his shuttle, awaiting rescue.

He was sure he was somewhere close by, probably hunting them down already with shuttles and with tanks. It was only a matter of time until he tracked them down again.

The shuttle lifted straight up like an elevator until they were just higher than the top of the cliff. Then it plunged out over the jungle, hugging so close to the treetops Elyot was sure they were striking branches. He could see the mountain ahead of them with the city walls just visible atop it, but the pilot banked slightly, following a path around the mountain rather than up to it.

The jungle petered out here, becoming a grassland dotted with occasional trees. The trees were immense, with widespread arms that shaded large parts of that grassland even though they were widely dispersed. But Elyot saw Alextra shudder and realized those were likely the same sort of tree that had tried to kill her days before.

The pilots were chattering into their comms and with each other, but too low for Elyot to catch more than the occasional word. He gathered they were working out just where to drop them off.

The shuttle banked again, this time taking them straight up against the side of the mountain. Elyot wished he could see straight up. He knew the Commonwealth ships were up there. But so were shuttle patrols. The pilots must have all that on their scopes, but he wished he could see it for himself.

"We can drop you pretty close, but you'll have to run for cover the minute you hit the ground," the copilot turned in his seat to tell them. "We're going to drop down. The minute we stop falling, you need to unbuckle and jump out the back. Then run clear. Fast."

"Wayde and I have been here before. We can get them inside without delay," Laera assured him.

"Just avoid the trees," he said as he turned back to his control panels.

Elyot didn't need to be told that again. He had seen for himself what those trees could do if disturbed. The rain of spiders that had turned out to be harmless had been horrifying enough.

The shuttle suddenly dropped straight down, like a plunging elevator, then halted just above the level of the grass. Elyot threw off his restraints then followed the others to the back of the shuttle. It was a bit more of a jump than he would've liked, but after hopping around the access passages in the flagship, he was starting to get used to landing from tall heights. He landed well enough, then rolled clear as the shuttle at once gunned its engines to rattle its way back up into the sky.

"Move, move, move!" Wayde was yelling, grabbing Elyot's elbow and dragging him into the shade at the side of the mountain. Then he pushed Elyot to the ground, all but smashing his face into the dirt.

Elyot lifted his head to see Alextra and Keani also pressed low under the waving heads of grass, Laera with a hand on each of them. Then he heard the sound of a Commonwealth shuttle passing overhead. Its well-tuned engine hovered over them for a minute, then abruptly dashed off in the same direction their shuttle had gone.

"It's following them," Elyot said.

"That's the plan," Wayde said, pulling him back to his feet. "We have to get inside before it comes back to look for us again."

"Where's inside?" Alextra asked.

"Through there," Laera said, pointing at what, to Elyot, looked like the side of the mountain. An unbroken stretch of rock, too steep to climb, with not a single hint of a cave.

But he had learned not to trust what he saw. He just followed Laera and Wayde up to that rock wall. Then he, Alextra, and Keani huddled together, waiting and watching as Laera and Wayde spread out, touching the rock face with their hands.

But nothing happened.

"It was more over this way, I think," Wayde said, heading more to the left.

"No, I recognize that twisty tree up there," Laera said, moving more to the right.

"Hurry. I hear that shuttle coming back," Alextra said.

Elyot heard nothing, but he moved closer to the rock face himself all the same. Keani and Alextra followed his lead, and they were all touching the rock now, desperately searching for an opening covered with a holographic disguise.

"Elyot. Good to see you," Calrin said, his head appearing out of nowhere. His face had the hint of a smile on it, but then he noticed the shuttle bearing back down on them. "Quickly," he said, taking Elyot by the hand and dragging him through the hologram.

Elyot blinked, then found himself standing in a large, square space carved out of the rock. A stack of storage containers stood against one wall, and some sort of hover-bike was parked on the other side. Nothing looked like it had been touched recently, and the floor was covered with the dried remains of grass blown in from outside.

Then Alextra and Keani emerged beside him. All three of them stepped forward as Wayde and Laera joined them.

Laera reached into her pocket at once and thrust the drive Elyot's mother had given her into Calrin's hand. "From Valria," she said.

"Excellent," Calrin said, tossing the drive into the air and catching it again. "Come on. Let's get this to a computer."

"There's more," Alextra said even as they all started walking at a fast clip across the squared-off room and into a smaller corridor beyond. The corridor took an immediate turn to the left and followed the side of the rock face, going up at a steep angle.

"We can get to everything in good time," Calrin told her as the corridor took a hairpin turn then continued up again, higher into the mountain.

Elyot really hoped they weren't going to walk all the way back up to the city. Because that would take hours.

"But this is important," Alextra insisted. "I can stop everything going on here with one call. That means your freedom without any kind of war."

"That would be lovely," Calrin said, but Elyot could tell he didn't believe Alextra at all.

The corridor turned again and kept climbing.

"Listen to me, the Commonwealth has no right to be here," Alextra said.

"That we all well know," Calrin said.

"I'm not talking morally or whatever. I mean legally. By intergalactic law. And they have to respect that," Alextra said.

"Intergalactic law? That's a thing?" Calrin said, still disbelievingly.

But before Alextra could speak again, the corridor took one last turn then ended in what looked like a motor pool. It was an artificial cavern within the mountain, no access to anything that Elyot could see, and it was only half-filled at the moment. But it had to be the rebellion motor pool. There were more hover bikes like the one he had seen at the bottom of the mountain, and there were carts and vehicles like he was used to seeing up in the city.

There were even a few tanks, although not as nice as the ones Koltn Ward had commanded when he was chasing the trio through the jungle. These looked like they weren't even operable.

But Calrin didn't head towards any of those vehicles. Instead, he led them across the center of the space, to a more brightly lit area still within the same cavern. This was walled off with the exact kind of temporary building materials Elyot had seen in the spaceport.

Calrin continued on down a long central corridor. Other people walking through the corridors stopped and stepped out of their way. They watched the group pass with curious eyes, but no one said a word to them.

Then they were in another command room with tiers of computer workstations. It was larger than the similar room in the spaceport. Elyot realized he was looking at the heart of the rebellion.

It was ridiculously undersized compared to the bridge of the Commonwealth flagship. So much so it made his heart sink. How could any of them believe they stood any kind of chance in a fight? Alextra's way was the only way.

"Valria's intel," Calrin said to the room at large as he plugged the drive into the command workstation. The central screen in the front of the room switched from some sort of tracking of all shuttles around the mountain to a menu screen of options from the drive.

"How long until he admits what she told us, that this is all bad news?" Keani whispered to Elyot.

"She should've come down and told him herself," Alextra said. "There's no more good she can do up there."

"She must've had a reason," Elyot said. "She knows more about her business than we do."

The three of them leaned against the wall at the back of the room, staying out of the way as the rebel leaders present all hovered around the command station and argued about what they were looking at.

Nearly an hour later, the conversation was clearly spiraling around the same talking points over and over.

"They are doubling their numbers," a gray-haired woman that

struck Elyot as the most sensible one present said, pointing up at the screen. "Twice the number of ships, twice the number of shuttles, twice the number of tanks. And triple the number of enforcers. We can't win this, people. We just can't."

"We always knew we were outnumbered," Calrin said for, by Elyot's count, the eighteenth time.

"So our only hope is to strike now, before the reinforcements get here," said the younger man that Elyot had decided he kind of hated.

"We're still scrambling from the loss of the spaceport. That's only destined to fail," Calrin said. Again.

"Look, isn't it time for you to listen to Alextra?" Wayde said, loudly before any of the others could repeat their favorite points again.

"That really is a pipe dream," Calrin grumbled.

"No, it's all true," Alextra said. Then she pinned Calrin down with a cold look. "You know who I am. You know why I'm here. Why would you think that I'm wrong about this?"

"She has a point, Calrin," the gray-haired woman said.

"I don't understand her point," the youngish man said dismissively.

"Allow me to explain," Alextra said, and pushed away from the wall to stand in the center of the command area. All eyes were on her. Even the people working on the computer stations on the lower tiers stopped murmuring to each other.

"Go ahead," Calrin said.

"During our return flight from the flagship, I saw the unmistakable sign of a Horus Corporation logo from the shuttle as we cruised over the desert," Alextra said. "This is a corporation that has existed for millennia within the Union of Free Worlds. The Union of Free Worlds is a collection of independent planets that exists over most of this quadrant of the galaxy. As small as this world feels standing up against the Commonwealth, the Commonwealth is far more dwarfed by the size of the Union of Free Worlds."

Elyot kind of admired the way Alextra kept anticipating questions and answering them before anyone could interrupt her. She dominated the room. Of course when she was done talking, it was good odds that they'd all just start arguing again about what it all meant.

Like Alextra, he was kind of wishing his mother was here. But

Alextra was doing a pretty good job of redirecting their energies herself.

"After the shuttle crashed, we headed across the desert to the logo I had seen from the air. I've never seen one myself, but I've read about them while living in the imperial palace. Logos in the Commonwealth are much like they are here, a marking on a package that tells you at a glance who created the item you're holding. But the Horus Corporation creates planets. To see their logo, it has to be big enough to be seen from space. But as long as they're making it that big, they also make it something to be experienced at a human scale. Like a pleasure garden in the middle of a vast, lifeless desert."

"I don't get your point," the irritating youngish man said.

Elyot expected Alextra to glare at him, but she wasn't in member of the imperial family mode. She was in smooth negotiator mode. She gave him a nod of acknowledgement for his question.

"Within the pleasure garden is a rock, and on the underside of that rock, protected from the rays of the sun, is the serial number of this world," she said.

That exploded the room. They were all talking at once, some disbelieving her words, as if the idea that there was a number written on a rock was the one improbable thing they just couldn't buy.

But others were more questioning. Still not getting what it all meant. With all the talking, none of their individual words were clear, but Alextra gave them each a nod, anyway.

"Please, people," she said, holding up her hands in a silent request for quiet. "It means your planet was terraformed by the Horus Corporation."

"So, what?" the youngish man asked. "We're employees of some intergalactic corporation and we don't even know it?"

"Maybe it means we're property," someone else said, and then the crosstalk in response to that made everything unintelligible noise again.

"What it means," Alextra said, loudly, and they all fell silent again. "What it means is that the Commonwealth cannot colonize you. You have rights, as citizens of the Union of Free Worlds."

"To be colonized by them?" the gray-haired woman asked.

"Only if you choose to be," Alextra told her. "They lost contact with you for millennia. That makes you independent from the Horus Corporation now under the Union laws."

"How do we know any of this is true?" Calrin said. "Haven't you spent your entire life within the confines of a palace? You've never even been to this Union of Free Worlds, have you?"

"No, I have not," Alextra admitted. "When I was young, I wanted to run away there. I read everything about the place I could find. But I've never been there."

"So we just need to make a call?" Elyot said. Someone had to get the conversation back on track. "To this Union of Free Worlds?"

"Yes, but for that distance we'd need an ansible," she said.

"What's an ansible?" Keani asked.

"It's a form of communication that is instantaneous no matter the distance between the two devices," Alextra told her.

"Oh," Calrin said, as if suddenly realizing something. Then he felt eyes on him and explained, "when the Commonwealth ships here send communications back to their home world, there is a significant delay between sending the message and receiving the reply. Usually more than a week." Then he flushed a little red. "We thought the imperial command was mired in bureaucracy."

"It is, but mostly it's the distance between star systems," Alextra told him. "They have satellites that fire the communication signals through wormholes, but even then there is a delay."

Elyot was pleased to see that everyone around him looked just as confused by her answer as he felt. With the possible exception of Calrin, who had a look on his face like he wanted to sit down under a tree somewhere and really think about that sentence until it made sense. Even if it took weeks.

"I'm guessing this means you don't have an ansible," Alextra sighed.

"No," Calrin said, but slowly, like he was thinking.

"They are rare even in the Commonwealth," she said. "My mother has one, a gift from the Union of Free Worlds, actually. But she never uses it. She's convinced they gave it to her to spy on her. It's in a locked room in the palace."

"If she has the only one in the Commonwealth, what are we going to do?" Calrin asked. Not in a panicked voice. By this point he understood Alextra well enough to know she never would've brought it up in the first place if she didn't have a plan.

"I can try to get access to my mother's ansible," Alextra said. "But let's call that Plan B."

"Okay," Calrin said. "What's Plan A?"

But before Alextra could answer, the sound of alarms filled the air, followed all too quickly by the sound of laser fire.

"The motor pool has been breached," the gray-haired woman said. "How?"

"Koltn Ward," Alextra said. Which on the one hand didn't answer her question, but on the other hand it totally did.

"They came down the tunnels from the city," someone else reported.

"We've been betrayed," Calrin said. He sounded resigned, like he had expected this to happen for some time.

"I'm afraid it's my fault," Alextra told him. "As soon as Koltn Ward knew who I was, he knew exactly how to track me."

"Didn't he know who you were the minute he met you in the tavern?" Keani demanded.

Alextra actually blushed when she nodded.

Elyot briefly wondered what his life would be like now if Alextra had admitted she was caught the minute Koltn Ward sat down to talk to her. If she had gone along quietly with him and the other enforcers. Would Mama Scotti still be alive? Would he still have a sometimes job in the tavern? Maybe with Keani as a friend in the city? She would still have to hide out, but half of the city were hiding from the enforcers.

It would be very different from how his life was now. About to be mowed down by laser fire, or run over by tanks.

"Your people have no hope of winning this fight," Alextra said to Calrin. "Please, just tell them to surrender."

"Even if I did, they wouldn't do it," Calrin said. "They would call me a coward and a traitor, but they would never stop fighting."

"But it's all so pointless," Alextra said. Then she threw up her hands in frustration. "Fine. I'll deal with this myself."

And she turned and marched off, back towards the motor pool.

Elyot spun on his heel to follow her, but Keani caught his elbow. "What are you doing?" she demanded.

"I'm not letting her do this," he said, wrenching his elbow out of her grip.

"Do what? It's not like he'll kill her," Keani said. "Apparently he can't. She'll be fine."

"She's not going out there trying to get herself killed," Elyot said. "She's going out there to get herself caught."

"What?" Keani asked.

"That's the quickest path to her Plan B, wouldn't you say?" he asked. "She gets caught, taken back to her mother, and she's right there with the ansible. Just like she said."

"That's not what she's thinking," Keani said, horrified. But then she looked over at Elyot with huge eyes. "That's totally what she's thinking."

"Come on," Elyot said, and the two of them ran down the corridor towards the smoke and fire of all the burning vehicles in the motor pool.

This was even worse than the shuttle fire on the flight deck. That space had been quite a bit larger, and only one shuttle had been on fire. But this enclosed space was filled with dozens of vehicles in flames, their metal frames distorted slag now. The smell was intolerable, thick and foul. Even breathing out of his mouth, it was like he could still smell the smoldering metal and plastic.

"Here," Keani said, shoving something in Elyot's hands. It was a face mask. He fitted it over his face, and the instant it sealed across his forehead and just in front of his ears, it expelled all the smoke and he was breathing cool, fresh air.

He turned to see Keani taking another mask out of a compartment in the wall. She put it on over her own face, then gave him a nod.

He could breathe now, but his eyes were taking longer to recover from the burning of the smoke. Even when he blinked the thick tears away, he couldn't see more than a few meters. But he could tell where the action was.

He just had to follow the laser bolts back to their source.

He and Keani emerged from a bank of smoke into a relative

clearing in the air. Two large machines on either side of the space were responsible, sucking the smoke away from the enforcers front line. They could burn anything they wanted to slag and never have to breathe a bit of it.

Then he saw Alextra, standing alone in the very middle of that space. She had her tanjo in her hands, but it was in staff mode and just resting, its bottom point touching the floor behind her. She was leaving her whole front open. Anyone could shoot her at any time.

Elyot had no doubt she could spin that tanjo back around fast enough to deflect any barrage of needles. But lasers? He wasn't sure if the tanjo could even handle lasers.

"Koltn Ward," Alextra said. She was calling him out, but when Elyot scanned the line of enforcers on the far side of the clearing, there was no sign of the captain.

Elyot started to surge forward, to stand by her side, but Keani caught his arm and shook her head. They were standing half in the smoke; it gave them some cover. Out there, they would just be two more things Alextra would be distracted trying to defend.

But he looked around him, desperate to find anything that might prove a weapon. He had a needle gun in his hand, but if Alextra had taken out even one of the enforcers, there might be a laser rifle he could snag.

But all he saw was smoke and flame.

"I demand to speak to Captain Koltn Ward of the Empress' Enforcers of the Commonwealth of Planets of the Third Quadrant of the Kullab Galaxy, fourth squad, third division," Alextra said. Her voice rang out even louder than the continuing alarms.

"Who demands?" a voice called out. Elyot scanned the line of enforcers again, all standing with rifles at the ready. Still no sign of Koltn Ward, but that was definitely the voice he'd just heard.

"I am Imperial Princess Alextra Camdon-Elber of the House Camdon-Elber, Sixth iteration of Tira, Fifth issue of Izbella Camdon-Elber, Empress of the Commonwealth of Planets." She paused, then added, "I can give you my genetic identification sequence if that helps."

"No, I believe you," he called back.

"What's going on?" Keani whispered to Elyot. But Alextra must have heard, because the hand holding the tanjo behind her back spread its fingers wide, commanding them to stay where they were.

"You can stop all this nonsense, Captain Ward. I've done what I came here to do, and I'm ready to go back to the surface," Alextra said.

"Oh, you're going back further than just to the surface," he said, then finally stepped into view, climbing out of a more portable version of the tank he had chased them all around the jungle in.

"I happen to know exactly what your orders are, Captain Ward," Alextra said. "And you will not be detaining me."

"My orders are to get you back to your mother by any means necessary," he said as he strolled up to her, apparently unarmed. Elyot could just see the red pinpoints on his chest where she had shot him with the needle gun on the shuttle.

"No, your orders are to turn me over to a member of the Imperial Family," Alextra said.

"Same difference," Koltn Ward said, but this time he sounded wary. She was driving at something he couldn't grasp yet, and he didn't like it.

"Your orders," she said, and even with her back to him, Elyot could tell she was grinning, "are to turn me over to the most proximate member of the Imperial Family. And that is *not* my mother."

"The entire Imperial Family is back at the Imperial Palace on the Commonwealth home world," Koltn Ward said. "You and I will fly there together on my brand new shuttle—thanks for that—and whichever member of your family meets us first can have you."

"Not quite," Alextra said. "I believe you don't have clearance to know this, but I have family here on Adghal."

"No, you don't," Koltn Ward said at once. But he didn't sound sure.

"I do, actually," Alextra said. "I have a cousin. Well, we call her a cousin. It's a bit complicated, and frankly not for all ears."

"What are you talking about?" he demanded.

"Perhaps if we step back a bit, out of earshot of your enforcers, I can tell you. I trust you, Captain Ward, but this is a high-level imperial secret," she said.

Elyot watched Koltn Ward struggle with his options before finally giving her a short nod. Alextra turned, gave Elyot and Keani a reassuring smile, then led Koltn Ward back to where the two of them stood.

"You can't speak in front of my enforcers, but you can speak in front of these two?" he demanded.

"Your enforcers are subjects of the Commonwealth," Alextra said. "These two are not."

"You know that's not something we agree on," he growled.

"Do you want to hear what I have to say or not?" she asked sweetly.

Koltn Ward scowled at her. Elyot could tell just how much he wanted to grab her by the arm and drag her off. Aside from that being very unlikely to go the way he hoped, the desire to know what she was hinting at finally won out.

"Tell me," he said, wincing as if mentally chastising himself.

"You know, I assume, that all the princesses are born from eleven perfected genetic lines," Alextra said.

He nodded, motioning for her to get on with it.

"Those eleven were crafted after much meticulous research by top-level scientists in the Commonwealth. And they were as perfect as people can be created to be. But there was a twelfth line that was—how should I put this?—less than perfect."

"That's a rumor," he said, scowling at her. "That's just some conspiracy theory the uneducated bandy about."

But she just kept smiling at him until the scowl morphed back into that look of uncertainty.

"It's true?"

"Why take my word for it?" Alextra asked. "You and I can go up to the surface together and present ourselves to the planetary governor."

"Why would we do that?" he asked suspiciously. "The man is a puppet."

"Yes, a puppet. But one who will be happy enough to introduce us to his chief art advisor."

"You're making that up," he said. But, again, he didn't sound sure. And she just kept smiling at him.

"There's one way to find out," Elyot put in, winning himself another Koltn Ward scowl.

"If you don't agree she is who I say she is when we meet, she can certainly prove it," Alextra said. "And if she can't, then I am happily your prisoner back to my homeworld."

Elyot felt himself starting to grin and quickly put a hand over his face to hide it. Koltn Ward shot him a suspicious look, and he strained to make his own expression one of total seriousness.

"Very well," Koltn Ward gave in. "And I suppose it's all three of you, is it?"

"Is it?" Alextra asked them.

"Like we're leaving you alone with him," Keani said. Elyot just nodded.

"If she's wrong about this art person, you'll have to," Koltn Ward warned her. "I'm not taking you two with me when I leave this planet behind, that's for sure."

"One thing at a time, captain," Alextra said. She pulled her tanjo in two and stowed it, then gestured towards the mini-tank. "Shall we take your conveyance?"

"We'll barely fit, but it's a short ride," Koltn Ward said, and the two of them crossed the zone of cleared air towards the line of enforcers.

"Do you understand what's going on?" Keani whispered to Elyot.

"I think this is Alextra's Plan A, somehow," he said. Then he grinned at her. "I can't wait to see what that somehow is, though. I've never been to the governor's palace."

"Oh, I have, lots of times," Keani said airily, sharing his grin.

Then they ran to get to the tank before Koltn Ward could try to leave without them.

12   THE LAST DEPARTURE

UP UNTIL A FEW DAYS AGO, Elyot had spent his entire life within the city walls of the capital of the planet Adghal. He had climbed to the tops of those walls from time to time to look down at the jungles and grasslands that spread around the mountain the city was perched on. Not with any longing to leave his home, just out of a desire to look around.

But since the moment he had met Alextra and Keani in Mama Scotti's restaurant, it felt like he had been everywhere. Down into the jungles, up into space to the far side of the moon, then down again to the heart of the desert that lurked just beyond the horizon from the city. He had seen hidden rebel spaceports, killer trees, and the most magical of gardens.

So it felt a little strange, after all those wide-ranging journeys, to be back home.

Well, sort of. Elyot had grown up close to the walls on the western side of the city. Pretty much the poorest part of town. He knew that cluster of blocks intimately, every rooftop and every sewer grate.

But now he was in the richer neighborhoods. Koltn Ward's mini-tank roared through the wide, smoothly paved streets. From where he sat with Keani on the top of the tank, Elyot could see over the residential walls around him, into lovingly maintained gardens where brightly dressed children played with pets or toys. He saw people tending to vegetable patches or flowering shrubs. He saw houses that seemed to be built entirely out of glass, opaque in places to keep his prying eyes out.

He had never imagined people so close to him were living such very different lives.

And when he had lain on the rooftop that was his sleeping place, he had gazed up at the Commonwealth ships that never left the sky over the city. He had never more than noticed the tower that thrust up like a spear towards those ships. But that was where they were heading now, the tank following roads that spiraled ever higher up the slope of the mountain.

"Who lives in that tower?" Keani wondered as the tank rolled up to a gate in the inner city wall, the wall that divided the government buildings from the rest of the city. Enforcers quickly waved them through, Koltn Ward never even bothering to come to a complete stop.

"I don't know. To be honest, I never really thought about it. It was always just there," Elyot said. "I spent a lot more time thinking about those ships."

"Yeah, they're hard to ignore," Keani agreed. "I saw them from my prison camp, but they are so much bigger here. It feels like I could reach out and touch them."

"It's oppressive," Elyot said.

The tank engine quieted for a moment and they coasted along the road as if Koltn Ward was debating stopping where they were, or turning in through the open gates of the governor's mansion. But Alextra must have argued against it, and soon enough the tank was accelerating again, following the curve of the road uphill, circling around to the back of the palace and the highest eminence of the natural mountain.

And atop that eminence was the tower. It looked like some strange outgrowth of the mountain's rock, like it had just become smoother and more regular over time. Elyot's eyes followed the windowless stone walls all the way up.

It was like that tower was trying to spear the ship directly overhead. It had to be an illusion. There was no way that tower was that tall, or the ship that close. But it made his stomach queasy all the same.

The tank came to a halt where the road ended. Then the top hatch swung open and Alextra came out, followed by Koltn Ward.

"We walk from here," Alextra said.

At first, Elyot didn't see how that was even possible. But there was a path that started where the road ended. Not a formal, groomed path, just a rut formed by many feet over many years. Alextra led the way along that path towards the stone prominence, then up a very steep metal staircase that had lurked hidden between two outcroppings of rock.

Elyot didn't like how steep that staircase was, or the way it had clearly come loose from its moorings in the rock in several places. It moved underfoot as they climbed it. It even shifted a little in the wind. And already the tank parked at the end of the road looked tiny. It was a long way down.

The staircase ended far short of the door in the side of the tower, and they had to scrabble up a steep slope that was covered in loose gravel that slid and rolled under their feet.

"How can anyone live up here? Every time you would need to shop for food, you would risk death trying to get your shopping back up here," Elyot said.

"She doesn't come this way," Alextra told him. She was the first one to reach the door. It was a heavy thing of dark metal that came to a pointed dome on the top. There was a little barred window at eye level, but a shutter of the same dark metal was shut on the other side so they couldn't see in.

Alextra knocked, but the sound of her tiny fist on all that metal was laughably unnoticeable. She pounded with the side of her fist, which was only a little louder.

Koltn Ward sighed dramatically, then unslung the laser rifle from his back. He struck the door with the butt of the gun, making the door vibrate like an unmusical sort of bell.

"That should do it," he said, shoving the rifle back into place.

For a long time, nothing happened. The wind blew around them, spinning Alextra's hair like a banner and sending more bits of gravel skittering down the slope, but that was all.

Elyot was just about to suggest they try something else when they all heard the sound of footsteps approaching the far side of the door. The sound was muffled, but Elyot was sure he wasn't imagining it.

Then the door opened with a shriek of rusted, long-unused hinges. Whoever opened it had trapped themselves between the door and the wall, so they were all just staring at a tiny bit of space at the bottom of a long metal staircase that looked no more sturdily anchored than the last staircase they had climbed.

Then a woman appeared from around the door. At first Elyot thought she was a twin to Alextra. But then his eye started picking out subtle differences.

This woman was a bit older, although he couldn't quite decide how much older. It changed from moment to moment, how old she looked.

She was also just a little less… perfect. Her silver-blonde hair had just a little less luster to it than Alextra's. Her blue eyes were a slightly more ordinary shade of that color. Her features were just a little less immaculately arranged.

She blinked out at all of them, like after climbing down that long staircase she was still surprised to see anyone standing at her door. But she didn't say a word.

"Do you know who I am?" Alextra asked her.

The woman seemed to notice her for the first time, which was odd since Alextra was the one standing directly in front of her. The woman blinked again, slowly, but then nodded.

"I didn't expect you to come see me," the woman said. "But we have all been told to watch for you. Won't you come in?"

She stepped back from the doorway. There wasn't quite enough room for all of them at the bottom of the stairs, particularly not once that woman motioned for them to clear the way so she could close the door. Elyot and Keani climbed up the first few steps of the staircase to make room for the others.

Elyot looked up. The same metal staircase zig-zagged back and forth up the narrow shaft, up as far as he could see.

It was going to be another long climb.

"I'm not going to try to escape, but I would like to ask a favor of you before you send me home," Alextra said.

"A favor?" the woman repeated. "What favor could you require from the chief art advisor to the planetary governor of Adghal?"

"I need to use your ansible," Alextra said.

The woman blinked, this time in something like surprise. But then she just nodded again and brushed past Alextra and Koltn Ward to step onto the staircase. It was a tighter squeeze for her to pass Elyot and Keani, but they flattened themselves against the cold, slightly damp stone wall to let her by.

Then they were all climbing up that staircase, step after step. Elyot lost count somewhere after four hundred.

The stairs ended in another tiny room with an identical door of heavy, dark metal, almost too large to be opened into that space. When she swung it open, the sunlight beyond was almost blinding. Elyot had to stumble out into the open air then wait for his eyes to adjust before he could look around.

The minute he could see, he was instantly grateful he had only taken two or three steps while sun blind. If he had gone much further, he might have walked right off the edge.

They were standing on the very top of that tower, and it was all one open space with no walls, no railing, nothing between the five of them and a very long drop. The top of the staircase they had emerged from jutted out of the floor like a square work shed.

And at the very center of that circle of tower top was a cottage. It was circular, made of some sort of honey-colored wood, with round windows of frosted glass and a domed roof that came to an onion-like peak.

Whatever he thought he might find at the top of that tower, that hadn't been it.

And it looked really incongruous against its backdrop of Commonwealth ships with their bristles of armaments and rows of winking lights.

"You live up here?" Elyot asked.

"Yes. I like the solitude," she said with a sad sort of smile. Then she led them across the weather-worn stone of the tower to the cottage door.

The interior was all one room, with a galley-type kitchen tucked into one area and a bed and storage chest in another. But most of the interior was filled with art, both finished works and things in progress. There was a slanted desk covered with stacks of papers, drawings in various stages of completion. A half-painted canvas waited on an easel near one of the windows. There was even a block of marble with only a few roughed-out marks on it, although the twisty, surreal sculptures around it gave a hint at what it would someday look like.

"You realize I'm not capable of hiding you," the woman said to Alextra. "The imperial scientists put certain psychological triggers in me that I can't work around. I have to turn you in."

"I know," Alextra said. "I just need to use your ansible. If you need to call out on it first, I understand. But you should know that this man here is Commonwealth Enforcer Captain Koltn Ward, and I am already in his custody."

"Oh, is that the situation?" Koltn Ward said sarcastically.

"If you are already in custody, then nothing further is required of me. You may use my ansible," she said.

"Thank you," Alextra said. Then had to add, "where is it?"

The woman looked around the cluttered cottage, then clicked her tongue as she looked around again.

"What does it look like?" Elyot asked, hoping that the answer wasn't something indistinguishable from all the surrealistic art around them.

"No, it's over here," the woman said, and dropped to her knees to dig under her bed. She emerged with something the size of the palm of her hand that looked like an ornate mirror. She handed it to Alextra.

"Thank you," Alextra said, taking the mirror and looking into it. She pondered for a moment then spoke to her own reflection. "Liaison to the Commonwealth of Planets at the diplomatic corps of the Union of the Free Worlds."

The mirror in her hand chirped, but nothing else happened.

"You must take her to the planetary governor next," the art advisor told Koltn Ward. "It's protocol."

"That was my plan," he said.

"I will accompany you," she said. "I will summon my conveyance now while Alextra is on her call. It will arrive shortly."

"Thank you," he said.

"No one has knocked on that door since I arrived here. Strange that you did."

"I guess we didn't know about your conveyance," Koltn Ward said with a shrug.

Elyot was pretty sure Alextra had taken the long way because the shortcut started in the governor's palace, and if they had gone in there, someone might have stopped them from ever getting up here at all. Alextra would've been sent home without ever getting her hands on this ansible.

"Aren't those things supposed to be really rare?" Keani asked, leaning close to peer at the back of the ansible in Alextra's hand.

"Supposed to be? What a strange way of putting it," the art adviser said, bemused.

"I thought the empress had the only one in the Commonwealth and she kept it locked up or something," Elyot said.

"We're not in the Commonwealth," the woman said.

"Yes, but still. That just makes this thing being here even weirder. Doesn't it?" he asked.

She shrugged. "Art knows no bounds. It must be free to spread wherever it wills, all throughout the universe."

"The art goes through the ansible?" Elyot said slowly, desperately trying to make sense of what she was saying to him.

"She has art dealers in all known systems and doesn't like to sleep on buy offers," Alextra told him. Then the ansible in her hand chirped again. It was no longer her reflection in the mirror, but the face of an older man in an ivory-colored uniform.

"Hello? To whom am I speaking?" he said uncertainly, squinting out of the glass.

"I am Imperial Princess Alextra Camdon-Elber of the House Camdon-Elber, Sixth iteration of Tira, Fifth issue of Izbella Camdon-Elber, Empress of the Commonwealth of Planets," she said.

"Offer to give him your genetic identification sequence, why don't you?" Koltn Ward said lowly.

"Has there been a regime change? We haven't heard from anyone in your sovereignty in decades," he said.

"No, Izbella is still empress," Alextra said. "I'm actually contacting you on behalf of another sovereignty, one my mother is trying to colonize. Only she has no right to do so."

"How does that involve the Union of Free Worlds?" the man asked.

"The planet in question, Adghal, is a creation of the Horus Corporation," she said. "I believe it was lost track of some time ago, but the current population would still like to exercise their rights to be protected from aggressive colonizers."

"And you can prove what you say?" the man asked. He kept glancing down then up again, like he was logging her answers on a tablet just out of view.

"I can provide you with the entire serial number for the planet," Alextra said. "Ready?"

"Go," the man said.

Alextra then rattled off a long string of letters, numbers, and named symbols. This went on for some time. Elyot remembered touching the worn remains of the inscription on the underside of the rock. Not only had Alextra been able to make it all out, she had committed it all to memory.

When she finished, the man was already nodding. "Yes, it's in our system here. You are correct, it was abandoned after the sale fell through at the final hour. How imminent is the danger of colonization?"

Alextra didn't answer. She just stepped over to the nearest window and turned the ansible so that it faced out over the city, and at the flotilla of ships hanging above it.

"Right. We're on our way," he said.

"I regret I may not be here when you arrive, but there is an organization here that can work with you on the next steps. They are led by a man named Calrin," she said.

"Are you personally in danger?" the man asked.

Alextra glanced up at Koltn Ward, but only for a split second. Then she said, "no. I am quite safe. I just need to return to my mother."

"Understood," the man said. Then the ansible reverted to merely reflecting her own face once more.

"Why didn't you tell him you needed help?" Elyot asked.

"Because I don't," she said as she handed the ansible back to the art adviser. "I am going with Captain Ward willingly."

"But why? You can't be done with what you set out to do. You've only been to one planet," Elyot said.

"And you haven't even seen all of that yet," Keani added.

"Nevertheless," Alextra started to say, but then broke off when they all heard the sound of a loud engine approaching the cottage.

They went out the door to see a hovering platform emerging into view up the side of the tower. It bobbed up higher than the tower momentarily, and Elyot was nearly blinded again by the bluish-white light of its massive hover disk. Then it settled down at a point level with the top of the tower, like an elevator platform with no sides.

Four Commonwealth enforcers stepped off the platform first, taking up positions around the tower. They had laser rifles in their hands, but kept them pointed down at the stone floor.

The next person to step off Elyot guessed was the planetary governor. He was wearing a fancy suit that was cut like a military uniform but had no rank or service branch insignia on it. His hair was also too long for him to be an enforcer.

Then came a face he did recognize: the admiral from the Commonwealth flagship. He was scowling at them all, but relaxed visibly when he saw Koltn Ward standing beside Alextra.

Elyot looked at the remaining people on the platform, but it was only four more enforcers with rifles. His mother wasn't there. She must still be on the flagship. He hoped she was okay.

"Any particular reason you came up here to chat with my chief art adviser and not present yourselves to me down in the palace?" the governor asked.

"Are you a citizen of Adghal?" Alextra asked him.

He looked taken aback. "Well, young lady, you might say I'm the first citizen of Adghal," he said. The admiral hissed something at him, but the constant wind kept Elyot from making out his words. The governor flushed a bit, then turned his attention to Alextra again. "I beg your pardon, your imperial highness." But then he turned back to the admiral again to ask loudly, "but isn't she a prisoner? I don't get the protocol here."

"I have no desire to stand on protocol, sir," Alextra said. "But I do need a clearer answer to my question. Were you born on this world, or are you from elsewhere in the Commonwealth?"

"I was born here," the governor said.

"Then as a citizen of this world, and furthermore as its elected leader, you should know that this world is not subject to colonization by the Commonwealth or any other sovereignty," Alextra said.

The governor glanced back at the admiral, but the admiral just shrugged.

"She claims this world was created by a corporation, and that there is a logo for this corporation out in the desert," Koltn Ward told them.

"And I never would've found it if you hadn't insisted on flying us all the way out there. So thank you," Alextra said to him with a cheery smile.

Koltn Ward just stood there, jaw hanging open as he realized she was right.

But Alextra took another step closer to the governor and admiral.

"I assure you it's true. The Commonwealth needs to leave, at once. Remove the enforcers on the ground and the ships from orbit," she said.

"You can prove what you're saying is true?" the admiral asked skeptically.

"I can. But I'm sure you're going to want to argue about the veracity of my claims for as long as you can. So let me tell you now that the Union of Free Worlds is already on their way. Their delegates will be here shortly, and they will remain until they are satisfied that the free people of Adghal are being ruled by leaders of their own choosing." Then she gave the governor a pitying look. "I have a feeling that's not going to be you. My apologies."

"You're bluffing," the admiral said.

"We all heard it," Elyot said.

The admiral looked at Koltn Ward, who reluctantly nodded.

Then one of the other enforcers ran up to whisper in the admiral's ear. The admiral scowled even more darkly than before. "I guess that confirms it. But we're going to need some time to dismantle our bases here and move the equipment back onto our ships."

He had been speaking to Alextra, but it was the governor who puffed out his chest importantly and said, "of course. We completely understand. But in the meantime, if you could just have those ships pull back to a higher orbit? It's a matter of optics, I'm sure you understand."

"Behind the moon would work," Elyot volunteered. "I mean, your shuttles go that far routinely already."

"Yes, that sounds perfect, admiral. Behind the moon," the governor said.

The admiral glared at the governor, not liking this sudden change in the man's previous subservient demeanor. But in the end he just said, "very well. It will be done."

Then he and his enforcers retreated to the far end of the platform. Elyot could see the admiral already barking orders into a comm.

"You three are the ones who discovered the truth about our world?" the governor asked, looking from Alextra to Keani to Elyot.

"More or less," Keani said.

"We all owe you more than we can ever repay, the entire population of Adghal. But won't you join me at the palace as my very special guests? I'm sure there will be much to be done when the Union of whatever she said arrives, and I would love to count on you all."

"You'll need to work with the rebel leaders as well," Alextra said. "Calrin and the others."

"The rebellion?" the governor said doubtfully, but at Alextra's warning glare he blanched and quickly said, "of course! Of course! I shall send for them at once. In the meantime?" he swept his arm towards the platform behind him.

It didn't look remotely safe, but the idea of going back down all those rickety staircases had no appeal at all. Elyot shrugged at Keani and stepped onto the floating platform. She leaped on beside him.

"Can you believe this guy?" he whispered to her, rolling his eyes at the governor. The man was clearly trying to win Alextra over to his side.

"He was elected before, wasn't he?" Keani said. But then she shook her head in answer to her own question. "No, your mother said that was all rigged. But does anyone here know that?"

"They will, I'm sure, before it comes time for the next election," Elyot said. "If my mother knows, then Calrin knows. No, I think when all is said and done, Calrin will be governor of Adghal."

"He's a good guy?" Keani asked. "He seemed so every time we met him."

"I barely know him better than you do, but I would say yes," Elyot said. Then he looked at the governor again, practically foaming at the mouth as he tried to sweet talk Alextra. "I don't think we could do worse."

"With Calrin as governor, maybe they'll shut the prison camps down," Keani said. Then she did something Elyot had never seen her do before. She rolled back her sleeve to look at the counter on her arm, slowly ticking down an impossible length of time. "But I'm not a citizen of Adghal. My parents weren't from here. So I guess I don't get a vote."

"Lots of things are going to change," Elyot assured her. But he was worried too. In his case, he was worried about his mother. Would she know what was going on in time to get off the flagship? Or would she be trapped in her new identity, whisked away to some new star system and some new mission?

And if she was exposed now, could she still be executed as a spy? He didn't know the first thing about how laws like that worked. But he did know when an enforcer had a grudge against you, the laws served whatever end that enforcer wanted and not the other way around.

The platform set down in the middle of an immense pleasure garden, just on the shores of a perfectly circular pond. The admiral and his enforcers left without saying goodbye, marching double-time to a waiting shuttle at the far end of a grassy field.

Elyot watched them climb aboard and close the ramp behind them. Then he watched the shuttle lift up slowly then fire its engines to propel it up into the sky.

He lost sight of it pretty quickly from there, but only because he was distracted by the sight of the ships that hovered over the city.

They were getting smaller. Even as he looked at them, they were receding.

He heard what sounded like a soft roar in the distance. The roar grew in intensity, and then there were shouts and whistles. He was hearing the people of the city. Everyone was outside cheering and celebrating as the ships that had hung over all their lives for years finally, finally left them in peace.

"My friends, it is time for us to part," Alextra said to Elyot and Keani.

"You're just going to let her lock you and your sisters up in rooms in some tower?" Elyot demanded.

"Of course not," Alextra said. "But you don't need to worry about me. You're going to have your hands full here, I'm sure. The work is only beginning."

"Yeah," Elyot said, but he wasn't sure he meant it. Alextra might be someone who could see herself sitting at meeting tables, helping others to craft a government or whatever. But that wasn't him.

Not that he wanted to go back to sweeping floors and serving chai makhanis in a restaurant, although that hadn't been the worse thing in the world.

He suddenly realized he was free to do just about anything he wanted now. The only problem was, he had no idea what that was.

"I thought we were going to stick together forever," Keani said. "I thought we'd see the universe together."

"We still might, someday. But I have to deal with my mother first," Alextra said,

"You freed us but not yourself," Elyot said to her. Keani glanced at her counter again and he realized even that wasn't completely true. He was free, but his friends weren't. Not yet.

"It's time to go," Koltn Ward said impatiently. "My shuttle is parked just over there. It's time we were on it."

"Don't worry about it. I'm going to be perfectly fine," Alextra assured them both. Then she turned and left with Koltn Ward.

She never looked back.

"I wish we could sneak onto that shuttle," Elyot said to Keani.

"I don't think we'd get away with that," Keani said. "But there are other shuttles."

"What do you mean?" Elyot asked her. A blur of motion caught his eye, and he saw the planetary governor standing on the back steps of the palace, desperately waving for them to join him.

"I don't know about you, but I really don't think this is where I'm meant to be," Keani said.

"In the palace or in the city?" Elyot asked.

"Frankly, on Adghal," she said. "I was born in a prison. I never did anything wrong, not to earn that kind of sentence. I don't think what my parents did was so bad either. I should never have been born here. I should've been born somewhere else. Somewhere out there."

"Okay," Elyot said. So now both of his friends were leaving him. He was going to be all alone. Again.

"Do you really want to hang around here and be the governor's special pets? I mean, it's not like he really takes us seriously. Just Alextra, and she's gone now," Keani said.

"No, you're right," Elyot said. "Maybe when these people come from the Union of Free Worlds, we can talk to them. Maybe they can help us get somewhere else."

"Maybe," Keani said, too brightly. "But maybe we don't need to wait for them. Who knows how long it will take them to get here, anyway?"

"So what do you want to do?" Elyot asked.

"Do you see that shuttle over there?" Keani said, pointing to yet another enforcer shuttle parked in the gardens. "I think we should stowaway on that. All the shuttles are leaving. We'll be up in space in no time."

"And then what?" Elyot asked.

"One step at a time," Keani said. "We'll figure it out one step at a time. Unless you wanted to stay?"

"No, I don't really want to stay," Elyot admitted. "I want to get back to that flagship and make sure my mother is okay."

"I was thinking of your mother, too," Keani said.

"How so?"

"I was thinking, as long as she's pretending to be a commander in the Commonwealth military, she's our best chance at catching up with Alextra," Keani said.

Elyot looked up again and was startled to see all the ships were already out of sight. He could see stars. A whole dome of stars over the city. It was beautiful.

He was glad he got to see it just one time. Everything he had gone through over the last few days was totally worth it.

"What are you thinking?" Keani asked him.

"I'm thinking I like your plan," Elyot said. "Step one, get on that shuttle and hide. Step two…"

"Step two we figure out when we get to it," Keani said with a grin. She touched the hilts of the knives in her belt. "Ready?"

Elyot touched the needle gun in his pocket. "Ready."

They sprinted across the garden, away from the palace and the only world they had ever known.

But towards everything they had yet to experience.

One step at a time.

SCI-FI SERIAL PODCAST!

Check out my new monthly podcast of serialized science fiction: THE TALES OF THE CHAI MAKHANI TRIO!

Elyot loathes the massive Commonwealth ships that hover menacingly over his home world of Adghal. He hates the Commonwealth enforcers who harass the populace even more. But with his mother missing and presumed dead, Elyot keeps his head down and strives to avoid notice. And he succeeds until the day two strangers enter his life...

New episodes of this sci-fi serial drop every 1st of the month.

Now streaming on Apple Podcasts, Google Podcasts, Spotify, Stitcher and more. Also available in eBook and print everywhere books or sold. For a complete episode listing, check out the page on my website.

COMPLETE SERIES: THE TRAVELS OF SCOUT SHANNON

The complete six-book series THE TRAVELS OF SCOUT SHANNON begin with book one, Under Falling Skies.

Scout Shannon's whole family died the day the Space Farers dropped an asteroid on their domed city. Now she lives alone, out in the wild with only her dogs for company. She prefers it that way.

But Scout finds herself at a crossroads. One road leads back to a quiet life snug under the protective dome of a city. The other road leads to a life in the rebellion, a life of adventure and excitement but also danger. Dare she try to find the rebels hiding in the hills?

Then a chance encounter with a stranger from the other side of the galaxy threatens to derail what remains of Scout's life. The entire galaxy awaits her, if she survives the next four days.

"Under Falling Skies", a young adult science fiction novel, set on a remote planet with a distinctly Old West feel. For fans of gunslinging women and young girl assassins. And dogs.

Under Falling Skies, the first book in THE TRAVELS OF SCOUT SHANNON, available everywhere now.

NEW SERIES: THE RITCHIE AND FITZ SCI-FI MURDER MYSTERIES

The Ritchie and Fitz Sci-Fi Murder Mysteries starts with Murder on the Intergalactic Railway.

For Murdina Ritchie, acceptance at the Oymyakon Foreign Service Academy means one last chance at her dream of becoming a diplomat for the Union of Free Worlds. For Shackleton Fitz IV, it represents his last chance not to fail out of military service entirely.

Strange that fate should throw them together now, among the last group of students admitted after the start of the semester. They had once shared the strongest of friendships. But that all ended a long time ago.

But when an insufferable but politically important woman turns up murdered, the two agree to put their differences aside and work together to solve the case.

Because the murderer might strike again. But more importantly, solving a murder would just have to impress the dour colonel who clearly thinks neither of them belong at his academy.

Murder on the Intergalactic Railway, the first book in the Ritchie and Fitz Sci-Fi Murder Mysteries.

ALSO FROM KATE MACLEOD

Love heists and capers? Then check out my new series, THE VIC HARPER CAPERS. The action starts with the novella THE THIRD POLE JOB.

Vic Harper and her gang retired wealthy from their life of thievery and heists. Whether in a luxury condo overlooking the river in Minneapolis or in a modernist mansion built into the side of a mountain in Colorado, life comes easy now.

Perhaps too easy.

When an old friend asks for a favor his niece, Vic and her mentor Chase Woodward leap at the chance to relieve a little of the boredom. But a quick bit of B&E in a wealthy suburb of Chicago leads to an even greater challenge.

The prize? Nothing much. Just the opportunity to level a playing field for their friend's niece.

But the heist? May prove to be their toughest ever. Because to get to the prize, they'll have to climb a mountain.

And not just any mountain. Their prize waits on the summit of Mount Everest.

THE THIRD POLE JOB, the first novella in the Vic Harper Caper series. For those who love capers, heists and other impossible missions.

ALSO FROM RATATOSKR PRESS

Also from Ratatoskr Press, The Witches Three Cozy Mystery Series by Cate Martin, a mix of mystery and magic that begins with Book 1: Charm School.

Amanda Clarke thinks of herself as perfectly ordinary in every way. Just a small-town girl who serves breakfast all day in a little diner nestled next to the highway, nothing but dairy farms for miles around. She fits in there.

But then an old woman she never met dies, and Amanda was named in her will. Now Amanda packs a bag and heads to the big city, to Miss Zenobia Weekes' Charm School for Exceptional Young Ladies. And it's not in just any neighborhood. No, she finds herself on Summit Avenue in St. Paul, a street lined with gorgeous old houses, the former homes of lumber barons, railroad millionaires, even the writer F. Scott Fitzgerald. Why, Amanda can practically hear the jazz music still playing across the decades.

Scratch that. The music really, literally, still plays in the backyard of the charm school. Because the house stretches across time itself. Without a witch to protect this tear in the fabric of the world, anything can spill over. Like music.

Or like murder.

The complete series is out now, and it all starts with Charm School.

FREE EBOOK!

Like exclusive, free content?

To get two prequel short stories to THE RITCHIE AND FITZ SCI-FI MURDER MYSTERIES as well as a bonus prequel novelette to the completed six-book series THE TRAVELS OF SCOUT SHANNON, signup for my monthly newsletter at KateMacLeodWrites.com.

Thank you!

ABOUT THE AUTHOR

Photograph © 2016 Jonathan Conklin

Kate MacLeod has written stories which have appeared in Analog, Strange Horizons and Mythic Delirium, among other places. She is also the author of two young adult science fictions series: The Travels of Scout Shannon, and The Ritchie and Fitz Sci-Fi Murder Mysteries. She also contributes to a serialized science fiction podcast called The Tales of the Chai Makhani Trio. She currently lives in Minneapolis, Minnesota.

Find out more about the author and sign up for her newsletter at KateMacLeodWrites.com.

ALSO BY KATE MACLEOD

Novels

The Slums of the Solar System:

Mitwa

The Mars of Malcontents

The Whole World for Each

Books 1-3 Box Set

The Travels of Scout Shannon:

Under Falling Skies

In Quaking Hills

Among Treacherous Stars

Against Impassable Barriers

Over Freezing Altitudes

At Galactic Central

The Travels of Scout Shannon Books 1-3

The Travels of Scout Shannon Books 4-6

The Travels of Scout Shannon Books 1-6

The Ritchie and Fitz Sci-Fi Murder Mysteries:

Murder on the Intergalactic Railway

Murder in the Skies

Body in the Catacombs

Death on the Summit

An Undiplomatic Murder

A Lethal Betrayal

Sci-Fi Novellas

The Intergenerational Tree

I Rise into a Daybreak

Caper Novellas

The Third Pole Job

The Twelve Days of Christmas Job

10-Story Collections

Tales of Blood and Ink

Tales of Old Gods and New

5-Story Collections

Tales from Heian-Kyo and Others

Tales from the Edges and Ends

Tales from Forgotten Days

Tales from Ancient and Future Times